I0553537

Second Chances

Second Chances: The Courtship Wars
Copyright © 2008 by Regina Jeffers

Cover Design and Interior Format by Rebecca Young

All rights reserved. No part of this book may be reproduced or
transmitted in any form or by means, electronic or mechanical, including
photocopying, recording, or by any information storage and retrieval
system, without permission in writing from the author except in the case
of a brief quotation embodied in critical reviews and articles.

This is a work of fiction. Names, characters, places, and incidents either
are the product of the author's imagination or are used fictitiously, and
any resemblance to any actual persons, living or dead, events, or locales is
entirely coincidental.

All rights reserved.
First published in 2008 by Xlibris Corporation.
Re-edited and Released in 2012.
White Soup Press

Other Books by Regina Jeffers

Darcy's Passions
Darcy's Temptation
Vampire Darcy's Desire
The Phantom of Pemberley
Christmas at Pemberley
Captain Wentworth's Persuasion
The Disappearance of Georgiana Darcy
The Scandal of Lady Eleanor
A Touch of Velvet
A Touch of Cashémere
A Touch of Grace
"The Pemberley Ball" from The Road to
Pemberley
The First Wives' Club
Honor and Hope
Second Chances: The Courtship Wars

Dedication

We remember fondly lost loves
and chances for happiness.

To MP,
You know who you are.

"Time Does Not Bring Relief"
by Edna St. Vincent Millay

Time does not bring relief; you all have lied
Who told me time would ease me of my pain!
I miss him in the weeping of the rain;
I want him at the shrinking of the tide;
The old snows melt from every mountain-side,
And last year's leaves are smoke in every lane;
But last year's bitter loving must remain
Heaped on my heart, and my old thoughts abide.
There are a hundred places where I fear
To go, - so with his memory they brim.
And entering with relief some quiet place
Where never fell his foot or shone his face
I say, "There is no memory of him here."
And so stand stricken, so remembering him.

Chapter One

"JACKSON," LUCIAN DAMRON extended his hand as he maneuvered the man out of earshot of other conference attendees. "Any news?"

Jackson Ryder knew what Lucian wanted to hear. "We've made progress." Jackson dropped his voice. "Starline is developing a new reality show, and they want you as one of its medical consultants. If this one goes the way we think, they'll pick up the talk show format for the fall season."

"You're not kidding me, are you, Ryder?"

"We'll meet after your session, and I'll give you all the details." Lucian realized that Ryder lived for such moments–teasing his clients, dangling the proverbial carrot before them. "One of my other regulars could also be picked up by the show. Maybe we can all meet–hash out the details."

Praying she wasn't late, Gillian Cornell rushed into the civic arena's conference room only to find clusters of people standing around waiting for the session to begin. Out of breath from running through the concourse, Gillian stood, chest heaving, before making her way to the stage. She wondered if she'd made a mistake in accepting Jackson Ryder's proposal to be part of this conference round table. Her *science* wasn't the science of the rest of this crowd. Gillian practiced what most of the conference attendees would call "New Age Medicine," although Gillian certainly didn't call it that. In fact, that term was so passé. A sex therapist and relationship counselor, Gillian held hopes of releasing her first book soon. If Ryder's promise of the new Starline reality show came through, she could launch her book to a national audience.

~~~

As he settled into his place at the presenters' table, Lucian Damron's eyes surveyed the room before settling on the still open doorway. Riveted to the portal, he couldn't curtail his instinctive appraisal of a striking beauty rushing through the entrance: a bit disheveled in her appearance, but oh so breath-taking, he noted how a moment of insecurity played across her countenance. Unexpectedly, he found himself rising to assist her.

"Is there a problem, Damron?" the moderator asked.

"No...no. I was just looking for the water pitcher before we began."

"I will take care of it for you," the man offered, but Lucian merely nodded; his eyes still searched the room for the woman.

Then he found her, and an uncomfortable deep rush of blood to his lower body, as well as a lift of his brow accentuated the pleasure he experienced in watching the slender woman march purposefully toward the front of room. The conference participants blocked part of Lucian's sightlines, but he managed to find her immediately each time she reappeared from behind another cluster. He enjoyed this perverted game of hide-and-seek as the woman, zigzagged her way through the crowd. Then, she began to ascend the stage's steps. *So, she's part of the program,* Lucian thought. *Perhaps a late night rendezvous.*

As she settled her belongings under the table, a sensual delight in the woman's perfection–her thin, aquiline nose and lush lips–coursed through him. When her eyes narrowed in response to Lucian's stare, he turned his head quickly, looking the other way for several minutes; yet, those same magnificent eyes drew him back to the woman's countenance. It had been a very long time, if ever, for Lucian to be so instantly taken with someone, but, this auburn-haired beauty had left his senses rattled.

~~~

"Are you telling me...telling this audience, that you seriously believe we choose our mates by how they smell?" After several less than stellar presentations, the discussion had become a heated one between him and the pretty brunette. In the back of his mind, Lucian considered how tantalizing it would be to argue and then have make up sex with his opponent.

"Why not? Attraction must be based on something...an intangible," she retorted. Is science absolutely certain that it knows what attracts two people to one another."

Although her impertinence infuriated him, a crooked, boyish smile played across Lucian's face. "Maybe it is something as tangible as a person's looks." Her appearance had certainly piqued his interest.

The woman quipped. "Or their body odor." A snicker crisscrossed the room as Lucian felt a twinge of indignation; in claiming her own respect from the audience, she had dismissed his.

His voice rose with the embarrassment: No one spoke to him with such bravado, especially not a woman. He knew full well his appeal to women for he had used it to carve out his current success. No cheeky female, despite how attractive she might be, would show him up. "Then explain to me, Miss Cornell, why there are so many divorces if all we must do is sniff people to find our perfect mate. Maybe we should act more like dogs."

Incredulously, she flushed before saying, "Some women already think men act like dogs." Again, came the snickers of laughter. "In reality, it is not so *simple*."

Lucian leaned back in his chair, crossing his arms across his chest, symbolically closing off the discourse and denying her ideas their validity. "It never is." A look of amusement overspread his face, and the laughter accorded him lasted longer than what his sexy opponent had engendered.

Despite his being her target, Lucian liked that she did not concede defeat. It spoke to the type of woman she was. The type he normally avoided. Miss Cornell demanded, "Dr. Damron, do you challenge the existence of Nerve 'O'?"

"I am a man of science, Miss Cornell; I am willing to accept the possibility of what you purport." He thought he saw the flash of her eyes, and Lucian smiled as if they were already lovers.

However, the lady brushed off his overtures, a fact he duly noted. Obviously, the woman meant to spend her time discussing her research and placing her agenda on the table. She had no time for him, and Lucian wondered what if he had made a mistake in demonstrating an interest in the woman. "Reproductively speaking," she continued, "MHC may determine how healthy our offspring might be, and as far as our susceptibility to another person, it does appear, Sir, that next to our brain, our nose is a powerful sex organ." The crowd responded as tainted images drifted among the attendees. "Women in my research groups report a connection between a satisfying sex life and their guy's scent."

"Oh, God, save us from scent aphrodisiacs!" Lucian protested loudly.

"A study by the Berlinger Foundation discovered which smells increase a man's arousal by increasing the blood flow to the penis," she countered. "Would you be interested in knowing what those might be, Dr. Damron?" Her voice held its own taste of sarcasm.

"Of course, Miss Cornell, enlighten me. I may need to know what odors to avoid in the future." Smugness crept across Lucian's countenance.

Even though the lady apparently meant to put him in his place, Miss Cornell laughed, and Lucian could hear the seductiveness of it. "Turn up your attraction," she smirked, "by having your mate indulge in pumpkin pie or black licorice or a donut or lavender."

⌒

"You were magnificent," Charlotte purred into his ear as she laced her arms around Lucian's neck. "You had the entire audience hanging on your every word." She kissed him intimately behind the ear.

Lucian smiled, but his attention lay elsewhere. His eyes searched the room for the likes of Gillian Cornell. Once they had exited the presentation, he had watched her move from one group to another, relishing in the attention but not dwelling with any one person too long. Lucian had found he liked that idea. Unrealistically, the idea of her being with someone special didn't set well with Lucian. Charlotte moved closer and allowed her hand to caress his hip. For some nine months, casual sexual relationship had existed between Lucian and Charlotte Blakeley. The casual part had existed purely on Lucian's side: Charlotte held hopes of something more permanent. "You certainly put that Cornell woman in her place," Charlotte intoned in her best socialite attitude.

"That was never my intention." Lucian nonchalantly extracted himself from Charlotte's hold while he distractedly searched the crowd for another glimpse of Gillian Cornell.

Charlotte's apparent jealousy resounded through her tone. "You cannot possibly believe the woman's opinions hold any merit?"

"Of course, I don't find her opinions valid." Lucian's voice carried a little too far. "The woman is a sex therapist for Christ's sake," he protested.

"Actually, I am a sexologist." Lucian turned to face a furious Gillian Cornell. "That means I've a psychology degree–the same as you, Dr. Damron."

Lucian flushed at being caught calling forth his masculinity before his acquaintances. "I stand corrected, Miss Cornell." He made her an exaggerated bow before stepping away from the contrariness displayed on the woman's countenance. "Your advanced education is duly noted." Her cheeks began to burn, and for that he felt a twinge of guilt; but in reality, the lady had her life and so did he. Lucian purposely threaded Charlotte's hand into the crook of his arm as he walked away. From behind him, he had no doubt that it was the very correct Gillian Cornell that he heard growl, "Pompous ass!"

~

"Come on, Man, out with it." Lucian greeted Jackson Ryder as he slid into the booth across from his agent. He had wondered all night what deal Ryder had made with the network, and he wasted no time in broaching the subject.

"In a few," Ryder teased. "I'm waiting for someone else to join us."

"Who?" Lucian thought maybe one of the network executives.

Before Ryder could answer, Gillian Cornell rushed through the door. Despite their confrontation the previous evening, Lucian smiled as she approached. "I'm sorry, Jackson," she laughed at herself. "I couldn't find my house keys, and then I lost the card where I had written down the restaurant's name. I'm a mess today."

"It's okay." Ryder stood as she approached the table. He assisted her off with her wrap. "We were just getting ready to order."

"We?" She finally noticed Lucian half sprawled in the booth's other seat.

"This is Lucian Damron," Ryder said as he allowed Gillian to slide in on his side of the table.

A flash of repugnance preceded her hesitation. "We've met!"

"I forgot," Ryder laughed nervously. "You two were phenomenal last night. I rarely listen to that kind of crap, but you had the audience mesmerized. I actually paid attention for five or six minutes."

Lucian rolled his eyes. "Gee, that's comforting."

"You don't get it, Damron. I stopped watching you two and started watching everyone else watching you. The crowd couldn't get enough of your exchange."

"I'm happy we entertained you, Jackson." She reached for one of the honey-buttered hot rolls that the waiter placed on the table.

"Let us order, and then we have much to discuss." Rubbing the palms of his hands together in relish, Ryder offered them both a conspiratorial grin.

"You are joking!" Although he directed his words to Ryder, Lucian looked seriously at Gillian, trying to gauge her true response. "You expect Miss Cornell and me to move into a mountain resort with six couples for seven weeks."

Ryder finished off his glass of wine. "That's the gist of it."

"Nothing personal to Dr. Damron," the lady aimed half an apology in his direction, "but in case you didn't notice last evening, Jackson, the good doctor and I don't see eye-to-eye on how to treat our patients."

Her remarks should have offended him, but Lucian found the nearness of Gillian Cornell affected him in an unfamiliar way. He actually enjoyed watching the animated manner of this slender, petite woman. The restaurant's shadows cloaked the delicateness of her figure. When she had first sat down, Lucian had sucked in a stunned gasp, finally seeing Gillian up close and without distractions. Her auburn curls were gathered in a severe knot at her neck's nape, and her glasses continually slipped down to rest on her nose's tip. Yet, those glasses couldn't hide her eyes' pure cobalt of her eyes, the kind of eyes in which a man could lose himself and enjoy every minute.

The narrowing of those pools of blue color brought Lucian from his magnetic mist. Realizing he had stared at Gillian Cornell, he stammered, "Forgive...forgive me, did you say something?" Automatically, he offered up the smile he had used to charm his most critical opponents.

Unfortunately, his tantalizing enemy's gaze hardened. "See what I mean, Jackson. Dr. Damron finds me so inferior that he can't even pay attention for two minutes. His attention span is even shorter than yours!"

Deliberately, Lucian summoned a haughty manner, the one he knew would provoke a response from the lovely Gillian. "I assumed, Miss Cornell, that I could just wait to sniff you to see if we're compatible. No conversation is necessary."

Obviously ignoring his response, she confidently refused to rise to Lucian's bait, giving him an indifferent shrug instead. Meanwhile, with what could only be characterized as unchaste thoughts filtering across his mind, Lucian found himself lost in her eyes again. He held visions of Gillian arching beneath him in his bed.

"It is a wonder you have any business, Dr. Damron, if you treat all female clients as you treat me." Her dislike hadn't waned.

"I love it!" Jackson Ryder declared enthusiastically. "And so will the American public."

"Well, I'm afraid the American public will have to love only Dr. Damron. I have no intention of subjecting myself to such an ordeal."

Lucian snapped out of his revelry. "If this will earn me the talk show, I'll do it."

"Sell your soul to the devil?" she accused.

Lucian half chuckled with thoughts of how Gillian could hold her own with the devil himself.

"Look, you two, the bottom line is this. The network wants both of you *or* neither of you. Lucian, if you want the talk show, you'll build your fan base with *Second Chances*. Gillian, if you want the book deal, you'll sign on for the show."

"You're...you're serious?" Gillian stammered.

"The future contracts you want all hinge on your doing this show. Media groups control all the outlets. Either play their game or get out of the ballpark."

Jackson Ryder's words visibly stung Gillian's sensibilities. "I resent being blackmailed, Jackson."

"You can resent it all you want, but the bottom line is this: This is the best deal I can get you right now." Ryder opened his briefcase to find the paperwork. "I'll leave the two of you alone for a few minutes to discuss how you feel about the offer." Jackson slid from the booth and sauntered over to the bar.

Lucian shifted his weight in the seat to face Gillian head on. "Well, what will it be, Miss Cornell? Are you willing to sell your soul to the devil?"

"Wipe the smirk from your face, Dr. Damron." She leaned forward, a dark anger evident.

Lucian's expression hardened. "Why do you hate me, Miss Cornell?" he muttered before he could halt the words.

"I don't hate you, Dr. Damron; hate would mean that I thought about you, and I assure you, I never think of you."

Lucian chuckled lightly as if her cut actually amused him, when, in reality, it had stung sharply. "Maybe you should think of me; it seems we're about to commit to an exclusive seven weeks' relationship." He paused pointedly. "I don't hear your refusal any longer."

"I need this book deal." Gillian gave a rueful shake of her head, "But I don't think I can swing this."

The woman puzzled him. "Why not?"

"I've other responsibilities, Dr. Damron."

Lucian's voice softened. "You have a family then?" A voice grimly whispered in the back of his mind, *Please don't let her have someone she loves in her life.*

"I don't have a husband or kids if that's what you mean."

"Boyfriend?"

"Negative."

"Girlfriend?"

"Negative once again." Gillian flushed at his close inspection and his insinuation.

A smile touched Lucian's lips. "Then what's the problem?"

"It's really none of your business, Dr. Damron."

"Lucian," he corrected her.

The blue eyes stabbed him with a curious gaze. "Wh...what?" she stammered.

"Lucian. If we're going to work together we should be on a first name basis."

"Who said we're working together?"

"I intend to convince you," he said with an easy smile. "That is unless you've an objection."

"Certainly not. I just don't think I can do it. I can't be away from my home for that long a period of time," she confessed.

"Look. If you have an elderly parent or something like that, why can't you arrange some sort of extended care facility to take over until you return?"

"It's not that easy, Dr. Damron."

"Lucian."

"Lucian," she said awkwardly. "I really don't believe..."

"Miss Cornell, look at how much they're going to pay us." He shoved the contract across the table at her. "You could afford excellent care for your parent."

"Dr. Damron, there are some of us who think money to be the least of our motivations. The personal contact cannot have a price. I have struggled and sacrificed more than you or anyone else can imagine to reach my current status. I won't be bullied or coerced by you or the network execs."

Lucian wondered how she had suffered, and compassion, along with a fierce fury, spread through his heart. Crazy as the idea was, he wanted to protect her to make certain Gillian Cornell never felt pain again. He wanted her to genuinely smile at him–to be happy to see him–to have her eyes light up when he entered a room. "I assure you, Gillian Cornell, I have never bullied or coerced any woman into doing something she didn't want to do."

Gillian reached for her purse. "Please mind you own business, and we'll both be happy."

Lucian placed a hand on her arm to prevent her departure. "I'm sorry." A wry smile touched his lips. "We've gotten off to a bad start. I do need this new gig, and it seems you do also. How might we pull this off?"

Gillian settled into the seat; her anger no longer evident. "Sometimes, I allow my anxiousness to control my tongue," she offered as a form of apology. "Dr. Damron...Lucian, I can't give you a definite answer at this moment. The only thing I can say is I'll try. Really I will. What is my time frame for a final decision?"

"We'll ask Jackson to join us."

Lucian motioned Jackson Ryder to the table. "Do we have an agreement?" Ryder rubbed his hands together, evidently a favorite gesture.

"An agreement in theory," Lucian offered. "Gillian has some issues with which she must deal before she can commit to the contract. When must you give the TV execs an answer?"

"I could probably stall until the end of the week."

"Thanks, Jackson, I'll see what I can do; honestly, I will."

"May I call you later in the week for your answer?" Lucian asked as he signed the credit card receipt.

"That's not necessary." Gillian reached for her purse. "I'll let Jackson know one way or another."

"I'd still like the opportunity to speak to you." Lucian's eyes searched hers for Gillian's approval.

"Okay...sure," she stammered. "Call me on Thursday."

As he watched her rush away, Lucian couldn't abandon the feelings, which had possessed him regarding Gillian Cornell. Rarely had he allowed himself the pleasure of "approaching" a woman; usually, he fended off their advances rather than making his own. Yet, a frustrated need had speared him as the voice of reason rose to destroy his images of her. Lucian fully understood that he couldn't become involved with the likes of Gillian Cornell. A man committed himself to such a woman, and Lucian couldn't risk such a relationship. An intimate, loving relationship could only survive if honesty existed, and Lucian could never have an honest relationship. He held too many secrets, secrets, which could destroy his reputation: destroy him. He should maintain his casual relationship with Charlotte Blakeley; Gillian Cornell offered too many dangers. However, what his head knew and his heart felt were in sharp contrast.

～

"Your agent wants you to do what?" Handing him a brandy, Charlotte incredulously took a seat beside Lucian.

"The show involves six couples who were once married and are now divorced. The contest involves which ones should remarry and which ones should stay separated. It's called *Second Chances*. The contestants would be secluded from everyone for seven weeks. I tenderly call it *Survivor* meets *Dr. Phil.*"

"You're not seriously considering this?"

"If I want the talk show in the fall, then I do this reality show; that's the deal."

"What's your role in this mess?"

"I provide counseling sessions, conduct observations, and that sort of thing." Lucian leaned back against the sofa, trying to relax as Charlotte stroked the side of his jaw.

"All alone?" Charlotte leaned forward to nibble on his ear.

"No..." he cleared his throat. "There are at least two other psychologists in attendance. One of them will be Gillian Cornell."

Charlotte sat up suddenly to look at him closely. "Why Gillian Cornell? She's worthless!"

"Well, I wouldn't go that far. Gillian works hard at what she does," he said without thinking.

Charlotte's eyes flashed with jealousy. "Gillian?"

"We have the same agent," Lucian explained quickly. "In fact, the network won't take one of us without the other. That's part of the deal."

"When were you planning on telling me this?" she accused.

Lucian stood to refill his drink. "Nothing personal, Charley, but I don't require your permission to make this contract." He purposely turned back on her. "We don't have that type of relationship."

She charged, "When will we have *that* type of relationship?"

"Maybe tomorrow. Maybe never. You knew that about me when we hooked up. If you want something more, then maybe you should look elsewhere." Over the past seven years, Lucian had said those same lines to more than one woman. He and Charlotte Blakeley enjoyed each other's company, and Lucian held no desire to discontinue seeing her, but he held no true affection for the woman.

Charlotte swallowed her retort. In some ways, Lucian wished she hadn't. He despised women who clung to some intangible hope that they might change him. "I didn't mean it that way," she rushed her apology.

"Of course," he said finally. "If you don't mind, I think I'll go."

"Please don't leave." Urgency crept into her voice. Lucian hated the sound of desperation in a woman's voice.

Lucian caught her hand. "It's been a trying day; I just require some down time. This was probably a bad idea in the first place; I've too many loose ends to consider before this contract is finalized. I'll call you sometime tomorrow."

She reached for his arm. "You will call?" she pleaded.

"I said I would, didn't I?"

"Yes," she whispered.

"Then I'll call." He lightly kissed her cheek and quickly let himself from her suite of rooms in an upscale hotel.

Yet, three days passed before Lucian phoned Charlotte. He had wanted to emphasize her place in his life, and permitting Charlotte to worry over his attentions would solidify that position. When he finally did call, Lucian only talked for a few minutes before feigning a pressing phone call from one of his work colleagues. He didn't phone her again the rest of the week. Over the past few days, he had decided to break it off with Charlotte before he departed for the reality show retreat. "She has served her purpose," he said aloud to his reflection in the foyer's mirror. Her social connections had opened doors for him, doors, which might have stayed closed without her, but now he required space. As he could not commit to Gillian Cornell, Lucian wouldn't allow Charlotte into his life. If Charlotte Blakeley knew all his secrets, she would broadcast his shortcomings to the world. He thought a woman like Gillian Cornell would stand beside him, but "Charlotte would find me quite repulsive," he concluded. "They are two different types, and neither is for me."

Lucian had waited until Wednesday before he sought out Gillian again. Having Goggled her name, he had spent several days discovering all he could of her. He knew, for example, where she had attended school, her recognitions, and her other accomplishments. He knew where she had lived, even succumbing to the temptation of using a satellite program to actually look at her residence. He felt a bit voyeuristic, but it didn't stop him from searching. When he discovered how both of Gillian's parents had died in a plane crash, a melancholy rushed over him. He had known her parents, and now he wondered why he had never made the connection; Lucian allowed fond memories of family to invade his most private moments. Her parents were well known for their social conscience. He thought it peculiar that she had led him to believe the reason she couldn't do the reality show had involved the health of a parent; yet, when he replayed the conversation in his mind, he realized that he had initiated the idea, and Gillian simply hadn't corrected him. Now Lucian wondered the real reason for her hesitation.

Planning to run some errands before her university lecture on the subject of MHC, Gillian stepped onto the busy street. Digging for her keys in her purse, an action, which plagued her several times per day, her attentions skipped a beat when Lucian suddenly stepped before her. "Dr. Damron," she gasped, reaching for her heart as if frightened.

"Lucian. Please call me Lucian." He reached out instinctively to steady her stance.

"Lu..Lucian," she flustered. "What are you doing here?"

"I know this is presumptuous on my part, but I wanted to see if there might be something I can do to help you settle your issues."

"How did you know where I lived?" she asked suspiciously.

Lucian smiled amusedly. "I am afraid I purposely found out what I could about you. I thought if we're to work together, it might be easier if we knew something besides what the lecture circuit told us."

"I suppose I should be flattered, but it's a bit disconcerting to know a stranger could find such personal information so easily."

"I was a bit tenacious in my efforts," he admitted before releasing his hold.

"I appreciate your concern, but I'm accustomed to handling my own problems," she announced.

Dr. Damron smiled, and Gillian realized it was a powerful one. *Deep-set dimples. Like those found on Clark Gable. God! To be the recipient of that smile on a regular basis would be heavenly.* "Of course, I have overstepped my boundaries; I apologize for intruding upon your privacy," he said dutifully.

"I am not offended, Doctor...I mean, Lucian." Gillian placed her purse across her shoulder. "I have taken care of my responsibilities, and I believe I'll be able to meet the contract. I just have a few small details to clarify, but now, if you'll excuse me, I must be at the university for a lecture soon." She looked around to hail a cab.

Lucian, realizing her intention, added quickly, "I've my car with me; might I give you a lift?"

"I wouldn't want you to go out of your way on my account." Gillian's eyes finally met his, and a tingle of anticipation rushed through her.

"I've nothing else planned, and it would provide me great pleasure to spend time with you." Lucian caught her elbow to lead Gillian to his waiting car.

The relatively short drive to the university didn't allow for much conversation, but Lucian used it to his advantage. "What's the lecture on?" he asked as he maneuvered through traffic.

"MHC."

"Is that the subject of your upcoming book?"

"It's a large portion of it, but there's more hard core honesty than many psychology based offerings currently on the market." A lull in the conversation ensued. Finally, she asked about the possibility of a talk show for him.

"It's my chance to market myself; I had hoped for something more along the lines of *Dr. Phil.* I want to take the high road—no fist fights, married siblings, or anything like that." Lucian turned to her suddenly. "Would you have lunch with me?"

Gillian stammered, "Lucian...I...I don't know whether that is wise."

"Why not? I'm not asking for an intimate evening. We'll have lunch and get to know each other. That's all I'm asking."

"I have the lecture."

"I'll sit in the back and listen. Then we can spend a leisurely lunch."

Lucian watched her closely. He could see the moment of indecision swaying in his favor, and he relished the idea. Finally, an aggravated sigh escaped her lips as she grudgingly turned to meet his gaze. "If you insist."

"Good." His eyes lit with anticipation. "Thank you, Gillian."

Good to his word, Lucian had sat in the shadows at the back of the auditorium, but that didn't keep him from Gillian Cornell's thoughts as she worked her way through the afternoon lecture series. "So, what makes two people fall in love?" she asked as she stepped from the podium and into the audience. "Have you ever been in love?" She thrust the microphone before the face of an obviously bleach-blonde co-ed.

"Sure," the girl's gum snapped as she answered.

"How did you know?"

"He was hot!" The crowd roared with laughter.

"Ooh, lust," Gillian purred. "Isn't it exhilarating?"

The girl giggled nervously. "Yeah, hot!"

"How about shared goals? Mutual interests?" Gillian moved on to an older grad student.

"Without that," he said what he thought she wanted to hear, "the sex is useless."

Gillian teased, "Well, I wouldn't go that far," she said seductively. "However, what if I told you an olfactory nerve discovered in a whale could be the real source of a person's attraction?" This time she turned to a jock type.

"You mean I just need to smell my girlfriend to find out if we're in love?" The guy blushed when his obvious girlfriend playfully slugged his shoulder.

Gillian's eyes rose to where Lucian sat in the shadows. "An esteemed colleague asked me a similar question recently." An enigmatic smile played across her countenance. "But the truth is a bit more complicated." Gillian returned to the stage to continue her thoughts.

"The truth is Nerve O has endings in the nasal cavity, but those nerve endings play a different role from what we might expect. Nerve O doesn't smell out the person to whom we're attracted, but it does identify sexual cues from all the thousands of potential lovers we meet on a daily basis. Family members, logically, have a similar chemical make up. That is nature's way of protecting close family members from procreating as we seek out those with a different chemical program."

"Unless you live in the South." A voice from the rear of the audience shared a bit too loudly.

"Hey, I went to school in the South," Gillian countered, shooting down the laughter before it began. "Nerve O also can be a cue to fertility issues, miscarriage, and infidelity. If your partner has similar chemicals, such problems may occur. This is where the old adage of opposites attract comes into play. And loading up on your favorite cologne won't change your love life, no matter what all the commercials tell you; our scents are natural and instinctive. You can't change the code. My last caution is to the females in the audience. Although I applaud your responsibility in choosing birth control, if you're sexually active, you must remember that birth control changes your hormonal makeup, simulating pregnancy, and, therefore, making your body seek out those with similar chemical programs, like family kinship, and not potential mates. Your choices for successful love may be affected by the pill."

A nervous giggle encompassed those in the room. "Before I leave you with this last lecture in the series, I wish to thank you for your participation in the program." A light round of applause spread across the room, but Gillian raised her hand to let them know she still required their attention. "I have contracted to do something else in the fall so I won't be a part of the series when you return to classes; I won't see many of you until the spring semester."

"Where you going?" A dark-headed prep shouted from the front rows.

Gillian glanced at Lucian once again. She hesitated before she offered an explanation. "Dr. Lucian Damron, whom I am certain many of you have noted in the lecture hall today, and I are working on a joint national campaign. That is all I am at liberty to tell you at the moment, but you'll be hearing about it before long." Gillian motioned for Lucian to come to the front. "Please welcome Dr. Damron. If you've questions for either of us, we'll be glad to address them."

Lucian self-consciously came forward as the audience applauded. He hugged Gillian quickly as he took the hand-held microphone from her and turned to face those gathered in the lecture hall. "How does she smell, Doc?" A sniggering voice penetrated the silence.

"Like roses," he responded with a light laugh.

Gillian corrected, "Actually, it's lavender."

"Well, that shows you I've no sense of smell." Lucian looked at Gillian with an amused smile. Then he turned to the crowd. "Are there any questions I *can* answer?"

For the next twenty minutes, they fielded psychology-based questions from those in attendance. During these brief moments, his admiration for Gillian Cornell continued to grow. She possessed a natural ease, which few could claim. People gravitated to her; they sought her opinions. Instead of finding her contentious, as he had first assumed her to be, Lucian realized how much she fascinated him. And that realization shook his world to the core.

Chapter Two

LUCIAN ESCORTED GILLIAN to one of his favorite Italian restaurants, not one where he normally took his "women," but one he frequented with friends. They ate, talked, laughed, and sat quietly enjoying each other's company.

"This has been a pleasant afternoon," Gillian offered as she sipped her wine.

Lucian saluted her with his glass. "You honor me." He automatically used one of his favorite come-on lines, but immediately felt a twinge of regret at doing so.

However, Gillian didn't respond as most of his previous tablemates might do. She ignored Lucian's seductive tone and continued their "academic" banter. "You went to school in California?" she asked, leaning forward in interest.

"Yeah. I earned all three degrees within a hundred-mile radius of home. What about you?"

"Obviously, I don't have my Ph.D., but both my bachelor's and master's came from the University of Georgia."

"Why no doctorate?" he wondered out loud.

"Couldn't afford to–too many responsibilities–not enough hours–too expensive." Her honesty shocked Lucian; people who regularly announced their own greatness had become his acquaintances. Gillian Cornell didn't fit that description.

Lucian refilled his wine glass and offered some more to her. "May I ask," he began, "to what responsibilities you refer? When we met with Jackson I thought you had ailing parents, but then I discovered your parents died in a plane crash." He let his voice rise in question.

Gillian didn't want to answer him, but she abhorred liars, and she wasn't a very good one. She valued two things in her life: her privacy and her independence. Now, she foolishly allowed a flamboyant man to question both. She instinctively knew she should keep Lucian Damron at arm's length, but when she looked into his eyes, she saw something she thought she could trust as being real. "This is not something of which I share easily; it is very difficult for me. I lost both of my parents six years ago. They were two of the most compassionate people God ever placed on this planet. They had tried for years to have a child of their own, but to no avail. When their hopes went unfulfilled, they opened their home to foster children. At one time or another over one hundred different abused or neglected children lived under our roof. We never had less than a half dozen in residence at any time. Then seven years into their love fest with "state" children, my mother found herself pregnant, with me. I was brought up in a house full of love, but that ended tragically with their deaths."

"My deepest sympathies." Gillian recognized a moment of regret, which crossed his countenance. "I can see how you are moved by their loss."

For a moment she hesitated, noting real concern in his voice, but Gillian wouldn't tell Lucian the whole truth of her life. Hers wasn't the kind of secret to which men readily took, and Lucian's quiet sincerity brought tears to her eyes. She took another sip of wine to busy herself. "What about your family?" she asked to distract him.

Lucian paused momentarily, but then he delivered his well-rehearsed reply. "My parents are both deceased, and I've no brothers or sisters. Where your parents were benevolent, mine were control freaks. I never ventured out much as a child. They home schooled me. I can count on one hand how many parties and gatherings I attended throughout my youth. I'm lucky therapy works, or you would be looking at one messed up guy."

"Then you're not messed up, Dr. Damron?" Gillian mocked.

A half smile played with the corners of his mouth. "No more than the average American male."

"Then the Lord knows you're beyond help." Gillian's taunt earned her a full smile.

"We'll see about that, Miss Cornell."

The remainder of the meal passed in joined congeniality. When Lucian escorted Gillian home, they had tarried in his car before saying their farewells. "Thank you, Lucian, for one of the most enjoyable days I've had in a long time."

"It's I who should be thanking you. It's been too long since I've been in the university classroom, and I had forgotten the exhilaration found there. Follow that with intelligent conversation, and the day was complete." Lucian turned his head to look carefully at Gillian Cornell. In that moment, he knew he wanted her, but not necessarily purely in a sexual way. Although he desired her body, he wanted other things, intangible things from her.

"I suppose I should go." Gillian reached in the back seat for her purse and laptop. "Thank you again, Lucian. I'll see you soon."

He caught her arm just as she reached for the door. "Would you have dinner with me on Friday night?"

Gillian bit her lower lip. "Why, Lucian?"

"Why not? You must eat; I must eat; we enjoy each other's company—all of the above." He noted how Gillian nervously shifted in her seat. "A relaxing dinner is all I ask, Gillian."

"Lucian, this afternoon was great fun, but I don't understand why you're giving me so much attention." She flushed. "I've seen the type of women with whom you associate. I'm not them."

A slight smile curled his lips. "Maybe I'm trying to seduce you, Gillian."

She pleaded, "Lucian, be serious, please."

"What's wrong, Gillian, has no man ever seduced you?" His self-assurance dripped into his speech. He had no right to pursue her. Lucian held too much baggage to even consider a woman like Gillian Cornell, but the elusive "carrot before the horse" syndrome had lodged quite solidly in his heart.

"Of course, I've had...I've had several...I've had serious relationships!"

"Then you'll know when mine turns *serious*," he challenged.

Every sense inside him sharpened as he waited for her response. The woman had already made inroads into his psyche. He watched a full gamut of emotions sweep across her face, but then he saw the softening in her eyes, and Lucian breathed a bit easier. He would win this test of wills. "Explain to me why you want to spend time with me, Lucian, and please tell me the truth."

He laughed. "I like you, Gillian. I enjoyed our day, and I want to know you better. Plus, we agreed it would make our time on the show easier." He knew he was in over his head, but Lucian thought it a lovely way to die.

"Friday night, then," she said reluctantly. "We'll see what happens after that."

When Lucian opened the door to his apartment, finding Charlotte on his threshold took him unawares. "Charlotte, what a pleasant surprise."

She stepped past him, and her expensive perfume left a trail where she had walked, wafting over him when she stopped to caress his jaw line. "I've missed you, Lucian." She kissed his cheek before indicating he should close the door.

He followed her into his living room and watched as she settled her leggy form on the love seat. "Charlotte, you should call before you come here," he reprimanded.

"I called, but you didn't answer my voice mails." Charlotte crossed her legs, purposely pausing to give him a glimpse of her upper thighs before closing them again.

"I will call when I'm ready to see you." Never coming near her, Lucian still stood in the doorway.

"It's that Cornell woman, isn't it?" Charlotte's tone changed to accusation.

Lucian returned her anger. "That, dear Charlotte, is none of your business."

She stood at that point. "I saw how you looked at her after the conference. You couldn't remove your eyes from her."

Lucian smiled with a remembrance of Gillian Cornell's eyes. "Again, Charlotte, whom I see is my business. Miss Cornell and I are scheduled to complete a program together; I told you that before."

Charlotte walked to where he stood; she laced her arms around his neck, but Lucian offered her no encouragement. "She's out of your league," she hissed.

"I know." He refused to look at her.

"Then why are you putting yourself through this?" Charlotte's mouth was inches from his face. "Take what's here and now."

"She's different." This time Lucian turned to look at her.

"It won't happen. Those types never fall for people like us."

"People like us?" Lucian didn't understand.

Charlotte smiled deviously. "Users. That's what we are—you and I. Users. We use other people; we use each other." She caressed his cheek once again as she leaned closer. "I don't mind being used." The heat of her breath lingered on his neck.

"I'm not in the mood, Charlotte." Lucian's voice held no regret.

She rested her hand on his chest. "Are you certain?"

"I'm certain. Good night, Charlotte."

"Call me when it falls apart." Charlotte kissed along his jaw line. "It will fall apart, Lucian."

"I know."

When she opened the door to Lucian, Gillian couldn't help but notice how roguishly handsome he was. "Good evening, Gillian." Those were the words he offered, but the tone involved closeness and warmth and intimacy. "Are you ready?"

Ready for what she wondered as she allowed him to lead her to his car. He clasped her hand in his as they went down the steps. "Where are we off to?"

"Some place special." He whispered into her ear as he held the door for her. Gillian felt a rush of heat spread through her entire body.

"I imagine, Dr. Damron, you make all those in your presence feel special." Gillian looked up at him with wide, innocent eyes.

"As long as you feel special, Miss Cornell, I'll be happy." He hovered over her as he braced her hand, and she pivoted in the seat to bring her legs into the car.

They had dined in a French restaurant known for its fine wine and exquisite cuisine. The bartender and waitress knew his name, calling out, "Hey, Doc D," upon his entrance. The hostess showed them to a darkened booth.

"It seems you are a regular," Gillian spoke with genuine pleasure, taking on a teasing tone with him.

"But I've never brought someone else here," he confessed.

"Not even that wisp of a woman clinging to your neck at the conference?" Gillian could not stifle her curiosity.

Lucian laughed, a low, husky, seductive laugh. "I am flattered, Miss Cornell; I thought you didn't notice me."

Gillian felt her insides quiver as he leveled a taunting smile on her. "I noticed, Lucian. How could I not? Every time I turned my head you were staring at me. At first, I thought I had something embarrassing like toilet paper stuck to my shoe, but then I couldn't resist returning your interest. You'll find that I love a challenge." She had told herself before he had called that she would not fantasize. If anything were to happen between them, it would first start with honesty.

"I guess I was pretty obvious." He looked a bit shamefaced, something definitely out of character for him, and then he gifted her with a full smile. *Those dimples again. Damn!*

The man across from her sent chills through Gillian. She sucked in a breath, afraid to release it. Lucian's mouth, so perfectly masculine, fascinated her. He sat relaxed against the booth's backing–sturdy and strong, muscular in every way. He came off as a bit arrogant, but she suspected that he had a right to be so. Lucian was strikingly handsome. "I wonder what you thought of me that night."

Her bluntness had taken him by surprise, and he hesitated, apparently collecting his thoughts or rehearsing his lines. Gillian wasn't certain which, and that fact troubled her more than anything else about this "date." Finally, he caught her hand in his, engulfing hers and intertwining their fingers. "I thought you were perfectly beautiful and perfectly insensitive to the fact."

Gillian's eyes dropped with his words, and she played with the band of his watch. "Please cease with the flattery, Lucian. I own a mirror, and I know where I rank beside women like your friend that evening."

"Nonsense!" he demanded.

His gaze fixed on her mouth, and Gillian found it hard to swallow. She eyed him, discomfited–afraid to withdraw her gaze from his. Lucian made her feel all out of kilter, thoughtfully aching. "Lucian, I don't want to play games; I'm level headed and independent," she whispered hoarsely.

"Who says I'm playing?"

"Of course, you're playing; you can't help yourself. Men like you have their way with women; it's natural for you," she tried to convince herself as much as him.

"Is that how you actually see me?" He looked fiendishly irreverent.

She reasoned, "You do have quite a reputation, Lucian."

"I find it hard to believe that you would give such rumors credit." Playfully, he reached out to trace her jaw line.

His gesture sent fire through Gillian. "What should I believe then?"

"Upon whatever both your heart and your mind agree. Do you think I could hurt you, Gillian?" Lucian offered an enticing, sensual smile.

Swallowing hard, she said, "Not on purpose. But I am quite certain you'll hurt me, Lucian. It's in your nature." She witnessed the effects of her words in the slump of his shoulders, and somehow that pained her.

Lucian became more alert. The teasing tone had disappeared. "Then you'll refuse to see where this takes us."

Gillian paused. Her heart pounded so hard that she didn't understand how he couldn't hear it. What would he say if she did refuse? Yet, both of them knew she wouldn't. "We'll take it slow."

"How slow?" he taunted.

"Very slow." Instinctively, Gillian imagined being spirited away by Lucian Damron. Being in his arms. Having him touch her intimately. It might be a slow trip–a slow trip to heaven.

⌒

"Gillian, hi, it's Lucian." He lay across his bed. "I hope I'm not disturbing you." He had waited for two days before calling, but it had taken all his will to do so.

"No, it's okay; I'm just beginning to unwind for the evening."

"Did you have a busy day?"

"The usual weekend errands–you know what I mean."

Lucian loved the sound of her voice over the phone. He had anticipated speaking to Gillian all day. The past few nights he had slept restlessly, waking often. Her voice had created a need in his body; he could have Charlotte or any other of half dozen different women; yet, finding solace with another woman didn't interest him; he wanted Gillian Cornell. "Yeah, I know. What did you do?"

"You really don't want all the boring details," she teased.

"You'd be surprised."

Nearly two hours later, Lucian realized he should allow her to hang up, but he didn't want to break the connection. However, he could hear Gillian yawning on the other end of the line. "I suppose we should say good night."

Gillian admitted, "It's been a long day."

"Good night, then." Reluctantly, Lucian ended the call. Thoughts of Gillian had consumed him; he wanted to get past this masquerade in which he found himself. He wanted to learn something of the woman beneath. To see if Gillian could learn to care for him. *Could she care for the man he was and not the image he let others see?* Pausing, he considered the avalanche of feelings she had created in him. *Could I be seriously considering of a life-long connection to Gillian?* She never pretended, and he was a walking "pretense." *Am I capable of nurturing the love of such a woman?* "Damn it to hell!" With an inarticulate growl, he wrapped himself in the bed linens and dreamed of Gillian Cornell.

On Tuesday morning the mail brought her a surprise in the form of an invitation to sit in a private box at the Kentucky Derby. The invitation had indicated that the show's producers owned the box; Gillian had never expected such luxury. Before she could digest what this meant, her cell rang. "Hi, Lucian," she sounded out of breath.

"Did you receive an invitation to Kentucky?" Lucian's voice shared her anticipation.

"Did you know about this?" For a split second, she wondered if he had manipulated her.

"It's a surprise to me too. You'll come, though?" he pleaded.

Gillian trembled inside; his voice did that to her. She cocked her head to one side, listening carefully for what he didn't say. "I don't know, Lucian. It doesn't seem proper. I'm thrilled by the opportunity, but you and I going off together just doesn't seem right."

"I'm not certain the producers would be happy if we refused. To me, the invitation seemed more like a summons. Maybe we should check with Ryder before either of us refuse. Remember, we're a packaged deal." A pang of regret stabbed her chest.

"I've always wanted to go to the Derby," Gillian said wistfully.

"We'll have fun; I promise." Lucian's voice encouraged her to accept. "Please come."

His tone made her heart turn flip-flops. Gillian swallowed hard, literally shuddering with delight. "If Jackson says we should go, then I'll go."

"Good," Lucian began, "if you had refused, I'd have to kidnap you and take you to some place secluded."

Gillian giggled nervously. "You jest!"

"Do I?" Lucian's voice took on his usual seductive tone. God only knew what his tone did to her private places.

The image conjured up by the insinuation in Lucian's voice caused Gillian to catch at her breath. She suppressed the warming sensation moving through her body. "We have to be aware and avoid a scandal. The producers want us as opponents, not as friends."

"I don't want to be your enemy, Gillian. In fact, I want to be more than friends."

Gillian wondered what it would be like to be with such a man as Lucian Damron. She had never considered such a thought. She had always assumed she would choose a man of sensibility. Of course, she had wanted someone attractive, but she had never expected to consider choosing eye candy, and Lucian was definitely eye candy. Her priorities had lain in companionable contentment. Lust and passion didn't exist in her world. However, with Lucian, Gillian could easily imagine taking pleasure in his arms. *It might be interesting to practice what I preach.* "Agreed. But you must promise not to try anything."

"I'll do no more than you feel comfortable."

Carefully choosing her wardrobe, Gillian had anticipated the trip. A svelte, clinging floral print dress and coordinating hat had created quite a stir. A pale blue colored frock. It had amplified her breast line while minimizing her waist. The off the shoulder design had caressed the softness of her creamy skin. "Wow!" Lucian gasped when he had seen her. They had agreed to meet at the track rather than traveling together. "You are breathtaking!"

Gillian had prayed for this reaction. Although they had spoken on the phone daily and had enjoyed a couple of leisurely lunches, almost two weeks had passed since they had gone on their "date," and Gillian had wondered if Lucian's interest had waned. Yet, when they met, his eyes had assessed every inch of her, searching her face before settling on the fullness of her breast. "Shall we find our seats?" Childishly, she felt joyous just being on Lucian's arm.

He led her to the seating enclosure. "You look delicious," Lucian whispered into her ear as he assisted her to her seat. "You sparkle; a man could get lost in the vibrancy of your eyes." He handed her a tall tulip-shaped glass filled with the traditional mint julep. "Upon which horse do we bet?" Lucian asked as he seated himself beside her.

"I've never made a bet." Gillian laughed nervously. "I wouldn't know how."

Lucian took the lead. "Let's use some of your woman's intuition. We'll make small bets on each race; it'll be fun, and we won't lose our shirts." Without having a clue as to what she was doing, Lucian allowed Gillian to pick horses in each race. Generally, she scanned the names on the list before choosing one based on her gut feeling. "What about in the last race?" Lucian teased.

"I want Tonka."

"Why?"

"The animal is named after the only survivor of Custer's last stand. There's got to be a significance in that."

"You amaze me." He brought her fingers to his lips and kissed the back of her hand. "I'll place the bets and then be right back."

The bright-jewel silks of the jockeys peppered the emerald green of the field. Lucian, looking debonair in a black suit and perfectly coiffed hair, slid back into the seat holding a handful of betting tickets. "Are you ready for some excitement?" The sensation found lurking in his voice alerted her.

Gillian unconsciously emitted a soft groan. "I've never done anything like this."

"Then it's about time, Gillian Cornell, that you start treating yourself better. You take on everyone else's responsibilities and leave no time for yourself. You deserve some of the good things in life." Lucian's voice reminded Gillian of how the serpent in the Garden of Eden must have sounded to Eve, but try as she may, Gillian could no more resist Lucian than Eve could the snake. "I'd like to see you truly happy this weekend." Lucian whispered softly in her ear.

"Well, here's our two newest celebrities," Sam Cuttles, one of the TV execs said as he and his wife slid into the seats before Gillian and Lucian. "We're glad the two of you could join us." He made the appropriate introductions.

"We're happy to be here; this was most generous of you to include Miss Cornell and me." Lucian's fine-tuned manners took over.

"We expect great things from you two. Now don't get too cozy during this weekend; we need that spark between you for the show. We're banking on your arguing about how to treat the couples we've chosen."

"Don't worry, Mr. Cuttles, Miss Cornell and I know what's expected. We can still respect each other as people and disagree on medical procedures." Lucian allowed his knee to rest against Gillian's as an indication he said only the words the execs wanted to hear.

Their attention was drawn to a coal-black filly with a star-shaped white marking on its muscular hindquarter. "She's beautiful," Gillian gasped. As if the horse could hear her, it strutted when it came directly in Gillian's sight lines.

"Rising Star might be a pretty piece of horse flesh, but she's a long shot at best. She barely made the cut." Sam Cuttles belittled Gillian's lack of knowledge.

"We certainly hope you're wrong, Mr. Cuttles," Lucian gave him an amused smile, "because Miss Cornell and I've a small bet resting on Rising Star."

"Then be prepared to lose your money," Cuttles added incredulously.

"We'll see." Lucian squeezed her hand. "Anything can happen." A thrill ran through Gillian. Horses continued to parade through the ring, circling before entering the chutes, but her senses remained on the man at her elbow.

"They're off!" Cuttles's wife yelled as the chutes finally opened. Lucian pulled Gillian directly before him, resting his hands on her waist. "You can see best from here," he whispered into her ear and then handed her his binoculars. "You deserve a close up of your first race," he said a bit louder in case anyone listened to his conversation.

Rising on her tiptoes to get a better look, Gillian placed the binoculars to her eyes. Almost as if in slow motion the scene enfolded before her. Clods of dirt flew from the horses' hoofs as they pounded their way around the track. The jockeys rode with fluidity, synchronizing their movements with those of the horses. The crowd roared with excitement. "Rising Star is in the lead pack," Lucian spoke to Gillian alone. Then, caught up in the excitement, they both screamed and danced around. Lucian pumped his arms, urging the horse toward the finish line, and Gillian squirmed about like a new puppy. But, all the cheering was for naught. Although she took third, Rising Star didn't win.

"I told you," Cuttles smirked, "although I admit your horse did better than expected. Unfortunately, I picked the real winner." He waved his winning ticket in the air.

Gillian looked dejectedly at Lucian. "I'm sorry; you should never let me choose." Tears welled in her eyes. "I'll pay you back what you lost."

"First, I would never take your money; I'm not that sort of man. Neither am I a serious gambler. When I bet, it's within my range. Plus, who says we lost. I placed a 'show' bet, and with Rising Star's odds, you and I, Miss Cornell, made a few hundred each."

Gillian eyes grew in size. "We won?" she nearly shouted.

With a conspiratorial tone clearly in his voice, Lucian's remarkable composure showed. "I am afraid we did."

Gillian squealed, and before Lucian realized what she did, she jumped in his arms, lacing her hands around his neck. He lifted her to him and kissed her lightly on the cheek. It was a quick show of affection, but not uncommon among the audience in the viewing stands. Yet, their eyes locked and held for a long moment before he sat her on the ground again.

"Congratulations, Miss Cornell," Cuttles intoned, "it seems you're extremely lucky." He excused himself to claim his winnings.

Lucian leaned across where he could speak to her alone. "Extremely lucky and extremely beautiful. It is nice to see you smiling, Sweetling."

She laughed nervously, but Lucian thought he had never heard anything so musically perfect. "Thank you, Lucian, for sharing this with me. This was phenomenal."

"The weekend isn't over; we still have more first time experiences to share."

Gillian felt a flush creep up her neck at his brazen words, but she summoned her nerve and gazed into his eyes for a long, private moment. "We said slow, Lucian." The words nearly stuck in her throat.

Lucian instinctively lifted his hand and touched two fingers to her temple and slowly drew them down her cheek, letting the warmth linger on her jaw line. Her breathing stopped, and his became suddenly labored. "We're involved whether we want to be or not, Gillian, and believe me, I'm trying to take this slow." The sunlight, quite unceremoniously, shone directly on them. Then he withdrew his hand and resettled himself into the seats. "We should claim our winnings. Do you have any preferences as to what you would like to do this evening?"

"Could we celebrate some place special? Besides wanting to spend time with you, I want this to be a night different from other nights." Gillian felt very bold admitting her interest to Lucian.

"Did you bring an evening dress?"

"Yes, I think I've something appropriate. What did you have in mind?"

"Jackson says the network is having a Derby party tonight. We could go; we've been invited. They'll be lots of celebrities and lights. I thought you might like that; it's definitely different."

"Do we have to socialize with TV people?"

Lucian slid an arm around her waist, pulling Gillian closer. "Not if you don't want to."

"I don't want to. I want to spend my time with you." As he tightened his hold on her, Gillian thought her heart had stopped the world's spin, and only the two of them existed.

Lucian knocked lightly on the door to Gillian's hotel room. They had rooms only a few doors apart on the same floor. When Gillian opened hers, Lucian nursed the desire to scoop her into his arms and carry her to the bed. "Gorgeous," he declared freely.

Gillian's dress of royal blue silk and lace left her shoulders bare, falling in soft folds to a princess length in the front and an inverted train in the back. Her hair hung loose, and she wore a single pearl-drop diamond necklace, which caressed the indentation of her neck. "Do you approve?"

"I may have to fight off more than one gentleman tonight."

"Don't tease me, Lucian. I have never dress up like this. It frightens me to think we'll be hobnobbing with celebrities. I'll be thankful not to shame you."

It was charming in a way. Her not understanding how strikingly beautiful she was. "You may, Miss Cornell, speak to other gentlemen tonight, but you must remember you are mine, and you will wound me greatly if you give your regard elsewhere."

His declaration sent of jolt of panic across her countenance, but she announced with a false bravado, "I believe I will be perfectly satisfied to give you my complete attention, Dr. Damron." She offered him a full, beautiful smile.

Her face lay only inches from his; the corners of his mouth curved up a fraction, and then his grin deepened. "If you're satisfied, then I'll be satisfied."

Chapter Three

THEY WALKED THE CARPETED entrance to the private venue. Surrounded by television personalities, Gillian giggled. "I feel like a real star."

"You're more beautiful than most of them, and who knows, by this time next year, you and I could be household names." Lucian cupped her hand and held it tightly in the crook of his arm. He felt her arm tense. "Relax, Sweetling, I've got you."

"I'm counting on that," she whispered.

They sat close together, speaking quietly only to one another. The room had overflowed with celebrities and wannabes. Normally, Lucian would work this room, turning on his natural charm to play to people's vanities and to find a way to use them. He had learned those finely tuned skills since the passing of his infamous *friend.* He had learned when to smile and when to flatter. Yet, tonight was different for him. Lucian wanted only to speak to Gillian.

"Hey, you two," Jackson Ryder sauntered over.

Lucian stood and shook the man's hand. "Nice to see you, Jackson."

"I've been watching you, Lucian, for well over five minutes, and I don't think you particularly care to see or to speak to anyone but Miss Cornell." Gillian blushed fully with his words. "It's good to note you two getting along at last."

"Do you have a problem with our spending time together?" Lucian accused defensively.

"Personally, no. However, the execs liked the way you mixed it up at the conference. That's what they bought."

"So they sent you over to warn us not to be friends," Gillian protested. "I resent the implication, Jackson!"

"Easy, Gillian, Your personal life is yours. In fact, if things work out, I'll take my ten percent of your children. I admit I've no scruples; they're not assets for an agent."

"We assured Cuttles earlier today that we know what is expected for the show. We'll meet our legal obligations." Lucian took Gillian's hand in his.

Jackson lowered his voice. "The show's success depends on your opposition."

"We understand, Jackson. Now if you'll excuse us, Gillian and I were about to take a turn on the dance floor."

"Sure, Lucian," Jackson called to their retreating forms.

Lucian gathered Gillian close to him. The tension remained from their confrontation with Jackson. "Forget him," Lucian whispered.

"Dare we?" Gillian allowed her eyes to drift to Lucian's face.

"Didn't you once tell me the personal contact was more important than the money?"

Gillian smiled. "I didn't think you paid attention to what I said."

Lucian gave her a secretive smile. "I assure you, Sweetheart, there is very little about you of which I take no note."

Gillian instinctively moved closer to him, allowing her body to mold to his. He could hear her heart beat erratically as he allowed his hands to drift to her hips, pulling her closer still. A little shiver ran through her. She fit perfectly against his form, as though God had created her for him. Without considering what she did, Gillian snuggled into his chest, and waves of desire made his mouth go dry. Lucian rested his cheek next to her hair. "You smell so good." He allowed the music to take them where they wanted to go, swaying rhythmically. She openly trembled again, and Lucian noted her breathing changed. "Gillian..." he rasped.

"Lucian, please don't," her voice barely audible as she closed her eyes to the desire flooding both of them.

"Look at me, Gillian."

Her eyes to met the intensity of his gaze. "I can't...I can't."

"That's funny," his voice held seductive overtones, "for I can't remove my eyes from your form."

Slowly, her eyes caressed his face. Lucian wanted to kiss her so badly; her sparkling eyes entranced him. He ached to touch her. "May we leave soon?" Lucian swallowed hard.

She didn't respond, but she released her hold on him and turned decisively to the exit. Catching up to her, Lucian draped his arm over her shoulder as he maneuvered the way through the crowd, but once outside, Gillian slid her arm around his waist and rested her head against his shoulder. They walked the three blocks to their hotel. Neither of them spoke; truth was, Lucian was lost to the anticipation of Gillian's next move. Finally, entering the elevator, Gillian reached for the floor button without thinking. The rapid rush of their ascent caught them both off guard; the movement threw her into his arms, and Lucian steadied himself by grasping the side railing. Impulsively, he reached over her shoulder and hit the "stop" button. The elevator lurched to a halt.

"Lucian?" her voice rose in inflection.

"I must kiss you, Gillian." Moments hung–unmoving, until he lowered his mouth to hers. Chaos and desire raged through him. Just as he predicted, the kiss was perfection. He couldn't resist the texture and heat of her mouth.

Sweet heaven! He squeezed her buttocks gently, as Gillian unconsciously clawed at his chest to get closer. On and on they kissed, his tongue exploring her mouth–long and deep. He felt his erection buck against her, but Lucian had no shame. He pressed her against the side of the elevator and ground his hips harder. He wanted desperately to touch her–to feel her soft skin under his fingers–to caress her breasts. To bury his face in her soft auburn hair. Finally, their lips parted, his hovering lightly above hers. "So good," he whispered huskily. He held her close, and Gillian rested her head on his chest. Her breathing came in ragged spurts against the underside of his jaw. Lucian caressed her neck before releasing the "stop" button. He stared at the flashing number lights as they moved closer to their floor.

The door glided open, and they stepped into the carpeted hallway. Lucian held her hand and reluctantly led Gillian to her door. He found it amusing how she fumbled in her evening bag for her key card until Lucian took mercy on her and pulled Gillian close for a kiss her. He tipped her chin upward, kissing her gently this time. When he withdrew,

Gillian spoke the words he had desperately wanted to hear. "Do you want to come in?"

At first, Lucian had no voice with which to respond. A nod of his head was all he could manage. He accepted the key card from her trembling fingers, swiping it and opening the door fully. Stepping inside, they stood by the closed door, neither of them taking a step into the room. It was a minute before he could find his voice. "This is awkward," he said at last.

"Please have a seat." She motioned to the pillow-endowed love seat. Removing his jacket and tossing it across the back of a chair, Lucian settled himself on the furniture. He sat back, laced his fingers behind his head, and closed his eyes as if getting comfortable, but he was anything but. The friction between him had Lucian fighting to keep his arousal under control. Gillian followed, seating herself beside him. Immediately, Lucian brought her into his embrace, where he might kiss her again.

"Lucian, is this right?" She presented him a rueful grimace.

He waited a moment before he answered. "It feels right to me, but if you have qualms, I understand. I want you, Gillian. It is my intention to make you mine."

A small smile followed the narrowing of her eyes. "You seem very assured," she half teased, although nervousness showed in the tension found in her body.

"Not really. I recognize you're not as certain as I, but I'm willing to take a chance. You still think of us as strangers where I believe we're destined to be together."

"Destiny, is it?" Lucian could see the wheels turning as Gillian sought a reason for his attentions. He loved how she bit her bottom lip when she was deep in thought.

Lucian did not want her close examination. Having anyone truly *see him* was more than a bit disconcerting. "What are you really thinking?" His finger traced her chin line.

She shrugged her shoulders and smiled faintly. At last, she confessed, "I'm scared, Lucian. This isn't me; I don't have casual affairs. In fact, I don't have affairs. Period. Don't toy with me."

"I don't play games, Gillian," he assured.

"Lucian, I've seen you turn on the charm. Women fall all over you. I don't want to be one of your groupies." She made an effort to straighten her bunched up skirt.

"Gillian, that man isn't me; it's what I do to survive–to prosper–to make my living in this world. Yet, it's not me. You've seen the real me; you listen when I speak; you understand my true nature. I've never felt that you have judged me on my appearance or any other superficial element. In fact, when I turned on *the charm* you so describe, that's when you called me to task." Needing to convince her of his sincerity, Lucian moved closer and smothered her face with kisses. His hands caressed the soft skin of Gillian's back. When he finally released her mouth, Gillian arched toward him, begging for more. He kissed her more gently this second time, allowing his fingers to trace a line down her throat and across her neckline. She leaned her head back to give him easier access. "I want you, Gillian," he whispered.

In a lust-induced haze, Gillian found her voice. "Lucian, I've never..."

"Never what, Sweetling?" His lips and tongue teased her ear.

"Never," she struggled to keep her voice even. "Never let myself..."

The realization of what she meant finally sank through the fog of desire, which had possessed him. "You've never been with a man?" His voice held both amusement and bewilderment.

Embarrassed, Gillian buried her face into the fabric of his shirt. "Is that so bad? I know it's not a choice most people make these days, but I wanted my first time to be with someone special." He could barely hear; she spoke so softly.

"But you're a sex therapist." The words came out as a question.

She demanded, "Any high school student understands the 'process' of sex. I don't have to be promiscuous to help my patients." She pushed away from him.

"I didn't mean it that way, but I can't help but wonder how can you speak honestly to your patients if you know nothing of the heat of a lover–of a passion which consumes you." His gaze drifted down to her breasts and then rested once again on her mouth. "You must learn to trust me, Gillian."

"Men promise women the moon but deliver bread crumbs."

"Not all men are the same, Sweetling." Lucian smiled wryly. "You could have any number of men with or without intimate relationships. Yet, you choose to become involved with me. You must ask yourself, Gillian, why is that? You know, as well as I do, there is something–something going on here–something between us. What do you choose?" He allowed his fingers to stroke her back and arm as Lucian nuzzled his lips against the side of her cheek before pulling back to look upon her countenance.

Gillian swallowed hard, and he could see her considering the giving of herself over to the dark passion they both desired. He could feel the warmth of her body along his side. He reached out to caress her face, but she forced him to break his hold on her.

"Lucian, there are repercussions for women. Our society accepts a man who has many sexual conquests, but for all our so-called modern thoughts, women are judged poorly for the same behavior. Plus, it's been a personal choice for me. Although I practice my beliefs, I don't see myself as highly religious; but it's an important choice for me. We've only known each other for a few weeks. I know nothing about your parents, your family, your interests other than your work." Lucian winced when she mentioned his family and personal history. "Sharing sexual relations seems to me to be something very personal. I can't look on it as a casual situation."

"I don't see us as *casual*," Lucian protested. Gillian's eyes darkened with the same intensity, which pulsed through Lucian's body. He couldn't imagine any man who had the opportunity to love her and didn't, no matter what restrictions she demanded. To allow Gillian to not know love seemed incognizant. He took her hands in his. "I know we're moving faster than we planned–than you wanted, but you can't deny what we're feeling."

"Lucian..." she gasped.

"Let me love you, Gillian. Let me show you how passion is supposed to feel. Let me give you pleasure." His voice grew husky in anticipation. Lucian's mouth closed over hers; a deep moan started in the back of his throat and ended in hers. His arms encircled her again, tugging her closer to him. Uncompromising, he held her to him, needing to feel her body molding to his. His kisses increased in intensity, and Gillian whimpered with delight. Lucian pressed her against the settee, cushioning her neck in his hand while allowing his lips to travel along her chin line and down the vein of her neck. Instinctively, his free hand slipped up to cup her breast; his thumb teased her nipple, sending sensations through her. The sensations shook him, as it did her, but Lucian put his own pleasure aside. He must teach Gillian about passion. The more he kissed her–the more he massaged her breast–the closer she came to abandoning all thoughts of stopping him. A shudder wracked his body. "Come, Sweetling," he said as he stood. He scooped Gillian into his arms and carried her toward the bed.

She laced her arms around his neck. Her voice offered a mild protest, "Lucian?" Yet, her body clung to him.

"Shush, Love," he whispered in her ear. "Tonight is for you alone; tonight you will know the pleasure of being loved by someone who cares more for you than he could ever tell you." Gillian placed her fingertips to his mouth as he laid her against the bed pillows. Lucian seductively kissed the pad of each finger before sucking the tip in an intoxicating taunt. He shifted Gillian's weight in his arms and unzipped the back of her gown, first, lowering it to her waist and, then, shoving it away from her body. "God! You're so beautiful." A rosy blush covered Gillian's skin. Slowly, tempting himself with the action, Lucian removed her lace bra and panties. He avidly surveyed the fullness of her breast; her nipples responded by standing taut. He took both in his palms feeling the weight of them in his hands; then he rotated his open palms over the nipples, teasing each tip. He drank of her beauty in the reflected lights of the room; Gillian resembled a Greek goddess comes to life. The auburn curls having come loose and now draped over the pillows spread out like ethereal wings. He thought her the most beautiful woman he had ever seen. Quickly, he removed his shirt, needing to feel skin on skin.

He lowered his mouth to one of her breasts, circling the tip with his tongue, tantalizing her with pure pleasure. Lucian moved to take the nipple into his mouth, suckling it gently at first and then making a more intense demand on her body. His erection bulged, but he refused to remove his slacks, knowing if he did, he would be tempted to take her in other ways than he had promised. He forced his own needs to subside; tonight he pleasured Gillian; tonight it was for her. Reclaiming her mouth while trailing fingers lightly up and down her arms and chest, he felt Gillian shiver.

Instinctively, she encircled his neck, enticing him closer still and allowing her hands to become tangled in his thick hair. He could think of nothing but pleasing her. His mouth trailed along her neck before recapturing her breast.

With determination, his fingers began to skim her torso, searching for a way to bring her heat to a burn. Lucian caressed the mound of hair and then stroked the inside of her thighs. Her wetness already oozed from her point of desire, and he considered the pleasures a man could find there. He continued to suckle her breast, but his hand searched her tender flesh. His thumb massaged the sensitive nub as his fingers slipped into her cleft.

Gillian's body tensed. Lucian raised his head, moving to speak softly in her ear. "I won't hurt you, Sweetling; you must trust me. I want only to please you." His fingers slid in and out of her, the heat of her desire driving him on. "Watch what I do to you, Love. Open your eyes; feel–look–and enjoy." Gillian forced her eyes open. Lucian sat beside her on the bed. With one hand, he gently caressed her breast; with the other, he buried his fingers inside her. His thumb circled her pearly nub, faster and faster, sending impulses through her body. "Keep watching as I show you how much I adore you." Tension clamped her legs shut on his hand, but Lucian encouraged Gillian to spread them wider. "Let it happen, Gillian."

Her hips began to thrust against his hand. Lucian's mouth returned to her breast, increasing her need. Finally, the spasms of passion took control of her body, and Gillian convulsed repeatedly against his hand. He massaged her cleft, draining all desire from her body, but he slowed the tempo, allowing Gillian to recover. Fully satiated. Lucian's inflamed erection called for its own release, but he swallowed that demand. Finally, he removed his fingers from her dampness. "You are exquisite," he said seductively. "Did I please you, Sweetling?" Lucian whispered intimately in her ear as he settled himself beside her on the bed and adjusted Gillian in his hold.

She snuggled on her side, resting in the indentation of his shoulder. "I want to be no place but with you, Lucian."

"Are you all right?" Lucian required her assurances.

She half giggled, "Tingling all over."

He settled beside her, cupping her breast in his hand. They had reached a new level of intimacy. "I want you to be happy, Gillian." Lucian kissed the side of her face. He instinctively stimulated her nipple with his thumb.

"I'm not unhappy. This type of relationship is different for me, but you gave me a choice, Lucian; it's what I wanted." She hesitated; her brain had engaged in denial once again.

He understood. Never in his life had he fallen for a woman as he had with Gillian Cornell. Lucian could not recall a day when she was not the center of his universe. He felt her body withdrawing; her body said one thing, but her head had told her something was amiss. Her defenses had been erected. Lucian protectively tightened his hold on her. "Gillian, I know all this is fast–but, although there are times I feel we're learning about each other–there are moments like this when I feel you keep important things from me. Everyone keeps secrets–it's human nature; otherwise we'd be too vulnerable. But everyone also requires someone with whom he shares his secrets, a person he trusts with his innermost self."

Gillian shifted uncomfortably in his arms. She turned, lying flat on her back, speaking to the ceiling this time. "Do you share your secrets, Lucian?"

He sensed the contradiction in his words. Lucian could tell her the *secrets* of his life since the death of his *friend,* but the stories of his life prior to that time might be harder to explain. That life didn't belong to this Lucian Damron. "I've secrets I've not shared with anyone else, but that doesn't mean I don't wish to find someone with whom I can share those thoughts without fear of censure."

Her face took on a perceptive seriousness when Gillian turned her head toward him again. "Are your secrets demons which could destroy you?"

"Some," Lucian said tentatively, "could hurt my reputation as a professional; others are more personal–pains I revisit periodically to assure myself that I can survive the disapproval of human kind." He swallowed hard, wondering if he said too much.

"Mine are more the painful kind." Gillian stroked the side of Lucian's face. "I don't know whether I can share them or not." She whispered, "But I would like for you to be the one when I'm ready to share."

He released a breath, and his eyes darkened, while a hint of a smile turned up the corners of his lips. "Did I tell you, Sweetling, that I've other ways to please you?" Gillian flushed with embarrassment and desire, turning her body to bury her face into his chest. Lucian returned to caressing her breast; his attention drawn to the heat of her body. He wanted to touch her again–wanted this night to go on and on. "You understand, Love, we're not going back–from this moment, we're going forward wherever this takes us."

"That's what I want, Lucian."

Gillian sat in the hotel dining room enjoying the Continental breakfast. In reality, she had eaten very little of what rested on the table; instead, she replayed her night with Lucian. He had kissed her all over– literally, all over–up her legs, teasing her until his tongue invaded her most private places. Afterwards, she had taken his erection and stroked him to a full climax. Having never considered such an action before, she had tentatively touched him, watching as she brought him some of the pleasure he had given her. Then he had taken her hand and showed her how to move up and down him–how to caress his sensitive tip. She felt exhilarated by the power they held over each other. His eyes had flashed with the fire between them and it was oh, so delicious.

"Is this seat taken?" Gillian looked up to see the composed countenance of the man of her imagination.

She gifted him with a full smile. "I was waiting for Mr. Right," she teased.

"I'm afraid, Sweetling, you are stuck with Mr. Wrong." Lucian sat his coffee cup on the table and then kissed her cheek. "I'm glad to see you're still willing to speak to me after last night," he whispered in her ear.

"We didn't talk much."

Lucian's eyes blazed with remembrance. "Ah, Love, you shouldn't say such provocative things to a man craving your every attention." Lucian touched her cheek with his fingertips. "Don't make me start singing *Memories.*" Gillian laughed aloud, and Lucian made his way to the breakfast bar.

A few minutes later, he returned. "How, Miss Cornell, may I ask do you manage to look so breathtakingly beautiful after such a long night?"

"I'll probably sleep on the plane," she confided with a blush.

Lucian refilled his coffee cup. "I couldn't talk you into staying an extra day?"

"I wish I could but..."

"But you have responsibilities." Lucian's tone held irritation.

Gillian's ire began to rise. "Yes, Lucian, I do have responsibilities." Then she hesitated and made a decision. "May I tell you something of a private nature?"

The abrupt change in her tone caught Lucian off guard. "Of course, you can tell me anything."

"You asked for secrets so I'm going to give you one of mine." Gillian's voice took on a wistful attitude. "When I told you about my parents, I left out a major fact."

Lucian reached for her hand to offer encouragement. "Go on."

"I told you how my parents thought for years that they couldn't have children and how they took in lots of foster children." Lucian shook his head in affirmation; he knew the story well. "What I didn't tell you is three years before I was born, my parents took in a child they eventually adopted as their own. My *responsibility*, Lucian, is my sister Barbara."

"I don't understand; if Barbara is several years older than you, how is she your responsibility?" Lucian traced her palm with his fingertips.

"It's true Barb is six years older than I, but she is *special*; Barb is a Downs Syndrome adult. That's why I still take care of her."

"Does she live with you?"

"When my parents tragically passed, I became Barb's legal guardian; she's the reason I debated whether I could be gone for seven straight weeks. I can't in all my heart place Barb in an institution. She spends time in a day care facility designed to meet her needs." Gillian shifted her weight and squared her shoulders, preparing herself for the usual barrage of criticism offered by most people upon hearing her story.

However, Lucian offered her no censure. She watched as his mind went someplace else for a moment: She thought he must have recalled his own family. Finally, he said earnestly, "You're one of a kind, Gillian. I admire your tenaciousness. Helping those who cannot help themselves says a great deal about your personality."

His remarks had surprised Gillian. "Most people think I have wasted my life and my youth with Barb."

Lucian looked at her in a way she had never experienced when discussing her mentally challenged sister. Pity often came; sometimes she experienced incredulity, but never admiration. "That's ridiculous," Lucian quickly added. "You're doing one of the most compassionate things of which I have ever heard, especially considering Barbara is not your natural sister."

Gillian blushed under his close examination. "Thank...thank you for understanding," she stammered.

"Now I'm really honored," Lucian added with a genuine smile. "Will I meet Barb sometime?"

"She doesn't normally do well with strangers, but I can introduce you to her in stages if you're patient. In fact, I'd like for you to see what an exceptional person Barb is."

"How could she be anything but exceptional raised in a house so full of love?"

Wednesday found Lucian in L.A., serving as a consultant to a renowned "prima donna" in the entertainment industry. As her physician, Lucian spoke to the media hounds about the woman's latest stint at a drug and alcohol center. And he was very good at his job. He had always had a natural way with people, something he never understood because it was not as if he had had any role models in his life who showed similar tendencies. He supposed he had had to fend for himself so long that he had developed a smooth manner. Lucian wasn't a man who was easily satisfied with the mundane. That was why many of his clients were celebrities. It was all about "having arrived." Eliminating the dead weight from his existence and using his ever present ambition to rise to the top. Just today, he had appeared on two of the early morning news shows and on *Entertainment Tonight*. At one time, Lucian had relished the spotlight as much as had his client, but now he felt the tediousness of these commitments. When his cell phone rang, noting Gillian's number, he settled into the hotel room sofa for a moment of peace. "Hi, Gillian, what an unexpected surprise."

Her tone sounded tentative. "Did I catch you at a bad time?"

"I always have time for you." The sound of her voice lessened some of the tension he had experienced since hanging up the phone from their last call.

"You've been busy today. It seems every time I looked at the TV, you were there." Gillian's voice took on a teasing tone, one he really enjoyed and one that created an ache in Lucian's body.

"I wish all the women with whom deal possessed your good sense," he declared.

"Stressful day?"

"Why does money drive some people mad?"

"If they weren't mad, you and I would be out of a job," she reasoned.

Lucian half chuckled. "I told you, you're the practical one." He paused before adding, "I've missed that practicality."

Gillian laughed too. "I shouldn't keep you, but I've a proposal for you."

"Are you on one knee? I never accept proposals without a person dropping to one knee." Lucian taunted.

Gillian's voice held both her embarrassment and joy. "Don't tease me, Lucian."

Lucian cleared his throat. "I'm being serious, Miss Cornell."

Gillian began anew, obviously a bit flustered by his words. "This Saturday is the Special Olympics; I had hoped that you'd consider going with Barb and me. You said you'd like to meet her, and I thought this would be..."

"Gillian, it's okay; I'd love to go; you don't have to convince me." Lucian laughed lightly.

"I do run on sometimes."

"What time?"

"It's an early day for Barb—unfortunately, an all-day affair, but the love in that stadium is unbelievable. You don't have to come for the whole thing if you don't want to."

"It would please me to spend the day with you and your sister. Just tell me what time, and I'll pick you up." She had opened the door a crack. Lucian recognized how dangerous this was: To step into Gillian's world. Could he survive among those of her kind? Could he become the man he had always wanted to be? "Only time will tell," he whispered to the empty hotel room. "A little more time..."

⌒

Early Saturday morning, Lucian parked his car before Gillian's townhouse. Knowing he would see her this weekend had made the end of the week more tolerable. Now, he anticipated what the day would bring. "Hey, Lucian." Gillian gifted him with a full smile when she answered the door.

"Are we ready?"

Gillian stepped to the side and gestured him into her home. "Come meet Barb first. I've been telling her about you all week. She's anxious to see what you look like."

Barb Cornell giggled like a preteen when Gillian introduced Lucian. She loudly told her sister, "He's cute," much to the embarrassment of both Gillian and Lucian. "Gilly, is he your boyfriend?"

Lucian shot Gillian a quick glance as she stammered to answer. "Lucian...is just a friend, Barb."

"He's a boy," her sister insisted, "and he's your friend. Lucian's your boyfriend. He's my boyfriend too."

"In that case, Lucian is my boyfriend." She gave Lucian a furtive glance to see how he would react to her words, but he took it good-naturedly. Then Gillian assisted Barb with her sports pouch. "Do you have your water?"

"Yes, Gilly."

"Then let's go."

A local high school hosted the games. National Honor Society students served as "buddies" for each special athlete. Throughout the parade of participants and the many events, Gillian kept up a running commentary of what Lucian should expect. "It sounds like you've done this before."

Lucian supported her climb of the bleachers where they could watch the events and wait for Barb's performance. "Barb's been participating for years. My parents brought her; now it's my responsibility." Lucian looked at her; tears shimmered in his eyes, and he could easily note the tension in Gillian's body. He understood that this day held an importance, and, instinctively, he cherished her loyalty and her love. Although the grief of losing both of her parents still remained, she recognized her duty to her sister. He said nothing, but Gillian allowed him to hold her hand lightly in his, offering some comfort. Lucian thought about his own childhood. He wondered if his mother had ever loved him; it was a question he had asked repeatedly as a young adult. For years, he had let those feelings of loneliness drive him to his current success. Now, he questioned whether he really ever overcame them.

When Barb prepared to run, Gillian and Lucian moved down to the track to be close by and to offer her support. "I run fast, Lucian." Barb looked at him honestly. Her lopsided grin had earned her a place in his heart.

"I bet you do." He pinned the race number on Barb's singlet.

"Do you like Gilly?" Lucian let his eyes search out Gillian along the sidelines.

"Yes. Yes, I do."

"Good. My Gilly is sad; she's not happy like me." Barb's innocent remark struck Lucian; he looked at Gillian once again. He would like to make her happy. Yet, he wondered if he possessed the capabilities to give a woman like Gillian what she required in life.

Noting Barb's interest in his reaction to Gillian, he purposely changed the subject. "You run your best. Gillian and I will be cheering for you."

Barb gave him one of her best smiles. "I like to run, Lucian."

He kissed her cheek. "Run fast, Sweetheart." Then he left her to line up with the others.

Gillian grabbed his hand when he approached. "I get so nervous for her."

"She'll do fine." However, Lucian didn't release Gillian's hand. In fact, he pulled her closer.

When the race started, Barb easily took the lead. Gillian and Lucian screamed for her throughout–every step bringing her closer to a victory. Tears streamed down Gillian's cheeks, and Lucian jumped up and down, pumping his arms and willing her on. Then the unthinkable happened. Gillian watched in horror as Barb stumbled just short of the finish line. The crowd grew silent as they watched the drama.

Lucian scrambled to reach her and help her up, but he stopped short when he heard Gillian scream "No! They'll disqualify her. Let her get up on her own." Lucian backed off a few steps. Gillian dropped to her knees beside Barb. "Come on, Baby Girl, you can do this," she pleaded.

"It hurts, Gilly." Tears appeared in her sister's eyes.

A catch came in Gillian's voice, but she never allowed Barb to witness her concern. "You have to finish, Baby Girl. Mama and Papa always said that you have to finish the race. It's only another ten steps, Barb. I'll count them for you. Get up, Barb. You can still get a medal if you go now." One runner crossed the finish line, and another turned the corner for the home stretch.

"Lucian will catch me?" Barb questioned, looking at Lucian's constricted face.

"Lucian will catch you." Gillian gestured, pointing him to the finish line. "Now get up, Baby Girl." As Barb fought to right herself, the second participant crossed the line. When she took off again, the crowd roared with approval. "Ten. Nine. Eight," Gillian called out as Barb pushed forward. "Come on, Baby Girl. Five. Four. Three. Two. One."

With that, Barb crossed the finish line and fell into Lucian's open arms. He supported her, caressing her head as he pulled Gillian's sister to his chest. He looked to see Gillian shoot a quick glance heavenward. "You were magnificent—absolutely magnificent," he whispered softly. After a few intense seconds, Lucian began to coax Barb out of his hold as Gillian joined them for a group hug.

Her tears reflecting her joy, Gillian said, "I am so proud of you, Barb."

"Mama said I had to finish every race." They led her toward the staging area. "You must finish, Barb. No one can stop now." Gillian slipped her arm around Barb's shoulder. A race volunteer hustled over with Barb's third place medal. "I got a gold medal." She shoved the ribbon award at Gillian.

"No, Sweetheart, it's bronze, but it does look gold, doesn't it?" Gillian laughed lightly as she shoved Barb's hair from her face.

"I never saw anything like this! This is better than any professional game I've ever witnessed! You gave us quite a scare, Barb." Lucian's adrenalin pumped. He couldn't resist picking Gillian up and swinging her around one time before placing her safely on the ground.

"Let's get you a bandage," Gillian said as she led Barb to the medical tent. "It's only a scrape, Barb. We will clean it and put medicine on it."

"It doesn't hurt any more, Gilly."

"Winning makes it feel better," Gillian assured her sister.

Barb watched as the medical staff cleaned off the wound. "Yeah, winning makes me feel good. I run fast, Lucian."

Lucian took her hand. "No one runs faster."

"I run one more time," she informed him.

Lucian looked at Gillian for confirmation. "Barb will run the 200."

"Then this time you win the real gold," he told her.

"The rules say I'm a winner if I just do my best," Barb corrected him.

Lucian appeared ashamed for allowing the hype of the competition to carry him away. "Just do as your parents said, Sweetheart. Finish the race. Gillian and I will be proud of you."

She smiled a beguiling smile. "You catch me again?"

"I will be at the finish line."

<hr/>

Lucian contentedly watched as Gillian refilled the drink glasses at the fountain drink dispenser. Who would think an afternoon watching exceptional children and adults compete in track and field events followed by pizza at a noisy, children-filled Chunky Cheese could be so satisfying? By now, he knew the curve of Gillian's neck, the smell of the lavender scent lingering on her skin, and the wistful expression playing across her lips. He was as contented as he ever had been.

"It's been a long day," she offered as she took the seat beside him while handing Barb another soft drink. "We certainly consumed your day." Gillian gave Lucian a great smile of apology.

"It's been one of my best days ever." Lucian nibbled on a slice of pizza. "What's next?"

Gillian looked about sheepishly. "I need to get Barb home soon. This is her favorite place. We'll play some skee ball, let Barb pick a prize, and then we'll head home."

"What about you, Gillian? Where is your life? I told you in Kentucky that you needed to consider yourself sometimes." Lucian knew he had no right to ask, but he couldn't stifle the words. She gave to everyone else, but he was smart enough to realize if Gillian was not willing to claim her own happiness, they would have no future.

She lowered her eyes. "Barb is my life right now. I know it sounds stupid, but my commitment lies with my sister. This is not a lifestyle I would have chosen for myself. I am definitely not my mother; in fact, often this lifestyle frustrates me. I want my own family some day, but I will live out the life I have inherited," she insisted.

Fascinated, Lucian stared with heightened awareness. Of late, he had thought about a family with Gillian; he had thought of taking her to his bed and making her call his name with passion, starting that family. His desire for her had counterbalanced the empathy for the situation in which Gillian found herself. She deserved more to life than what she had inherited from her parents. She deserved a man who would make her feel the things a woman was suppose to feel.

Back at her townhouse, Lucian spent what remained of the evening stretched out on Gillian's sofa watching cable movies and munching on microwave popcorn. Gillian had lounged in a recliner or was propped up on pillows on the floor throughout the evening. Barb, clutching her two medals, had gone to bed early. "I was surprised at how quickly Barb took to you. She's usually frightened of strangers." Gillian handed him a beer.

"I've always had a way with people, especially those who require my care," he said nonchalantly.

Gillian confessed, "I thought you were a player when I first met you."

Lucian spewed beer all over himself. "Thanks for the vote of confidence." Sarcasm dripped from his words.

"Well, I'm...I'm sorry, Lucian," Gillian stammered, "but that's the image you portray to the world." Despite speaking the truth, she couldn't shake the feeling of disloyalty spreading through her veins.

Lucian leaned against the padded back of the furniture; he looked at her intently. The truth of her words became evident. "I'm ashamed if that's how you saw me, Gillian."

"We just misconstrued each other." Impulsively, she reached out to caress his face. "I'm glad we started over." Lucian actually felt the pain of her words. He had wanted to start over–to start over with Gillian Cornell, but Lucian Damron was in too deep. Gillian stood slowly and crossed closer to where Lucian reclined on the sofa. She sat beside him and leaned down to kiss him. "I'm sorry if I hurt your feelings."

"If you continue to do that for a little longer, I believe I can find it in my heart to forgive you." His hand held her head where she couldn't withdraw.

She teased, "How long will it take before I pay my penance?"

Lucian's tongue tantalized her upper lip. "I cannot say for certain, Miss Cornell, but it may take some time."

"I suppose if I must pay, I must pay." Gillian deepened the kiss allowing her tongue to search his mouth. She rasped, "I thought, Dr. Damron, I might convince you to do something for me. I've been thinking of something special I've been wanting to do."

Lucian rubbed his lips across hers. "You know I'll give you anything I can. All you must do is ask."

Gillian kissed along his jaw line. "I've but one request, and only you, Lucian Damron, can give it to me. I want you to make love to me."

Lucian froze. "Are you certain, Gillian? This is not a decision you can take back."

"Any qualms I held you erased today when you welcomed Barb into your world. You didn't just tolerate her to placate me; you treated her with respect," she said definitively.

Lucian pulled her to him, and Gillian flattened her body along his. His hands searched her curves, pulling her hips in alignment with his. Lucian's breathing became ragged and shallow. He whispered, "You have no idea what effect you have on me."

She began to stroke his growing erection as she nibbled on his ear lobe. "I want to have an effect on you, and now, I want you in my bed."

"I thought men were supposed to be the aggressor." It was one of his affectionate barbs, but Gillian, unfortunately, took it personally. She started to withdraw, but he held her tight. "Don't…"

"Don't what?"

Lucian's breath tickled her skin when he spoke. "Don't withdraw. Don't keep me out." His lips searched hers again, and Gillian's breath audibly froze. "Did you say something about a bed?" he teased.

They rose, and Gillian silently led him to her bedroom. Once inside, Lucian closed the distance between them. The glazed over look returned to Gillian's eyes, and he found it both amusing and stimulating how she jumped when he inched closer. His proximity had driven her forward, and she slid her arms around his waist. Lucian's mouth returned to hers, needing to control the situation–needing for Gillian to be like all the others–needing to use his charms to possess her, but he knew in his heart she would never be like any other woman he had ever known. Her breath quickened when he lowered his head to kiss along her shoulder blade. Still in an embrace, he backed her toward the bed.

Gillian slipped her arms around his neck as he picked her up and placed her across the bed. Gently, he kissed her four times: her temple, the side of her face, the corner of her mouth, and her lips. Those lips parted, and Lucian quickly deepened the kiss, using his tongue to explore the warmth of her mouth. He cupped her face in his hands, and Gillian sighed. The sound teased a smile from his mouth. He would have her; Gillian would be his. Lucian controlled the situation as he had done everything else in his life. He loosened her hair from the ponytail she had worn that day, letting the curls spread across his arm, and then he ran his fingers along the length of it, amazed by the way the light played off the red highlights. He traced a line with his fingers from her temple down her face toward her neck. Lightly. Tantalizingly. Lucian stroked her arms, her legs–her torso, just touching her, enjoying the feel of Gillian's skin. Slowly, he unbuttoned her blouse and loosened the hook of her bra. During a kiss he slipped both off her shoulders and arms, tossing them on the floor. Now, he was free to touch her intimately.

Lucian released her mouth and trailed kisses down her neck and across her chest. When he caught one of her breasts in his palm, she instinctively arched into his hand, begging for more. Her nipple hardened, and Lucian squeezed it, rolling it between his fingers and thumb. She moaned when his lips took the place of his fingers; his tongue encircled the tip before he suckled gently at first, but then more demandingly.

Lucian inhaled deeply to control the passion rising too quickly between his legs. He unfastened the Capris she had worn and eased them over her hips. Then he stood briefly to divest himself of his own clothing. He reached for his wallet to retrieve a condom. Lucian sheaved himself in the latex protection before returning to the bed. Her panties had disappeared into the linens, and he paused before touching her again, suspended the significance of the moment.

She whimpered when he returned his mouth to her breast. Tauntingly, he drew circles across her stomach with his fingertips. His hand moved slowly, but he finally pressed two fingers into her folds. The wetness nearly sent him over the edge; she was ready for him so he massaged her nub with his thumb while continuing to dip his fingers in and out of her desire. Gillian drew a shaky breath and then squirmed, pushing her hips upward until his fingers sank deep into her sensual pleasure. The wetness—her response—the picture of her laying beisde him—all threatened to undo him.

Gillian's soft moans begged for fulfillment. Lucian had ached for this moment, had dreamed of it—had waited for such completion with this woman. He longed for her touch. That touch, her taste, her warm female scent combined, sending his senses into a fever pitch as he waited for the moment that she would desire him as much as he did her. Arching against his hard body, Gillian finally begged, "Please."

"Soon, Sweetling." She trembled, and Lucian fought the explosion consuming him. He led her hand to his erection. "I told you, you have a profound effect on me. I want you as much as you want me."

Gillian slowly caressed the length of him, coaxing small, strangled groans from him. "I want to please you, Lucian. I want to do this well." A ragged breath escaped his mouth when she stroked the soft rounded tip.

Her touching him had increased Lucian's need to plunge his fingers even deeper into her. His thumb circled her velvety nub, faster and faster. He recognized her growing passion—knew it was coming. Her body writhed, and her hips thrust upward seeking the relief only he could give. Finally, she cried out and convulsed against him; her insides contracting on his dripping wet digits. Spent and satiated, Gillian gasped for air, softly nuzzling into his neck.

A crimson haze overspread his body; every part of Lucian required her. He placed himself over her, lifting one of her knees. Then he positioned his erection. He closed his eyes as his tip slipped into her wetness. Her body tightened around him, wanting to draw him fully inside. Repeatedly, Lucian pulled out of her and then plunged in again. Each time, he went further than the last. A gentle lift of her hips encouraged him to continue. Finally, he pushed through her virginal barrier. Pausing to allow Gillian to adjust to the pain and to allow himself to take command of his out-of-control desire, Lucian resisted the wispy sensation to bury himself in her and never come out.

At last, she reached out to touch his face. The look in Gillian's eyes mesmerized him. She was perfection, and he would spend his life proving himself worthy of her. He bowed his head to kiss her again–his tongue snaking in and out of her mouth. He returned his attention to her breasts; instinctively, Gillian's hips moved against him. Lucian doubled his efforts, suckling her breast and thrusting into her. Her bare legs wrapped around him as Lucian drove harder. He released her breast; then he reached between them to stroke her faster and faster, bringing her along. Lucian felt the sensations coursing through her. Her hips rose as he pushed farther and farther. Reaching her brink, she called his name. She tightened around him; Lucian could feel her impulses all along his shaft. Seconds later, his own release followed an explosive ecstasy. He groaned from deep in his chest.

They lay limbs entangled waiting for their breathing to slow. He wrapped his arms around her, stilling the movement of their hips. He rolled onto his back, taking her with him, pulling the linens over them. Gillian snuggled into his shoulder, and Lucian stroked her arm. "Are you all right?" he asked at last.

"I feel so alive. You were magnificent," she whispered.

"Thank goodness you've no point of reference, or you might find me just as being adequate." He half chuckled as he pulled Gillian's body closer to him.

"Being average is under rated," she taunted. "However, you, obviously, are more than adequate." Gillian's hand lightly drifted down his body.

"You're a wicked temptress, Miss Cornell." A smile played across his lips as he kissed her.

"Now that I know what to expect, I might like to try this again." She caressed his half aroused shaft.

"Woman, you are unbelievable!"

Chapter Four

THE FACT THAT SHE HAD NOT seen him again for another ten days did nothing to lessen Gillian's feelings of happiness. They had made a commitment to each other. "He can't help it if he has to go out of town for a consultation," she told herself. Besides, she also had outside commitments also. However, if she admitted it, Gillian regretted her not accepting the invitation to the convention in Lake Tahoe. They could have spent time together if she had. Lucian was one of the keynote speakers, and it would have been wonderful to be discovered on his arm. Thankfully, he called her at least once daily, and on several evenings they had fallen asleep while talking on the phone. On one such evening, she woke with a start, but then upon listening more closely, Gillian could hear Lucian's light breathing on the other end of the line. She closed his eyes and imagined him lying beside her before drifting off to sleep again.

Searching for the perfect outfit, Gillian hustled through the shopping plaza. Lucian would return by late afternoon. She had never realized how dependent a person could become on another. Their night of passion still played vividly in her mind. In the past few days, she had surreptitiously made subtle changes in her appearance. She had wanted Lucian to look at her and to see a beautiful woman. She had a stylist highlight her hair and to give her a new look. She had visited a makeup specialist for some pointers and had purchased contact lens. Now, she was on a mission for new clothing items. When Lucian called later this evening, she wanted to wow him into submission. Deep in thought, she darted in the door of an upscale dress shop where she came face-to-face with Charlotte Blakeley and a few other socialite types. "Excuse me," Gillian mumbled, moving past the woman who had been Lucian's intimate until a month prior. Gillian wanted no reminders of Lucian's former conquests. She worried she would be found wanting.

"Well, well, what do we have here?" The woman blocked Gillian's way. "Miss Gillian Cornell isn't it?" Her opponent's tone held pure disdain, along with a large dose of jealousy.

Gillian ignored her and moved to go around Lucian's leftovers, but the other two women countered her efforts. "The lady does not seem to favor your company, Charlotte," the slender blonde mocked.

Charlotte Blakeley didn't remove her heavy gaze from Gillian's countenance. She towered over Gillian by several inches. "I am certain Miss Cornell wishes I didn't exist; I am a reminder of her foolishness."

"I am afraid," Gillian fought to keep her voice even, "that I've not had the pleasure of an introduction."

Charlotte's laugh reflected the irony. "Yet, you know who I *am*."

"I know who you *were*." Gillian returned the sneer.

"Sounds like a challenge," the blonde taunted Charlotte.

Charlotte didn't divert her eyes, but she spoke to her friend. "Miss Cornell is Lucian's latest conquest."

The blonde laughed out loud. "Her?"

"You should've seen her before." They spoke as if Gillian didn't stand before them. "She's evidently has attempted to make herself more appealing for Lucian's sake. However, when you're plain, no one can make you pretty."

Gillian's temper rose quickly. "Maybe Lucian is sick of artificial beauty–the best plastic surgery money can buy, is it, Miss Blakeley?"

Charlotte shot her a look of death. "Lucian didn't seem to mind when I saw him this week."

Gillian's mouth turned up in amusement. "You don't expect me to believe you? Lucian, for your information, has been out of town for two weeks."

The woman said confidently, "Lucian was in Tahoe, and so was I." She moved in to where her face was only inches from Gillian's.

"I talked to him every night–sometimes all night," Gillian countered. Her jaw clamped tight against the anger.

"You know how men are. Lucian's stamina increases with sex; I'm certain after we made love our Lucian crawled from my bed and made his phone call to you. He knows I'm a bitch without my sleep. I left him keyed up enough to entertain your long distance love affair."

Charlotte's words were barely more than a whisper, but they curdled in Gillian's stomach with the power of thunder. Could Lucian have done this? Why would any woman so defame herself without some measure of truth in her words? Gillian had known from the beginning that Lucian would eventually leave her, but she never thought it would be so soon. "I don't believe a word you say." Gillian mustered her courage.

"Don't you?" A smile crept across Charlotte's face. "We'll see, Miss Cornell. We'll see." Then she turned on her heels to leave Gillian standing wide eyed, tears pricking the backs of her lids.

By the time Lucian appeared at her door that evening, Gillian had experienced the full gamut of emotions: disbelief, bewilderment, jealousy, incredulity, anger. She had reasoned that she should trust him, but a part of her couldn't abandon her earliest qualms about Lucian's reputation as a womanizer. Everyone on the lecture circuit knew Lucian Damron as a professed bachelor. He loved the fairer sex, and he openly *professed* not to want a serious relationship. "I was a fool to think I could change him. It's every woman's dream to mold the perpetual bad boy into the perfect mate, but reality says it's not possible," she had reasoned aloud. When she had thought about it, Gillian realized Charlotte Blakeley and Lucian Damron were the same type. They had used each other–exploited other people for their own amusements. He had used her; she was exactly what Charlotte said: *Lucian's latest conquest!*

"Hi, Sweetheart." He kissed her cheek when he entered. Gillian smiled tentatively as she closed the door behind him. Lucian turned immediately and took Gillian in his arms, planting a lingering kiss on her upturned mouth. "I've been wanting to do that for two weeks. God, I have missed you."

"I'm happy to see you, too." Gillian broke the hold and led Lucian into her living room. She seated herself in one of the wing chairs while motioning him to the sofa. "How was your trip?" Gillian didn't look at him–couldn't make herself look him in the eye; instead she straightened the dart in the waist of her dress.

Gillian didn't fool anyone; after not seeing each other for two weeks and the intimacy they had shared in their nightly phone conversations, she knew that he expected, at least, several amorous kisses; yet, she kept her distance from him. When he finally asked, "Is something wrong, Gillian?" her heart nearly broke. How could she not trust him? Yet, she had no real reason beside her naïveté to believe anything he said. He had told her from the beginning that he would seduce her, and he had.

Gillian forced her eyes to take in the concern found in Lucian's. "There's nothing wrong."

"Are you certain? You're acting odd." She knew that Lucian would attempt to read her face for the truth. It was part of what a good psychologist did.

A constricted smile laced her lips. "Of course. What could be wrong?" Gillian grimaced with the knowledge of how foolish she acted; her inner voice demanded she reject Charlotte's insinuations. "It's just been a hectic day."

Lucian's eyes jumped with anticipation. As he leaned forward, he said quietly, "I can help you forget your day. Trust me; you'll remember the night though."

Gillian's heart jumped; she wanted what he offered; she wanted to become lost in his arms. "That sounds promising." She emitted a soft giggle and blushed.

Lucian moved immediately, pulling her to her feet and taking her in his arms. His mouth found hers. The heat rose quickly between them, and Lucian's hands searched Gillian's body. Finally, she broke the kiss, but not the embrace. Lucian continued to brush her lips with his. He growled, "I find you quite irresistible."

Unable to stop the desire climbing steadily up her body, Gillian clung to him. "Lucian, we must stop," she moaned.

Reluctantly, Lucian released first her mouth and then her body. "You take away my reason." He half chuckled as they straightened their clothes. "Maybe we should go," he offered shamefacedly.

"I think that's best."

The dinner, although more solemn than she had anticipated, passed quickly enough. Despite her earlier desire for Lucian, in the back of her mind, Gillian couldn't brush away her nagging doubts. As she sipped her wine, she asked innocently, "Did you meet anyone you knew in Tahoe?" She couldn't explain why she asked; she knew he wouldn't just come out and tell her he had slept with Charlotte Blakeley.

"The same old crowd–you know those out on the lecture circuit." Lucian circled the top of his glass with his fingertip.

"Then Howard, Peltiere, and Bradley were there?" She sipped again; Lucian frowned before he nodded in agreement. "With whom did you socialize outside the conference?"

Her ambiguity obviously puzzled Lucian. "No one really. I had dinner with Bradley twice. Mostly, I watched old movies and waited to call you."

"No conference groupies?" She half teased, but jealousy played into her tone.

"There is no one else, Gillian." Lucian reached for her hand, but she let it drop to her lap. "You know I desire you," he spoke in undertones.

She let her eyes follow her hand. "Everyone can see your desire, Lucian. What I don't see is a commitment to anyone but yourself."

Gillian's words had stung, and his voice rose in accusation. "What do you think I did in Tahoe?"

Gillian's insecurities rose with his questioning attitude; yet, she would not back down. "I understand that you had, at least, one visitor in your room while there." Her eyes demanded a response.

Lucian jerked his hand from the table, knocking a glass of water into his lap. He stood quickly, grabbing a napkin to mop up the excess water. He growled through clenched teeth, "I can't believe you think so lowly of me, but then you always did, didn't you?" His words felt like a slap across her face, and Gillian winced. "From that night at the conference, until now, there's been no one else–no one but you, Gillian, but I'll never be able to convince you. You're too righteous–too judgmental–too ready to believe lies when your heart knows the truth." He threw the napkin on the table. "Allow me the opportunity to freshen up this mess, and I'll take you home." Lucian strode toward the men's room, leaving Gillian dejected and confused.

She sat quietly for a moment before a flood of guilt overcame her. Quickly, she scribbled a message on a scrap of paper left it on the table, and ran for the exit. Yet, she was not quick enough. Lucian returned to the table before she cleared the restaurant's entrance, and he gave pursuit. Fortunately, Gillian climbed into the back of a taxi just as Lucian reached the street. When she turned her tear-stained face to look at him, Lucian screamed, "Gillian! Damn it, Gillian. Wait!"

Seconds later, Gillian's cell rang; the distinctive dial tone told her it was Lucian. She hesitated before answering it. Then with resolve and not giving him a chance to say anything, she pushed the "send" button. "Lucian, I can't do this. I can't be involved this way. Please don't call me again." With that, she closed the receiver and shut the phone off because she knew he would ring right back. Hugging herself for comfort she wasn't likely to find, she fought back the anguish already lodged in her heart.

∼

His hand clenched about the report he had casually removed from the stack on his desk. It had been more than eighty hours since he had last seen Gillian, and still Lucian held no idea what he had done wrong. What had caused her to run from him? Dear God, he had thought for a time that he would finally know happiness. That he could have the family he had always desired. A family with the most trustworthy and loving woman of his acquaintance. He could have Gillian welcoming him home from a day's work. Gillian sitting on his lap on a chilly winter's evening. Gillian heavy with his child. Gillian in his bed. All of it. The perfect scenario. Every man's ingrained desire to mate and to know contentment. Yet, somehow it had all slipped through Lucian's fingers.

For three days, Lucian had left her multiple messages on her cell phone, on the voice box of her land phone, and in her email inbox. He had even spent some ten minutes pounding on her townhouse door, but Gillian had pretended not to be at home. Odd as it may sound, he could feel her through the door. Feel her anger and her disillusionment, and the thought had stayed his hand from knocking again.

Gillian had listened to each voice message and had saved each email to her documents, but she didn't answer his pleas for an opportunity to talk. Lucian had continued to claim that he held no knowledge of her accusations. She thought that if he had admitted his wrongdoing and if he had apologized, that she would have forgiven him for his indiscretion; but

Lucian's refusal to admit his tryst with Charlotte Blakeley meant Gillian couldn't forgive him, nor could she forget.

After three days the pleading stopped. He had left her one final message. "Gillian, listen to your heart." The words ripped the said organ to shreds. Like it or not, she had fallen for Lucian Damron. And like it or not, she was under contract to spend seven weeks with him during the show? She was doomed.

⌒

When Lucian read her short note at the restaurant, he had panicked. For unknown reasons, Gillian had withdrawn from him. He had to fix it; whatever it was, he was at fault. He knew that without a doubt. He was a moron. A jerk. He had to make Gillian look at him. Their truths lay within their eyes. She couldn't deny him if she would just look into his eyes.

For three days, Lucian didn't leave his apartment. He wanted to be home when Gillian returned his call, but the call had never come. "Damn her!" he protested one minute, but the next he was begging for divine intervention to bring Gillian to her senses. "She is the most hard headed woman I know," he declared to the empty apartment. "Yet, she is the only woman who has ever stirred your soul." He closed out the storm of emotions when he shut himself in. His work lay strung out across his desk, but concentrating on such mundane matters wasn't of importance–only Gillian mattered; he had made a mess of his life, and all his maneuvering and his intelligence couldn't fix it. Repeatedly, he paced the length of the apartment and then again, hoping a solution would show itself, but nothing came.

Muttering a senseless prayer, he had sunk to his knees in supplication, begging for a god he had rarely worshipped to assist him. Gritting his teeth against the pain, the realization slapped him coldly in the face: He had no future with Gillian Cornell, but he had bought into the dream, thinking that just this one time that God would allow him to know true happiness.

When his doorbell rang, Lucian raced to answer it, hoping against hope, that Gillian had forgiven him, and that she was on the other side of the door. Scruffy from not having shaved since that the night at the restaurant, he paused only briefly before opening the door to his future.

"Hello, Lucian."

Routinely, at breakfast time, Gillian picked up the morning newspaper and settled into the breakfast nook to start her day with the latest news, accompanied by her favorite homemade protein shake. "Let us see what is happening in the world," she mumbled aloud as she turned the page.

However, reading about the Presidential elections wasn't part of today's agenda. Today's news rested purely on Lucian Damron. He was all she thought of. The phone calls and the emails had stopped. Gillian didn't know whether she had wanted them to, or whether she had wished them to go on. Despite her best efforts not to do so, she had wondered where Lucian could be. She regularly considered what he might be doing. And she had chastised herself for being so foolish. "I should call to apologize," she had told herself. "I know the real Lucian, the one who treated Barb as she should be treated. The one who made love to me so tenderly." Her skin flushed with color every time she thought of their lovemaking. "How could I have been so cruel to accuse him without even giving him time to respond?"

Then her eyes fell on a picture in the society pages. It was from a gala fund-raiser in the "arts" district. Several well-dressed patrons of the arts smiled for the camera, but her attention rested only on one face. Lucian stood among the cluster posing for the lens. He smiled and laced arms with the others. Finally, Gillian's eyes took in the whole picture. Standing beside him, arms laced about his neck, was Charlotte Blakeley. A soft moan escaped Gillian's lips before the tears tripped down her cheeks. "Damn him!" she uncharacteristically swore. Well, she now understood why the phone calls and emails had stopped. "Out of sight; out of mind," she murmured. "I had hoped for absence makes the heart grow fonder. You're an idiot!" she admonished as her eyes rolled upward in frustration.

Barb slid onto the breakfast bench beside her, and Gillian quickly used the knuckles of both hands to wipe away the tears. She purposely took a long drink of the shake, attempting to drown the pain with a sense of normalcy. Barb's eyes, like Gillian's had earlier, finally focused on the news page. "Look, Gilly. It's Lucian." Her sister pointed to the page.

"Yes, Baby Girl, it's Lucian." Her pain unbearable, Gillian could barely speak the words.

"He's sad. Lucian's sad," Barb pointed to the picture again.

"No, Sweetheart," Gillian mumbled, "Lucian's happy. See. He's smiling." Reluctantly, her fingers traced the black and white image.

"That's not Lucian's happy smile," Barb insisted. "His happy smile looks like this." Barb then demonstrated what she interpreted as Lucian's true smile. "The picture smile is the one Lucian uses when he's trying to be nice. Like when you say you like someone's cooking but don't mean it. See, Gilly, Lucian's not happy." Her sister's innocent belief in Lucian's goodness touched Gillian despite the anger and the sense of betrayal coursing through her.

Grinding her teeth together, Gillian counted to ten and then again before attempting a smile for her sister's benefit. "That may be, Barb, but Lucian has chosen to spend time with people other than us." Despite her best efforts, Gillian's tears had returned.

Seeing her sister so upset and not knowing the true cause, Barb's tears came too. "I'm sorry, Gilly. Lucian didn't like me; Lucian didn't want to be my boyfriend. That's why he won't come to see us anymore."

Gillian embraced the girl in a tight bear hug. "No, Barb," she offered, "it was me he didn't like. Didn't love. Lucian is still your boyfriend, but because of me, we probably won't see him for a long time."

"You'll be sad again, Gilly. I don't want you sad again," Barb protested

Gillian pushed strands of hair from Barb's face. "I won't be sad, Baby Girl; I have you. How could I be sad if you're in my life?" Then she rocked her sister in her arms, seeking comfort that would not come for either of them.

"These are the six couples the show's producers chose for the finals. Each brings a unique perspective to the program, and each will have the viewing public championing his winning, as well as demanding his going home." The show's director Michael Hood explained to a number of key people involved in its success. Four weeks passed since their argument, and Lucian could barely keep his mind on the specifics of the couples. Gillian was in the same room with him at last, and all he wished was to be alone where they might talk and settle this madness. He watched as she avoided his continuous stare.

"Each week the couples will participate in some sort of romantic challenge. One week, for example, it will be learning to trust one's mate again. We'll do one of those Outward Bound scavenger courses or something similar where the couple must work together to win the challenge. Whoever wins earns a prize–an in-home renovation, a dream trip–that kind of stuff. Another week it will be a ballroom dance challenge.

"Then you three will provide the hidden motivations and secrets with your analysis and consultations. Dr. Damron, we expect you to provide the overview of the couples each week–turn on the charm–the animal magnetism. Dr. Stryent, you will be the medical liaison, the one who brings the show its medical legitimacy. Miss Cornell, you are our secret weapon. You've got those all-American girl looks–the touch of innocence, but when you start counseling these couples sexually, you'll blow the American viewing public away.

"Because of the *sensitive* nature of what we'll be discussing, the show is playing to the cable audience in the nine o'clock time slot, but I've no doubt you'll win the ratings' war with the network shows. We're looking at Tuesday night–no sense in competing with Monday USFL, which is a staple on TV. The show will be live; the mountain home is ready for us. Consultants, I want to remind you there are cameras throughout the house, including a few in your wing. That way the public can see that we have nothing to hide; what they see is what they get; just make certain they don't see you running around naked." Everyone in the room let out a nervous chuckle. "The public will vote for who stays and who goes home weekly. The winners will earn a quarter million dollars and a dream wedding.

"I have included a file on each couple for the therapists. That way you'll know something about the people we've chosen. Maybe you can gleam some details, which will make good TV. Are there any questions?" Hood glanced about the room, but he obviously had no intentions of entertaining questions. "Doctors, I would like to meet with you exclusively next Thursday. It will be an all-day affair so come prepared. We'll be leaving for the mountains on the twentieth of next month. We'll be gone seven weeks. No one gets voted off the first week. Week one we'll feature three couples; on week two, we'll feature the other three. The public will vote each of those two weeks. Whoever has the least votes goes home after week two. Then a new couple every week after that until the finals. My staff needs to report back here after lunch. The rest of you are free to go."

As quickly as he could maneuver through the people scrambling for lunchtime, Lucian caught Gillian's elbow. "Do you have time for lunch?" He had missed her desperately.

"I don't think so, Lucian. We have nothing to say to one another." She pulled her arm from his grasp.

If that were true, it would be the first time. He and Gillian had spent countless hours just talking. She was a woman with lots of opinions—some of which he vehemently opposed, but she was also a woman whose views he valued. She was likely the most opinionated woman he had ever met. Perhaps that was part of the attraction. Most of the women Lucian met would try to ingratiate themselves to him by agreeing to everything he said. "Gillian, please. I don't know how to fix this, but I'll do anything," he whispered so the others couldn't hear.

"There's nothing to fix," she insisted. "It was great while it lasted, but we both knew we weren't meant to be. We realized that from the beginning."

"Yes, we are, Gillian," Desperation insisted.

She turned on him then; cold steel pierced his heart. "If we're meant to be, then how could you turn to Charlotte Blakeley four days after our argument? Four days, Lucian! Within four days you found solace with someone else. That doesn't sound like a man who believes the words coming from your mouth. If you don't believe it, how can I?"

"I didn't..." he protested. "I made a commitment months prior."

"I don't want to hear it!"

"But you must." He blocked her retreat.

"I said I don't want to hear it!" She shoved his hand away and disappeared into the group exiting the room.

Before Lucian could respond, Dr. Stryent caught up to him. "Say, Damron, do you think we could talk?"

Anxious to follow her, Lucian looked after Gillian. "Sure...sure, what do you need?" He answered, but his attention still rested on Gillian's retreating form.

Michael Hood strode up and down the room. He was a man who thought out loud, who planned out loud. Stryent, along with Lucian and Gillian, sat in a small conference room, listening to Hood's plans for the show. "I assume at this point you're familiar with each of the show's participants. Again, I want to caution you to not choose favorites; you cannot sway the public's vote. I want to portray each with as much honesty as we can."

"What if someone honestly should not be together?" Lucian asked. "Don't we have a responsibility as medical professionals to let that be known?"

"Of course," Hood added, "but we must offer counseling without bringing down public censure."

"There are a couple of people in this mix who've some unsavory characteristics." Gillian snarled her nose.

"Of course, Miss Cornell, we have to have someone interesting, someone the American public can love and someone they can hate," Hood reasoned.

"It seems Jenkinson's been a womanizer for years," Gillian interjected. "Such men should not be encouraged."

"Maybe you jumped to an unfounded conclusion regarding Mr. Jenkinson," Lucian challenged. "It is possible, you know, that you might be mistaken about the man."

"I doubt it; the evidence is quite clear." Gillian knew they spoke not of Jenkinson but of their relationship.

Lucian apparently knew it also; he argued his points alone. "Miss Cornell, you're quick to judge people without really knowing all the circumstances. A man, for example, might find himself at an office party or a gathering of some kind, and some female may attach herself to him, but that doesn't mean he slept with her or had a relationship. He could still be true to his wife–his partner."

Gillian forced her eyes to his. "What if the man had a history with the attached female? Wouldn't you agree, Dr. Damron, that it might look more than a little bit suspicious?"

Hood laughed. "Now this is the kind of interchange we'd had hoped from the two of you." Hood rubbed his hands together. "It's our desire to see you two mix it up–to disagree."

Amusement graced Lucian's lips, which only fueled her anger. "I can assure you, Mr. Hood, Dr. Damron and I rarely agree on relationships." Gillian offered up a new challenge.

Lucian gave her a smile, the one she remembered from their intimate encounters–the one she didn't expect at this moment. The impact of his smile sent a quick burning wildfire through her, and her hormones kicked into overdrive. "Oh, I don't know, Miss Cornell, I bet we could come up with a few things we both might enjoy–old movies, horse racing, or even something as simple as Chunky Cheese."

Gillian fumed. How dare he insinuate their memories into this conversation? She flushed with the implications. Her heart was too bruised to acknowledge his lasting authority over her ego. "You're right, Dr. Damron, every relationship has its moments when things seem so right. Even you and I have had times when we've called a peace treaty, so to speak, but that doesn't mean we could build the type of relationship that would last. A few brief encounters mean nothing."

Lucian laughed lightly, obviously amused by her implications. "That sounds like a challenge, Miss Cornell. We'll prove who is right on the show. You can prejudge everyone, and I will withhold my opinions until I have all the facts."

In anger, Gillian slammed the folder closed. Lucian Damron infuriated her, but for a brief moment her heart still wanted to believe him. In that moment, she allowed the question of whether he could be right. Had she jumped to conclusions? She had thought that she knew Lucian, and that he knew her. Then the unwanted remembrance of Charlotte Blakeley's face and voice appeared mixed with Gillian's memories of Lucian's touch, and she knew that she was right. Lucian had abused her trust.

"Before you go," Hood added, "we have a couple of publicity gatherings scheduled. Stryent, you'll bring your wife. Dr. Damron and Miss Cornell, please choose someone to accompany you who will not bring controversy with them. That woman you did the fund-raiser with a couple of weeks ago looked good on your arm, Damron. Try for someone like that again."

Gillian saw Lucian flinch. Steeling herself, she said, "Yes, Miss Blakeley makes a suitable match for Dr. Damron. She'll do nicely, won't she, Lucian?" she taunted.

"Charlotte Blakeley is exquisite," he said. "I could do worse." She quickly noted his self-satisfaction at wounding her pride.

Gillian felt the tears prick her eyes' corners. "I'm certain, Dr. Damron, that Miss Blakeley is exactly what you require. You've made only a few mistakes, I can imagine, when it comes to choosing your companions."

"What about you, Miss Cornell, do you always choose well?" he challenged

"No, I'm afraid I'm better at helping my patients than I am in making choices for myself." Gillian's lip quivered with emotion when she looked at him. "You know the old adage about if you can't do something well yourself, you teach someone else to do it. That's me—unlucky in love." She continued to stare at Lucian.

"Well, either way, find someone who can escort you to these events, Miss Cornell," Hood demanded. "I'm certain you've someone in mind."

⌒

A woman on a mission, Gillian called her college roommate Susan when she arrived home. "Susie, do you suppose I could get your friend Daniel to escort me to several events over the next couple of weeks?"

"I don't know, Gilly. Why do you need a hot date?" Susan's interest piqued.

Gillian ignored her insinuations. "I just need an escort to some required presentations—that's all."

"Come on, Gilly, who are you trying to make jealous?"

"Nobody, really..." Gillian attempted to convince Susan, as well as herself, that her motivations were pure.

"Okay, you're not trying to make someone jealous, but you need a gorgeous looking guy as a date." Susan laughed lightly.

Gillian started her sales pitch. "Actually, I thought it might help Daniel too."

Her long-time friend's tone remained amused. "How may I ask will this assist Daniel? He'll want to know."

"Well," Gillian hem-hawed, "the required outings where I need a date involves a bunch of TV and media executives; Daniel could network; I know he's looking for something besides his *fallback* job."

"He'd like that," Susan mused.

Pleased with the plan, Gillian added, "Of course, I'll pay him, too."

Susan relented, "Daniel could probably handle it. When do you need him?"

"I'll email you all the details in a few minutes," Gillian reassured her.

"I'll call Daniel as soon as you send them."

Gillian hesitated. "Susan," she stalled, "do you suppose Daniel could pretend to be interested in me?"

Susan laughed out loud. "Gillian, you're precious. Daniel can make anyone jealous even if he wasn't trying to do so."

"Good! I'd like to make lots of people jealous."

~

Lucian watched her carefully at the meeting, and for a brief, fleeting second, he had observed the chink in Gillian's armor open and invite him in. That moment of hope he had recognized; he'd seen it in his own eyes occasionally. He would use that chink to win her back.

Lucian, therefore, positioned himself where he could see the door. To date, his efforts to earn Gillian's forgiveness had been fruitless. He grumbled, "Of course, it might help if I knew for what I should be apologizing." He realized that Gillian believed that he had seen someone else while in Tahoe, but Lucian didn't know how to convince her of the truth. "I don't know what the bloody hell she wants from me," he grumbled.

Charlotte, whom he had dutifully escorted to the function, brought him a drink from the open bar. She looked like she had just stepped from the pages of *Vogue,* but Lucian could care less. His eyes watched only for Gillian.

Literally, when the "tall, dark, and handsome" man stepped through the door, Lucian felt a bit inadequate, and then he realized, reluctantly, that the man held Gillian's hand, and he led her through the crowd. Seeing her with someone else ripped his heart open. To Lucian's horror, the man slipped his arm around her waist. Gillian smiled at him and touched his lips with her fingertips. Then the guy lightly kissed the pads of her fingers. Not realizing he did so, Lucian groaned in defeat.

Charlotte noted the distress on his face and turned to see the object of his concern. "Well. Well. The ugly duckling landed a big catch," Charlotte snarled. She made the move to come closer to Lucian, but the look on his face told her to reexamine that notion. He wanted nothing to do with Charlotte at the moment. How could he? Gillian was in the room, and she was giving her attentions to another man. She was the most stubborn woman he knew. Stubborn. Argumentative. Sexy as hell. Without a word of parting, he walked slowly away from his date.

Circling the room to keep Gillian in view, Lucian examined his options. Gillian, much to her credit, looked ravishing. She wore a simple, clean-cut royal blue suit with a lacy black bustier underneath. It lifted her bust line, offering a hint of sexuality. Lucian held vivid images of caressing her breasts–the taste of them–the sensations he and Gillian had experienced. He had never felt jealousy, but tonight it coursed through him. The man leaned in to kiss Gillian's cheek, taking the opportunity to assess her attributes. Lucian would gladly flog the bounder to within an ounce of his life. The man plotted Gillian's seduction; Lucian recognized the look and the stance. He had used it often enough himself. His natural instinct was to join her–to take her away–to protect her from her escort. The only thing in his favor was that a quick talking scoundrel would not easily fool Gillian. Flowers and jewelry and smooth words would not sway her.

Slowly and nonchalantly, he worked his way through the crowded room, speaking politely to different show associates. In the back of his mind, he wondered if any of them would even acknowledge him if they knew his secrets. Of late, his thoughts of Gillian had made him question his life choices. She was that kind of woman–the kind, who made a man question his life. Lucian had always encased his heart in an icy vault; unfortunately, Gillian Cornell held the key. Amorous schemes to win her flashed through his mind.

Gillian's heart fluttered alarmingly when she spotted Lucian's methodical approach. He cut a fine figure, and Gillian had found pleasure rising inside her merely by looking at him. When they finally locked eyes, they shared a moment of remembrance, one of the times they had made love. She felt it deep within her, the way his hands searched her skin, and she had given him her secrets. A flush kissed her cheeks with color, and the flicker of recognition played across his face. Every sense memory she had was tied to Lucian Damron.

Reluctantly, Gillian tore her gaze away from his. She readily accepted Daniel's hand and started toward the buffet table. In some ways, Gillian wished she had found Daniel attractive and his attentions pleasing, but she feigned her interest in the man, the same way he had pretended to be interested in her. No "lightning" existed when he took her hand. Moments ago, she felt Lucian's touch from across the room. She couldn't resist searching the room for him again. He leaned against the doorframe, looking relaxed, but Gillian thought him to be anything but.

Lucian's eyes narrowed. Gillian's caress of the man's arm did unusual things to his composure. They made an attractive couple; Gillian would fit nicely into the bounder's embrace. Lucian swallowed hard, fighting back the bile rising in his throat. He had fought the urge to demand that she be his. He had wanted desperately to see those blue eyes staring back at him with desire—her lips swollen and parted. It made him hard just thinking about it. Obviously his plan to give Gillian time to come to her senses about their relationship had backfired for now she enjoyed the attentions of another man. Had she forgotten him so easily? His fantasies involving Gillian had dwindled with these new realities. He could tolerate it no longer; he insinuated himself between Gillian and her date. Only inches from her, he could feel the heat of her body. "Gillian." He could only speak her name.

"Excuse me, Dr. Damron." She attempted to sidestep him. Lucian noted that on some level, her susceptibility to him remained, and it gave him a flicker of hope. It seemed she was not so unaffected by him after all.

Lucian caught her arm. "Gillian, please, we must talk."

"There's nothing to discuss," she hissed in a sharp whisper. Then she offered her companion a half smile. "Daniel, may I introduce one of my colleagues, Dr. Lucian Damron?"

"Nice to meet any friend of Gillian's." The man extended his hand to Lucian.

Numbingly confused, Lucian shook hands out of politeness. "How long have you known Gillian?" he mumbled.

"It seems like forever, doesn't it, Gilly?" He reached out to pull her to his side. "Her former roommate Susan and I grew up together. Gillian and I have been thrown together on and off for years, but we recently found each other again. Isn't it marvelous how some simple act such as buying groceries can change one's life completely?"

Jaw tight, Lucian asked Daniel the question, but his eyes searched Gillian's face for the truth. "So, you met at the supermarket?"

"Yeah, over the fresh cantaloupes. Who would think it?" The man's enthusiasm seemed a bit too lively; Lucian wondered of the interloper's sincerity and was just about to say something to that effect when a hand touched his shoulder.

"Marcus? Marcus Chambers? It is you." A man of medium build spoke to Lucian in a familiar manner.

Lucian tensed for a brief second, but then recovered. "I'm ...I'm afraid you've the wrong person," he stammered.

"You're not Marcus Chambers? Unbelievable! You look exactly like him; at least, like he did back in high school," the man insisted.

"Still not him," Lucian added more emphatically.

"Gee, I'm sorry." The man gestured in surrender as he stepped back. "I guess we all really do have a twin somewhere. Sorry about the mix-up."

Daniel expelled, "That was weird."

Gillian had noted how he remained deceptively upset by the encounter. For once, he wished they did not hold a special connection. Despite his best efforts, his well-honed composure flashed with agitation. "Are you all right?" she whispered softly.

Lucian's eyes drifted to her countenance. "Yeah. I'm...I'm fine. Thanks."

She stepped closer. "Are you positive? You appear upset," she continued to whisper. He stared into the calm blue pools of her eyes. "Is there something I can do?"

Lucian wanted to take her in his arms and lose himself in the heat of her body. It would be so easy to do; she stood so close. His hand reached for her cheek, but someone grabbed it in mid air.

"There you are, Lucian." Charlotte's sugary tones set his nerves on edge.

Reality had arrived, and the moment had escaped them. "Oh. I see you brought Miss Blakeley, Lucian. How unusual!" Sarcasm dripped from Gillian's lips. The door that had been opened by her concern for him had quickly slammed shut again, and this time Gillian bolted it in place.

Charlotte wrapped her arms around Lucian's waist and rested her head on his chest. "The queen of mundane. Imagine. It's Gillian Cornell."

Daniel extended his hand to Charlotte. "It seems Dr. Damron and my Gillian have both forgotten their manners. I'm Daniel Lewis."

Charlotte loosened her hold on Lucian. "Charlotte Blakeley." She accepted his hand. "What do you do, Daniel? I mean for a living."

"I'm an accountant by trade–boring stuff–handling other people's money." Gillian took a long look at Daniel, and Lucian wondered if something was not amiss.

"Any famous accounts?" Charlotte leaned in to tease Daniel with her sexuality.

"Now, Miss Blakeley, you know I can't compute and tell." He returned the taunt. "But I'm sure you'd recognize some of my clients by name."

"Well, Mr. Lewis, you could be interesting after all!" Charlotte cooed as she let her eyes drift over Daniel's lanky frame, as an insult to Gillian. Lucian recognized Charlotte's "claws" fully extended.

"Excuse us," Gillian said, pulling on Daniel's arm, "we'll see you later." She took Daniel's hand, and he eased her into him as they walked away.

Lucian stood staring after her. "Come on, Lucian," Charlotte forced him to look at her. "She's moved on. When will you accept that? I'm still here."

"I know, Charlotte." Lucian's eyes returned to Gillian's retreating form. "I apologize for putting you in this position. You deserve better than this."

Charlotte leaned in closer. "I deserve you, Lucian."

"No one deserves me," he mumbled. "I'm not worth it."

"Stop it!" Charlotte demanded in exasperation.

"Stop what?" Defeat cloaked his shoulders. Lucian had known for a long time that when he fell, it would be a long suffering descent to the bottom. He held too many secrets. Too many lies. There was no way out for him. He would be forever on the outside looking in.

"Stop moaning after that little nothing! She's not even in your league!" Charlotte insisted that he look at her again. She tugged insistently on his arm.

"You're right. Gillian Cornell's out of my league, but it is I who should be thankful for any attention she sends my way."

At the next two "required" appearances Lucian came stag while Gillian still kept company with Daniel. At each event, Lucian's eyes followed every move Gillian made; he allowed himself the pleasure of drinking in the sight of her. Occasionally, he caught a glimpse of *his* Gillian, and then she would replace it with the mask she wore of late. Lucian had decided after the first night's disaster and his unusual self-loathing that he could win Gillian's affections again. He recognized that they shared a mutual desire–a searing endless heat–and he would use it against her. Everything in her still wanted him. He was sure of that fact, and Lucian was willing to "sacrifice" himself to fulfill her passions.

She stood some five feet away from Daniel, who was making small talk with a couple of the show's assistants. Lucian had waited patiently for his move. Anticipating the end of the conversation, Lucian stepped before Gillian for a face-to-face. The smell of her lavender wafted over him, and he fought every urge not to drop to his knees before her and plead for her forbearance. Instead, he smiled and murmured a greeting, "Gillian, long time since we have spoken."

Slowly, unwillingly, she settled her gaze upon him. His eyes held her in an intimate moment. Social conventions would require her to acknowledge his presence, but Lucian noted the angry frustration evident in her body language. "Lucian, how pleasant to see you again." She said the words loud enough for those milling about to hear. She leaned in for the obligatory "air" kiss. Yet, Lucian had no intention of wasting a kiss when Gillian stood this close. Instead of a warm breath on her cheek, Gillian felt the warmth of his lips on hers. The kiss was brief, but it had served its purpose as a reminder of their time together. "Was that necessary?" she snarled, obviously alarmed by his closeness.

Lucian offered a teasing smile; he leaned closer so only she could hear. "I was just wondering, Sweetling, if your friend Daniel or anyone else in this room, besides me, knows you have a mole on your right hip bone? I doubt it."

Gillian flushed with color; her cobalt blue eyes flashed with passion. She moved away from him as quickly as possible. "You should not say such provocative things," she whispered hoarsely.

"Of course, I shouldn't," he chastised himself, "but that won't keep me from doing so." Lucian strolled away; he would seek her out again later. He ordered a beer from the cash bar. His instincts had proved correct. He loved the reaction he had received from her; Gillian Cornell's indifference to him lay shallow. He may be out of her life, but their affair was never far from either Gillian's or his mind.

Just to reinforce his power over her, Lucian stepped behind a potted palm and hit the button on his cell phone that was preprogrammed for Gillian's number. From the shadows he watched her grimace when she recognized his number on the screen display, but rather than make a scene, Gillian stepped away from the others to take the call. "What is it now, Lucian?" she said testily.

"I thought I might offer myself up as proper escort rather than that popinjay to whom you cling," he said teasingly. "You would look so much better on my arm."

"Things have changed," she declared defiantly.

He smiled inwardly. She was trying so hard to convince herself that what they had was over. "Did I ever tell you that I like a woman with a bit of spunk?" he said seductively.

"God, you are egotistical!" Gillian accused.

"Not so," he countered. "Yet, of late, I have wondered why you become so flustered in my presence. Before, we had an easy give and take. I gave. You took. You gave. I took. It was perfection. You do remember perfection, don't you, Gillian? You and me together."

Throughout the conversation, she had searched the room for him. Finally, her eyes found his. The woman was dangerous to his peace of mind. "Lucian, please…" she whispered.

"I love it when you say 'please,' Darling." He hit the "End Call" button, but Lucian did not look away. Gillian remained locked in his gaze until a stranger stepped between them. "Oh, yes, Darling, I love it when you say 'please,' and I plan to hear it again very soon."

⌒

Gillian had hated her response to Lucian. As often as she had schooled her feelings for him, his presence always played havoc with her composure. His smile sent a hunger through her. She shivered, recalling her reaction to him; he had sought her out and had purposely enticed her with the seductive timbre of his voice and the promises in his gaze. He was Temptation in its worst form. She had wished in some ways he wouldn't pursue her, but, in other ways, his continued attentions made her glow with happiness. "Our affair was too hot not to cool down," she had told her mirror's reflection only this morning. "I can't seem to resist his charm."

As Lucian walked away, she deliberately inched closer to where Daniel stood; he had worked the crowd, networking. The show's producers liked his looks, and at the last gathering, they had asked him to audition as the program's host. Since then, Daniel had showed her little attention; instead, he groveled for the gig. Listening to him "perform" had made her want to leave immediately, to escape this *circus* she had created. However, she had remained dutifully at Daniel's side; a smile plastered to her face, Gillian nodded at all the right times, pretending to be interested in what he said. Yet, being ignored completely, she slunk away to nurse her bruised ego and to reflect on her earlier encounter with Lucian.

She bought a white wine at the cash bar. Taking a sip, she allowed her eyes to search the room. *Where was he? Where was Lucian?* She made polite conversation here and there as she circled the room slowly; no matter how she had attempted to remain indifferent, her whole body cried out for Lucian. Therefore, it was no surprise when, as if by magic, he materialized at her side. "Come with me," he demanded, leading Gillian toward an abandoned room. Heat from his body wormed its way up her arm and into her chest.

Without thinking, she followed his lead until the door closed behind her, and then Gillian panicked. "What do you think you're doing, Lucian?"

"I wanted to speak to you," he said in a low, controlled voice, "and you refused my request."

"You'll screw it all up–my book deal–your TV show! You'll destroy us," she reminded him angrily.

"Talking won't destroy us, Gillian!" Frustrated, he ran his hand through his hair.

She insisted, "If they find out about us, it could!"

"You didn't care before. Why do you care now?" he barked out.

"Before, I thought we had something worth more than the media contracts, but now I know it was all part of the act!"

"Damn it, there is no act!" Lucian wrapped his arms around her and dragged her body closer. She started to protest, but he smothered the sound with the pressure of his mouth on hers. The kiss started as a battle of wills, but being pressed against his hard, muscular body did things to her. Lucian assailed her mouth–tasting and teasing, his tongue stroking her. She couldn't get enough of him–didn't think it possible to ever have enough of Lucian Damron. Then the intensity of the kiss changed from a battlefield to slow eroticism. Blatant lust in its purest form. Fog invaded her mind, and Gillian gave herself up to the moment. His tongue slid in and out of her mouth, mimicking what had once been her greatest pleasure, creating an intense yearning, and she arched toward him. In a sound between a groan and a whimper, she surrendered, and Lucian deepened the kiss. Just like that, she quit being angry; she wanted him as much as he had wanted her. She clung to his neck, helplessly raising her hand to his thick black hair before she melded into his body. The strap of her cocktail dress slipped from her shoulder. She shuddered with the onslaught of desire.

When his knuckles brushed the fullness of her breast, it was as if she had found her way home. This man was home, in its truest sense of the word. He shifted his hands to her nipples, forcing the bud to its hardness. She moaned with the pleasure. Yet, his betrayal remained a stumbling block between them. She could not face the pain of his withdrawal again. The protest returned. Valiantly, she pushed against his chest. "Lucian, we can't do this."

"Why not? We're great together." He pulled her close again. And he was correct. If Gillian lived a thousand years, she would never know this type of pleasure again. Only in Lucian's arms had she felt whole.

"It doesn't matter," she insisted. Gillian fought her way free of his embrace. "I'm not the kind of woman who gives her affections easily.

You're not the kind of man who gives his affections at all. No matter how great we are, there's no future for us, and I can't do casual sex. It is just not my style. Let's just go back to the way we started–contesting each other on the lecture circuit." Lucian released her without protest, but something told her that his restraint had been worn thin.

"Gillian, I can't do that! It's out of the question! We've come too far," he argued.

Moving away abruptly, Gillian stepped around him. She shot him a dismissive glance. "Lucian, we cannot continue our relationship. You have to accept that."

Chapter Five

THE SHOW'S CREW, ALONG WITH Dr. Stryent, Gillian, and Lucian, arrived at the mountain retreat a few days before the participants. The technicians had set up the lighting and the sound, stocked the place with food and supplies, and finished off the last minute details. Once again, Michael Hood met with the three psychologists for their last briefing before the taping began. "The couples will arrive tomorrow morning," he began. "I know we've been over the parameters before, but I want to review them again. First, each of you understands your role in this process. You will counsel the couples in groups and as individuals. We'll tape each of those sessions. The couples know they're being taped so it will be up to you to pull them from their self-consciousness. We assume some will be uncomfortable at first. You'll need to make them forget the camera's rolling.

"The cameras are everywhere–that means even in your private quarters, but not in your bedrooms. Remember to cover up before you step from the bathroom. We wouldn't want pictures of you out there on the various social medias." Hood let out a light laugh.

"Why are we being watched?" Stryent demanded.

"It's to assure the viewing public none of this is staged. The only part of your tapes we plan to use is if you discuss your findings about the couples. We'll tape 24/7, but we'll only use sixty minutes per show. Of course, the first two weeks are ninety minutes long. Then there's the first elimination. It is possible for a *Second Chances After Dark* on one of the premium stations, but that's not definite. In that, we'll use scenes not seen in the regular cable slot.

"Now let's discuss some security issues. As explained earlier, your personal communication will also be monitored. That means your phone calls, text messages, emails, and stuff like that. You may only use the phones and computers given to you by the show. We don't want to censure your talking to love ones, but nothing about the show or the participants may be discussed. So, for example, Miss Cornell, you may speak daily to your sister's medical facility to assure yourself that her care is meeting your specifications, but we will use a 'delay' broadcast, so to speak, where we will monitor whether you share information on the show. The same type of monitoring will occur on your emails and your text messages. We will not allow news leaks to occur regarding the show's outcome.

"Just relax and enjoy yourself this evening. Review the participants' portfolios. I would suggest that you meet after lunch to exchange ideas and information on the couples. For the show itself, some activities will be preplanned–things like the dance lessons and the obstacle course, but we can also facilitate extemporaneous activities. If you think of some sort of therapy from which the participants might benefit, then we'll go with the flow. Any questions?" He paused to survey their faces. "Okay, then, I'll be around if you need me."

Gillian sat in a comfortable chair in the lounge area; the portfolios for each couple scattered on the floor at her feet. She thumbed through one of the folders, making notations on sticky note tabs. Engrossed in what she read, she took no notice of the man when he approached her. "Excuse me, Miss Cornell, have you seen Dr. Damron?"

Gillian looked up to see one of the show staffers. "No, I'm afraid I haven't," she assured him. "I believe I heard him say he wanted to check out the grounds before we meet later this afternoon. Is there something I can do to help you?"

The thing that made Gillian so successful as a psychologist was her look of innocence. She possessed an air where a person wanted to confide in her–to be her friend, and she used it to her benefit. The man looked sheepishly around. "I just wanted to show Dr. Damron this picture from my high school yearbook. I thought Dr. Damron was a guy I went to high school with. Of course, he isn't, but I wanted to show him his twin; that's why I brought my annual with me."

Gillian remembered the incident. It was one of the few times she had seen Lucian visibly shaken. Something in his reaction acknowledged that Lucian hid the truth. Curious, she asked, "Might I see the picture?"

"Sure." The man laid the book open on the low coffee table before them. Gillian dropped to her knees to get a closer look at the book. "See, here's a picture of Marcus Chambers. Doesn't he look like Dr. Damron?"

The face was younger and a bit more naïve looking, but the resemblance was uncanny. She observed the same dark eyes, eyes that could look into a person's soul, and the same enigmatic, nearly wicked, smile. "He does favor Dr. Damron," she mumbled. "Are there other pictures of Marcus Chambers in here?" She flipped a couple of pages, searching for the familiarity within the faces.

"Yes, Ma'am." The man smiled. "Marcus Chambers was a bit of a loner; I don't know much about his family. Someone once said that he lived in a foster home. He worked part-time at the local hospital. It was a small town; everyone knew everyone else's business. I just remember how smart he was. I never once asked for anything from him that he didn't try to do. Of course, with his looks he was popular with the girls, but I don't think he saw any one for very long. A real ladies' man!" As he spoke, he pointed to club pictures and leisure shots containing Marcus Chambers' image.

"Well, I agree with you. Dr. Damron has a twin." Gillian gave a light laugh. "I hope he finds this amusing."

Her tone made the man look up suddenly. "Do you think I might offend him? I wouldn't want to do that; Mr. Hood would have my head."

"Maybe you should put the book away. Let me see how Dr. Damron reacts. If I think he'd like to see the pictures, I'll let you know."

"Gee, that's nice of you, Miss Cornell. I just thought he'd think it was funny; I mean, I wanted him to see why I made a mistake at the party." The man seemed nervous. "This is my first major show; I sure wouldn't want to muck it up just because I offended someone."

"It's okay," Gillian assured him. "I know Dr. Damron would probably laugh this off. I think we're all a bit stressed, hoping for the show's success. I'll let you know when he's ready to see the book."

"Sure. Thanks, Miss Cornell." The man closed his yearbook and stood to leave. "It was nice speaking to you."

After his exit, Gillian returned to her chair and her files, but she no longer concentrated on the portfolio contents. It was the image of Marcus Chambers, which fascinated her.

⌇

Stryent led the discussion, but all three contributed to the discourse. "Let's review what we know about each group. We should be familiar with each couple's background and their looks. We can't be walking around scanning their files for information."

"Can we use our personal communication devices to record our observations?" Lucian asked as he straightened the folders on the desk.

"I assume, but maybe we should speak to Hood just in case. He said something about screening calls and information. Now, what do we know about Gary Jordan and Melinda Salyer?"

Gillian explained, "They were married in college–freshman year, I believe. They divorced eighteen months later. However, they have remained *friends* over the years. Neither speaks poorly of the other. They've both been married and divorced from other people."

"How old are they?" Stryent asked.

"It appears they're in their early to mid-forties. They've been separated over twenty years."

Stryent looked confused. "Is there another couple who's been separated for a long time?"

Lucian flipped over another folder. "Mary Nelson's not seen her ex-husband Bruce for ten years. He went out for a drink with friends one evening and just didn't return home again. Bruce left her with nothing; she worked two jobs to raise their child. I'm not sure why she has agreed to be part of this show; it doesn't appear that she wants him back. I would venture that she's doing the show for the money or some sort of revenge. He was gone for seven years before she even applied for a divorce, and even then she kept his name."

"Many women keep the man's name, especially when children are involved," Gillian offered, but Lucian intentionally ignored the hint of a challenge in her tone. He meant to keep her a kilter as far as their relationship was concerned. Arguing with her had only added to Gillian's image of him as a self-serving scoundrel. Instead, he would reason with her and seek out opportunities to prove himself.

"Yvonne Curry Griffin and Sean Griffin have an unusual situation," Stryent changed the topic. "They don't seem to want to be together, but their families and friends believe they're the ideal couple. They've been apart for five years."

"Then we've got the infamous Theo Jenkinson," Gillian intoned. "He has several illegitimate children; Grace Blunt Jenkinson supposedly caught him more than once with other women."

"Don't forget we cannot prejudge," Lucian cautioned.

"I just hate when a man cannot be true; he made a commitment to Grace and their child," Gillian reasoned.

"You don't know the man, Gillian; maybe he's changed. Maybe he now realizes what he lost when he abandoned Grace." Again, Lucian used Jenkinson as a way to speak about their relationship, and despite her strong resolve, she allowed Lucian to hold her gaze for an extended moment before she looked away.

"Once a man has a reputation as a womanizer, it seems he takes great pride in it," she said softly. "He doesn't think about the people he hurts." Gillian let her eyes rest on her hands, which were folded in her lap. Lucian watched as she swallowed hard, evidently, trying to keep the pain from showing, but the moisture pricking at the corners of her eyes was apparent even to the casual observer. Lucian instantly wanted to take her in his arms and comfort her and assure Gillian that he had never meant to hurt her and would never hurt her again. He would rip out his own heart first before he would see harm come to her. Yet, he made himself stay the course. Time would arrive for such declarations, but she had to relearn to love him.

Stryent interrupted the moment. "Let's move on. We shouldn't spend all our time on Jenkinson. We have Andrew Belden and Ada Colton Belden. What do we know about them?"

Gillian swallowed hard again, and her resolve returned with a shift of her shoulders. "They were married less than two years. He broke it off when he found out that before the wedding that she had slept with her sister's fiancé."

"Maybe I should prejudge her," Lucian disputed.

"Leave it, Lucian; you've made your point," Gillian hissed. "Both sexes make mistakes."

"Does Belden still love her?" Stryent wanted to know.

Lucian added, "His pre-show interview indicates as much."

Gillian laughed awkwardly. "It's like that movie *The Wedding Date*."

"What?" Stryent asked.

"Oh, it's what gentlemen righteously call a *chick flick*, but that's the sub plot of the movie. The girl getting married slept with her step sister's fiancé," Gillian explained. "A bit ironic, isn't it?"

"I doubt if it's ironic," Lucian mused. "The show's producers likely chose the Beldens specifically for that point. We have to remember the producers picked each of these couples for a particular purpose. They weren't chosen randomly."

Stryent added, "You're right. Thousands applied, and only these six were chosen. I am certain the producers are looking for a certain amount of drama. Okay, who's last?"

Gillian looked about nervously. Constantly aware of the slightest change in her demeanor, Lucian couldn't help but to respond. "What's wrong?"

"I'm just beginning to feel very voyeuristic. I feel like we're spying on people, striping them naked before the American viewing public."

"Remember that they made the choice to be here, Gillian—the same as did we." Lucian instinctively leaned in to protect her from something neither of them could explain. Casually, he squeezed the back of her hand as it lay across her lap under the table, and Gillian impulsively cupped his hand to hers with her free hand; it was the briefest of gestures, but for both Gillian and Lucian it was a flicker of what once lay between them.

As he did earlier, Stryent didn't observe what was occurring between his colleagues. He continued to analyze the files while ignoring Lucian's body language. "The last couple married after only dating for three weeks. The marriage wasn't much longer—less than six months. They've been apart for three years. Neither of them is currently in a relationship. Well, I guess that's the competitors for the courtship wars," he added without a smile.

"I like that," Gillian giggled self-consciously, releasing Lucian's hand. "Maybe the producers should subtitle the show *The Courtship Wars*." She moved one hand through the air as if seeing the words on a marquee.

"Courtship Wars," Lucian whispered. His thoughts had returned to his relationship with Gillian. *That's exactly what this is for me: a courtship war.*

"Do you understand, Barb, that we'll talk to each other every night over the computer? I'll be able to see you, and you'll be able to see me." Gillian adjusted the screen.

"This is fun, Gilly; it'll be just like a space ship–like on TV." Barb came in close to the screen and made silly faces for the camera.

"If things aren't good, Baby Girl, you need to tell me, and I'll come home. Okay?" Gillian instructed.

"Okay, Gilly."

"You can see me on the real TV some too. I told Mrs. Stafford to allow you to watch before you go to bed. Of course, that's only once a week."

"I want to see my sister on TV." Barb laughed loudly before mugging the screen again.

A soft tap on the door drew Gillian's attention away. Lucian stood in the half-opened doorway. "I'm sorry, Gillian; Hood wants to see you for a minute."

Gillian looked longingly to the screen and then to the door. "Barb, I guess I'll have to hang up."

"No, don't," Lucian stopped her. "If it is acceptable to you, I'll talk to Barb until you return."

She despised it when Lucian did the right thing: Gillian didn't know how to respond. She turned to the screen. "Barb, would you like to talk to Lucian for a few minutes? I must see what Mr. Hood wants; I'll be back in a jiffy."

"Sure, Gilly, I miss Lucian." Her sister beamed with happiness, and Gillian experienced a twinge of jealousy. Even with all his flaws, Barb would gladly accept Lucian. Her sister did not support Gillian's boycott of all things Lucian Damron.

"Okay, then." Gillian reluctantly slipped from the room. Meanwhile, Lucian took up his position.

Lucian assumed his smooth-talking persona. "Hi, my lovely, Barbara."

"Hi, Lucian. You shouldn't stay away. I miss you; so does Gilly." Innocently, her words flamed Lucian's hope.

"I didn't want to stay away, Barb; it's all a big mistake," he explained.

Barb accused, "Gilly says you don't love her anymore. Why don't you want to be our boyfriend?"

Her childlike words tore him apart. He felt about two inches high under Barb's questioning. "Barb, please believe me; I want both you and Gillian as my girlfriends again. Who said I didn't love Gillian?"

"Gilly said. I had told her that you didn't love me anymore, and that's why you were in the picture with the other girl." Not understanding, Barb's eyes filled with tears.

"Barb, please don't cry. I never meant to hurt you. I love you; you have to know that. Please still be my girlfriend," he pleaded.

Barb stifled her tears, wiping her face with her sleeve. "Tell Gilly, Lucian. She cried at the picture too." Lucian swallowed hard, forcing his self-loathing away. "Lucian?"

"Yes, Barb." He brought his attention to the screen. "I've a secret. Do you want to hear?" Total abandon played through her voice.

Although his mind raced to and fro, he tried to sound calm. "Sure, Sweetheart. Tell me your secret."

"I've another boyfriend. His name is Thad. You can meet him when you and Gilly return home."

Lucian teased, "I'm jealous, Barb. Is he as handsome as I am?"

"He's handsome, Lucian. With Thad, I'm his only girlfriend. You like Gilly too," Barb reasoned in her childlike manner.

"I do like Gillian best, but I still love you too, Barb. Don't forget it, okay?" Lucian fought back the anger, knowing he had hurt Gillian so badly. "Have you told Gillian about Thad?" he asked cautiously.

"It's my secret." She sounded like a spoiled little child at the moment.

Lucian worried, "Barb, people who love each other don't keep secrets. I won't tell her, but I think you should tell Gillian about Thad." Who was he to advise someone about keeping secrets? He was a walking conundrum.

"She might get mad at me," she insisted.

"Gillian loves you. Tell her your secret."

"Gillian loves you, too. Don't make Gilly cry again," Barb warned.

"I won't...I promise, Barb. I swear!" Lucian gasped at how simple she made all this sound; his heart beat a staccato in response.

Gillian reentered the room. Lucian bade Barb farewell and exited, as quickly as good manners would allow. He required time to mull over what Barbara had innocently confided. Gillian, obviously, felt more than she had pretended. Somehow, he would use this information to his advantage.

⌣⌒

The participants arrived, settling in for the competition. Much to Lucian's chagrin, Daniel joined them for the filming. Luckily, he would not be around on a daily basis. The producers would bring him in for the weekly commentary once they had edited the film for the broadcast. Just as luckily, Gillian threw herself into the counseling scenarios, keeping her from advancing her relationship with the hunky host.

⌣⌒

On the second day of filming, Gillian gathered all the "wives" into a session in the smaller study. She was excited about the possibilities, and her few interactions with the women had made her feel amazingly comfortable. It was only her reaction to everything Lucian Damron that troubled her. The staff had provided soft drinks and wine coolers along with snacks to make for a more relaxed atmosphere. "This is our first session," Gillian began. "These times are for me to get to know you better." She purposely didn't remind them of the video cameras. "I'm going to ask simple questions this first time." The ladies lounged on the sofas and chairs. A sense of nervousness flitted through the air, charging them with anticipation. The couples had arrived throughout the day yesterday. They had dinner together, along with the three show psychologists, but this was the first real opportunity to discover something of their competition.

Gillian cleared her throat for attention. "Ladies, over the next few weeks I'll be asking you some very personal questions. Sometimes you're going to feel a bit of angst and not want to answer; sometimes you'll bubble over with enthusiasm. I must insist for this process to work that you participate. So, when you feel the discomfort, push through it and share your thoughts. When you have a lot to share, we'll all listen. However, I must also insist that you allow others the opportunity to share equally. You don't judge, and you don't censure what your fellow competitors say. We will not attack each other." The women eyed one another, but they all agreed. "As I said before, my question today is an easy one. What do you miss most about your ex?" Gillian watched as the women shifted their weight, taking sips from their drinks, trying to stall before they answered.

Finally, Melinda Salyer found her voice. "Well, I guess I'll start." She rolled her eyes in embarrassment. "What I miss most about Gary is the heat of his breath on the back of my neck during the middle of the night. We always used to sleep spooned together. You know what I mean." Some of the others nodded in encouragement. "It was the thing that I missed when we were no longer together. That's the only time I ever felt safe–protected. When I was with Gary."

Gillian's mind flashed to Lucian; she missed him desperately, but she had forced the loneliness away. "That's potent, Melinda," Gillian barely whispered. "Did you ever tell Gary that when you were married?"

"Not really," Melinda half laughed. "The man already knew he had enough control over me; I always melted when he gave me one of his smiles. That's probably why we're still friends; I could never refuse him. Telling him something so secret would be too difficult."

"Yet, you tell perfect strangers," Mary added incredulously.

"I think I just finally needed to say the words out loud," Melinda spoke quietly as if deep in thought.

Silence prevailed for a few minutes before Nicole O'Connor's soft words added to the empathy all of them felt for Melinda. "Mark and I weren't married very long. Heck, we didn't even date very long, but he had a way of looking at me. I never knew what he hoped to see when he stared at me; yet, I admit I liked having him look." A hormonal sigh filled the room.

"They always look at you like you're special when you first meet," Mary nearly spit out the words, "but it's all part of the act. They never mean it; none of them do."

Gillian thought of how Lucian's eyes always found her in a crowded room. She would have to admit, his gaze created sensations that she would never forget. The group continued to allow Mary to rant for a few more minutes before Ada Colton cleared her throat to speak.

"I wanted Andrew from the moment I saw him. I screwed it up, but I did love him. I always knew he was the person who could touch that deep need in me, but I betrayed him, and he turned from me."

"Well, you have another chance," Gillian cautioned.

"I do," Ada offered, "and I don't plan to screw this one up."

"My Theo knows how to kiss better than any man on the face of the earth. Maybe that's why women throw themselves at him. I miss being held so close and that groan of his when he would sweep me into his arms. He's a very sensual man, and I miss his desire." Grace Blunt laughed seductively. "He's quite a lover."

The other women offered up looks of surprise and of admiration. Finally, Yvonne turned to the group. "I don't have anything so intimate to share. I just miss talking to Sean. We used to sit for hours and just talk. We're friends; at least, at one time we were."

Gillian laughed. "If men would simply learn we women think talk is sexy, the female population would be in great trouble."

"Amen to that," Melinda added.

"What about you, Mary?" Gillian turned to her hardest critic in the group.

"I can't think of anything about Bruce that I miss. Maybe I did at first, but when he didn't come back, I obliterated him from my memory. I was too busy trying to feed my child to miss Bruce any longer."

The women grew quiet. Melinda reached out and patted Mary's hand. A sisterhood of hurt developed. Melinda whispered, "Men have all the control; no matter how much women's lib we shout about, it's still a man's world."

Again, silence prevailed as lines of friendship formed. "What about you, Gillian? Do you have a husband somewhere? An ex?"

"No, I've never married." Gillian looked embarrassed under their close scrutiny. "I take care of my special needs sister; I haven't had much time for relationships."

"Surely there was someone important in your life?" Ada inquired.

Gillian let her gaze cloud over with memories of Lucian. "Yeah, there was someone with whom I thought of...well, you know what I mean, but he's no longer in the picture."

"What do you miss about him?" Nicole gushed. Instinctively, they all leaned forward to hear her secrets.

Gillian hesitated, not sure she wanted to open up the hurt again. The pain of losing Lucian was still too new—too raw. Finally, she described the instant she knew she loved him. "He had a way of coming up behind me, and I could feel his heat all down my back. I couldn't stop myself from leaning into him. When you ladies know me better, you'll find out I'm real into scents. My current research is on how we're all attracted to certain scents. Anyway, I would lean in, and he would whisper in my ear, 'You smell of lavender and vanilla.' He knew my favorite scents. I was hooked."

"I hear you're dating the host, Daniel Lewis." Melinda's statement came out as a question.

Gillian confided, "I went out with him a few times."

"Was it Daniel Lewis? Was he the one?" Nicole moved closer as if Gillian held the world's secrets.

"No, it wasn't Daniel. We're good friends, but he wasn't the one."

Mary asked, "Are you going to tell us who it was."

Gillian grinned, "I need some secrets, don't I?"

The women giggled, young girl giggles, like they were all fifteen again and discussing boys and crushes and first loves. "I think that's enough for today, Ladies. You're welcome to stick around and talk or head off to other activities."

"Thanks for sharing with us," Yvonne smiled as she made her exit. "It's nice to know you don't have all the answers either. It makes me feel less vulnerable." Instinctively, she hugged Gillian. "I will enjoy talking with you."

During her session, Gillian had forgotten the cameras rolled, but Lucian hadn't. He stood mesmerized, watching how quickly the women had taken to her. It was like she was their sister or their daughter or their neighbor. Gillian engendered confidence and sincerity. The women opened themselves to her immediately. He watched in delight, but when she spoke of her "secret love," he felt suddenly out of breath, as if he had run a marathon. She had spoken of him; her memory was of him. It was an honor that someone as perfect as Gillian Cornell would consider him worthy of remembering. In the past, Lucian had catered to the red-hot affair. One lasting a month or two with lots of sex and some sort of payoff for his career, but Gillian had never been that type of love interest.

There was lust. Lots of it. But there was something different about the woman. She spoke of home and family, and as much as that idea scared the holy crap out of him, Lucian secretly swore the memory Gillian had described to the contestants would not be the last one she held of him.

Sam Cuttles watched Gillian's session too. He also took note of Lucian's reaction. "Hood," he motioned to the man to follow him to a secluded area. "Have you noticed how much sexual tension there is between Dr. Damron and Gillian Cornell?"

"Not really," Hood replied.

"Well, there is. I saw it early on in Louisville. Trust me on this one, there is," Cuttles smirked. "We should use this to our advantage. Get tape of them together. Let's also have them participate in the challenges; then we'll see if the blogs light up the way I think they will."

Hood's attention rested on the video of Lucian's reaction to Gillian's session. "It won't hurt to watch them. You might've just figured out a way for us to win the ratings war, Sam."

Cuttles laughed softly. "My gut's never wrong. We thought the show's success depended on their opposition; now I'm of the persuasion to believe their desire for each other could be our trump card."

Hood laughed also, as if their discussion lightened his concerns for the show's success. "It'll be fun to watch at the very least."

"Guys, over the next few weeks, you'll be meeting with me, Miss Cornell, or Dr. Stryent on a regular basis." Lucian sat with the men in the late afternoon. "Sometimes your former wives will join us. Sometimes we'll meet individually. Many of the questions will be tailored to open up lines of communication. Dr. Stryent and I are psychologists; Miss Cornell is a sex therapist."

"Does that mean she'll teach us how to be better in bed? I'm already pretty good in that department, Doc." Theo Jenkinson grinned from ear-to-ear.

"Maybe she'll teach our ex-wives how to be better in bed. Maybe I might look at Yvonne more in that case." Sean Griffin slapped Theo on the back as he took a seat.

Lucian laughed too, but only to gain their confidence. "Actually, sex therapy involves more talking than anything. The discussions will be highly explicit. Miss Cornell might ask how often you masturbate or how quickly you have an orgasm. You might be asked to read appropriate material or watch a video." The sincere nature of Lucian's tone indicated he would broker no one not participating fully.

"Oh, good, porn." Theo sought the endorsement of the other participants, but all he received this time were disapproving stares.

Lucian leveled a look of "death" on the guy while the others shifted nervously in their seats. "We will take each of the exercise seriously," he warned. "Okay, today I want to know what turns you off sexually."

"You're kidding, right?" Sean stumbled across the words.

"Not really," Lucian nodded his head. "Come on, don't be shy." His question was met with total disbelief. The men slouched in the chairs, arms folded across their chests, shutting out the possibilities. Lucian waited, but nothing came. "All right so *what we have here is a failure to communicate.*" He laughed lightly at his joke. Still no one opened his mouth. Finally, Lucian tried a different tactic. "How about I start? For me, a big turn off is the woman who tells me how to make love to her. You know what I mean. Touch me like this. Don't mess up my hair."

"Yeah, that's bad, but it's just as bad if you have to do all the work," Andrew Belden blurted out. "God, this isn't the 1800s; so often I wished that Ada would respond or even be the aggressor."

Lucian said softly, "Would it have made a difference?"

"It might have made me think that she'd forgotten her supposed one-night stand." Andrew spoke aloud the doubts that he had felt forever. Lucian made a mental note to assist Andrew with this issue.

"What bugged me about Melinda is she always thought her body wasn't attractive. She would complain until we turned the lights off." He laughed lightly. "I always thought she was beautiful, but she didn't trust me when I told her that."

"Sometimes it's hard to convince them we mean what we say." Lucian spoke without thinking. Pictures of Gillian's face when she left him still haunted him. Her hurt so evident.

"Yvonne talked too much in bed. She wouldn't shut up; she'd go on and on about the house and her job and even the bills."

Lucian's head snapped up. "It's funny that you say this because I know many women starve for a man's attention." He recalled Yvonne's comment about missing Sean's company. "Did you realize how much Yvonne needed that downtime? Did you spend lots of time just talking prior to the marriage?"

"Yeah, but once we were together, there was no time. We worked different shifts," Sean reasoned.

"I don't know Yvonne, but I do know women think differently from men. Where we think spending what little time we have in a day intimately, they need time to decompress, just sitting together and hearing a loved one's voice. It sounds silly to us, but it works for them," Lucian assured him.

No one said anything, as if hearing Lucian for the first time. Finally, the floodgates opened. Lucian heard about women who after marriage let themselves go, women who fake it, and women who talk about former lovers. "I hate women who wear men's cut panties or even boxer briefs. Give me a woman in a thong any time." Theo Jenkinson pumped out his chest in a primal hunter move.

Mark Clayton turned to him. "Really? I prefer a high cut brief. A long leg is a turn on for me."

"A little lace–black lace–is nice." Bruce Nelson finally opened his mouth.

"Leather and lace." Theo smiled conspiratorially.

Lucian laughed. "We're different breeds. We men. Miss Cornell says we're turned on by weird scents. I once didn't believe her, but hearing how we differ on preferences in women's underwear, maybe I should take her more seriously."

Theo leered, "She's a looker, Doc. Why haven't you checked out this Cornell woman? She looks like your type. I noticed you aren't wearing a wedding ring."

"No, I'm not married," Lucian said distractedly, thinking about Jenkinson's observation. Had he been too obvious in his reaction to Gillian? "Do you think so? I mean, do you think she's my type?" He sucked in a breath almost afraid the others could read his mind. Lucian swallowed visibly, the tendons of his neck straining to push down the hope, which sprang into his chest.

"Sure, anything can happen," Andrew added. "She's not hooked up with anyone is she?

"She dated the guy who's the host for awhile. I'm not certain where that stands, though," Lucian shared in encouragement.

"Him? He doesn't seem her type." Gary snarled his nose. "Actually, I thought he was a homosexual; he's too pretty."

Theo laughed. "He is, isn't he?"

"Anyway, I shouldn't discuss Miss Cornell with you. We're not here for my relationships; we're here to assist you."

"We'll assist you too, Doc. You can be in the same boat as the rest of us poor losers," Mark gestured to the group.

"I think I can handle my own love life." Lucian looked around innocently, but images of Gillian's mouth, her full bottom lip quivering enticingly darted across his memory.

While Gillian and Lucian continued their sessions divided by gender, Dr. Stryent conducted individual evaluations of all six couples. Stryent's sessions would be the highlighted segments on the first two episodes. He would try to predict their compatibility with their ex-mates.

"The day of the show's broadcast we'll put the couples through the first physical test. We'll tape the event for the broadcast." Hood held his daily briefing.

"I thought the show is a live one," Stryent protested.

"We know all the couples may take more than the twelve minutes we've blocked for the event. So, we'll tape each stage; it will be just like all the other taped segments." Hood went over the show's format. "By the way, Damron, Cuttles has decided that you and Miss Cornell will take part in some of the challenges along with the participants."

Gillian's head snapped up. "Why just Lucian and me?"

"Because Dr. Stryent's age and health won't allow him to be a part of the physical challenges. It's too dangerous," Hood reasoned. "He'll do some of the others though."

"Why do we have to be a part of the challenges? This wasn't in the original contract," Lucian demanded.

Hood bestowed a smile on each of them. "First off, Doc, the small print says we can change the job description. Secondly, Cuttles thinks we need the participants to buy into the challenges; their enthusiasm will increase if they have confidence in you."

"I don't know," Gillian gasped. "I agree with Dr. Damron; we didn't sign on for all this."

"Well, Miss Cornell, the stakes have changed. We don't expect you to win the challenges. In fact, we don't want you to win, but we do want you to have empathy for the participants, and we want the competitors to see you as someone they can depend on."

Lucian looked at Gillian, but he spoke to Hood. "Are we partners or individuals in these challenges?"

"Basically, you're individuals, but sometimes we'll have you work together."

"I see," Lucian muttered. He wasn't certain forcing Gillian to be with him would further his cause to win her again. "Can we do this, Gillian?" He directed his attention to her, attempting to read her real thoughts.

"I don't like it." Gillian looked bewildered. "But I suppose it's possible; we just have to finish."

Chapter Six

THE SIX COUPLES, ALONG WITH Lucian and Gillian, made their way along the western foothills of the Highland Mountains south of Butte. The Humbug Spires loomed ahead. Fifty rock towers ranging from fifty to six hundred feet, the Humbug Spires also sported fragrant meadows and dense forests. Douglas firs and lodge pole pines lined the pathways and trails. The group made the nearly two-miles' trek toward the northeast fork of Moose Creek.

Daniel's voice set up the scene for the TV audience. "Our couples, along with two of our show's resident psychologists as their cohorts, will experience a modified Outward Bound type ropes' course. The purpose here is to develop trust because we all know for a marriage to survive, trust is a major concern. Our participants must make the gradual climb toward Moose Creek. It is a little less than two miles to this checkpoint. Here they will encounter a ropes and beams obstacle course suspended high above ground. The teams must overcome doubts and work together to complete the course. Both members of the team must complete the course together. There are no individual competitors. The couples must make decisions and compromises, as well as learn to rely on one another if they are to receive a second chance at love."

The viewing screen switched to the fourteen individuals setting out for the checkpoint. They each carried a preloaded backpack to make the climb more difficult. Each woman carried twenty pounds in her pack; each man packed thirty pounds. "Remember that you must stay with your partner. If he or she lags behind, you must give him support to catch up," Lucian called out. "Pace yourself; the purpose is not to finish first, but to finish. You must cross the end line together."

The first mile saw the group remaining very much together, but the weighted packs began to take their toll on the competitors. Melinda and Gary stopped to rest; when they started out again, she and Gary carried his pack together while he packed her load on his back; yet, they worked together–the ultimate rule of the challenge. The camera caught his caressing her cheek as they began the gradual climb once again.

Mark and Nicole laughingly teased each other throughout the climb. Athletically inclined, the trek didn't faze them; they offered each other assisted over obstacles and enjoyed points of interest together. The other couples did likewise at a more sedate pace. That is, everyone except Mary and Bruce Nelson. They walked together, but they ignored each other's needs. Bruce seemed exasperated by Mary's lackadaisical attitude, and Mary clearly loathed everything about her ex.

Lucian watched them warily from a distance. Walking at the front of the group, he and Gillian set a steady pace, but they didn't rush the climb. "I don't know why they were chosen," he said out loud, noting the Nelsons with a nod of his head.

Gillian's eyes drifted to where he indicated. "They, obviously, have no desire to remarry. I'm surprised the show's producers even located him. Mary's seen nothing of him for years."

"How does a man just walk away from his family?" Lucian's attention left Nelson's face and rested on Gillian's countenance. "I could never do that; I would stay and work it out."

Gillian's reaction to the soft timbre of Lucian's voice was as it always was. She reluctantly drew near him; her gaze trained on him. He caught himself wanting to touch her, but he shoved his hands purposely in his pockets. The cameras moved in to capture his face, as he climbed toward the turning point. "I can't imagine you ever being so cruel," she admitted reluctantly.

"I wouldn't mind coming here sometime and going fishing," Andrew called to Lucian. "I bet the trout are thick."

Ada moved up beside him, taking Andrew's hand. "I never knew you liked to fish."

"Yeah, I like it; it's quiet and peaceful. Maybe we could come here sometime; we could camp out, do some hiking–you'd like the waterfalls, I bet."

Ada dropped her eyes from his intensity. "I'd like that." Andrew instinctively raised her hand to his lips and lightly kissed her knuckles.

Approaching the turning point, Lucian saw fear suddenly encompassing Gillian's stare. Wanting to protect her from whatever frightened her, he moved closer. Instinctively, he took her elbow to support her. "What is it, Sweetheart?" he whispered close to her ear.

She swallowed hard, trying to steel her nerves, but her eyes grew as she saw the rope course. "I'm afraid of heights," she murmured urgently. "I can't do this!"

Lucian dug a water bottle from his pack to hand to Gillian to disguise their conversation. "The cameras are rolling," he spoke quietly as he turned his head to observe the show's staff focusing on the contestants.

"I can't, Lucian!" she hissed. "Why didn't they tell us? What am I going to do?"

"You're going to climb the ropes," he insisted. Before she could respond, he added, "I'll help you; you can do this. Your mother and father would expect you to try. Barb would try it. You can't always play it safe, Gillian; sometimes you must put your trust in someone else. You'll have security lines on you; you won't fall."

"I won't fall because I won't do it!" she insisted.

"Gillian, look at me. You're the bravest person I know. Trust me; I'll never let anything happen to you."

"You'll hold me throughout?" Her eyes pleaded for assurance.

Lucian fought the urge to smile. He also fought the urge to tell her he had wanted to hold her close to him for weeks now. Instead, he whispered in her ear, "I'll never let you go."

A similar reaction became evident when the other couples reached the first stage of the competition. Every woman in the group had a fear of heights. As the couples became aware of the unlikely coincidence of each woman having the same phobia, a new realization hit. The competitors were chosen for their similarities rather than their differences. Yvonne laughed nervously at the prospect of climbing the rope ladder to the first beam platform. Other women stared at the heights being asked as part of the challenge.

Daniel stepped into the mix. "Well, we do have a dilemma." He gave the TV audience a conspiratorial smile. "It seems our contestants have discovered a key component in their selection. All our women have a phobia about heights. That means they must trust their former partners and depend on their ex-husbands to assist them across. Let's get a comment from our resident psychologists before we start. What must our couples do to make this work?" He thrust the microphone at Lucian.

Lucian looked cautiously at Gillian. "It appears the men must step forward and prove themselves worthy of the trust they have asked the women to put in them."

"How do you feel about this situation?" Daniel turned to Gillian; he had no idea the turmoil coursing through her, and Lucian hated the man for his insensitivity.

"Everyone has irrational fears," she stumbled through the words.

Lucian realized the subtle change in Gillian's voice indicated her continued agitation. The tumult that beset her drained the color from her face, and she swayed unconsciously against him. Resting his hand at the small of her back to calm Gillian's growing anxiety, Lucian reached for the microphone. "Miss Cornell and I are going to demonstrate some techniques the men might use to assist the women. Gillian will play the phobia-ridden wife's part, and I will assist her up the heights and across the rope bridge."

Gillian looked at him in disbelief. She would permit Lucian to conceal her unreasonable fear, keeping it from the world's view. Taking her hand in his, Lucian led Gillian toward the rope ladder.

Looking upward at the swinging ropes, she turned to bury her face in the masculine line of his chest. "I can't...I really can't," she moaned.

"I have you, Gillian. Trust me." Lucian turned her around to face the rope ladder. He assisted the staff members with her harness and his. "Go ahead. I'm right behind you," Lucian encouraged.

Tentatively, Gillian began her climb. Lucian shadowed her; every time she stepped up a rung, he moved up behind her, protecting her body with his. He cupped her in his embrace at each rung, encircling her with his arms. Once they were far enough up the rope that the audio couldn't hear what he said, Lucian whispered in her ear each time he moved up behind her. Most of the time he only said things like "Good" or "You're doing great." However, the higher they climbed, his remarks changed to "I'm so proud of you" or "You're absolutely magnificent."

After the twentieth rung, Gillian's pace slowed to a stand still. Her fingers frozen on the ropes, she closed her eyes to quiet her fears. Again, Lucian cupped her body. "What is it, Sweetheart?" he murmured into her ear.

Gillian didn't open her eyes. "Lucian, I need to go back down!" She reached with her foot to find the previous rung. Of course, Lucian rested on that one. The shift of her weight knocked him from the support. As he struggled to maintain his position, the ladder began to swing from their sudden movement. The couples on the ground looked on in amazement; many of the women squealed in fright, burying their faces in each other's embraces.

Dangling from one arm, Lucian fought to right himself on the ladder. Gillian froze, but seeing Lucian swing back and forth in mid air, she forced herself to reach for him. "Catch my hand," she yelled.

Lucian grabbed her wrist. He saw her fright take a backseat to her need to save him. He had won the battle, and it gave Lucian a sense of purpose. Catching the rope part of the ascent, he wrapped his foot around the contraption, pulling himself close to the twisting incline. In infinitely long seconds, he recovered his position several rungs below Gillian. He caught his breath as the ladder stilled at last. Looking up, he realized Gillian had reached for him; tears streamed down her face–horror frozen there.

Quickly, he moved to her. She straightened stiffly to allow him room on the same rung. She looked at him in disbelief. "I'm sorry, Lucian," she moaned as she buried her face in his shoulder.

"It's okay, Sweetling. You can't get rid of me that easily," he whispered as he caressed the back of her head. Realizing the cameras still rolled, he released her. "We need to finish this, Gillian."

She didn't answer, but she nodded her consent. Tentatively, she stepped to the next rung; "Sweetling, we're going to cross the bridge. You will not look any place but into my eyes. Do you understand, Gillian?" She reluctantly shook her head in the affirmative. "We'll take it one step at a time–no rushing."

Gillian's mouth turned up in a hint of a smile. "You like to rush me, Lucian."

His grin turned into a full-fledged smile. He took a step backward. "It's your fault," he teased as he reached for her hand. "You're so irresistible; I couldn't control myself." A stumbling step forward and an expression carved with lines of determination told him they would succeed. "Follow me, Sweetheart," he encouraged her. "It's simple; you know I'll never let anything hurt you. Take another step forward. Let your foot find the support. Look only at me; we'll make it if you trust me." Gillian's gaze locked on his. Step-by-step they crossed the rope bridge, and then Lucian lowered them to the ground with the pulley.

"Wow! That was incredible," Ada gushed as the women surrounded Gillian. "I would've believed that you were terrified."

"I was...I mean I'm afraid of heights," she admitted as her composure returned.

Melinda spun Gillian around. "But you went anyway?"

"We all...we must face our fears," Gillian stammered. Knowing the cameras rolled, she quickly added, "Plus, I knew Dr. Damron would protect me. We're friends." She looked at Lucian, trying to express her gratitude.

Daniel squeezed between Lucian and Gillian. Handing the microphone to Lucian he asked, "What did you say to our Gillian Cornell up there?"

"I just told her that we'd take our time; I wouldn't rush her." Lucian hoped Gillian understood his double meaning. Originally, when Cuttles demanded that they participate along with the contestants, Lucian had disliked the idea, but he felt that he had made more progress with Gillian on that rope ladder than he had since their initial fight. He would embrace the idea of using the challenges to win Gillian's affection.

⌒

The contestant couples for the most part mimicked Lucian and Gillian's efforts. Each time, the men took the lead in helping their ex-wives—again, everyone except Bruce Nelson. He stayed behind Mary on the ladder and the rope bridge, but it was up to Mary to face her own fears. Surprisingly, she controlled her progress across the obstacles with a resolve not often openly demonstrated.

"Mary, I'm so proud of you," Gillian hugged her, once Bruce lowered them to the ground. "You were invincible up there."

"I did what I had to do...no more. As you can see Bruce doesn't know the meaning of the word *trust*." She turned her glare on the man who had once been her husband. "He continues to separate himself from me and our child."

Gillian didn't have an answer. The reason why the Nelsons participated in the challenge still escaped her. She admired Mary Nelson's determination and her independence, but as much as Gillian abhorred what Bruce Nelson did to his family, she could see how Mary could be a hard woman to love, simply because she was an inherently *hard* woman. Gillian would ask Lucian to conduct individual sessions with the Nelsons. "Come with me," Gillian led Mary away.

After the show's premier, Gillian sought out Lucian. She had wanted desperately to thank him for his assistance on the obstacle course. Yet, when she allowed herself to think on Lucian, it wasn't gratitude she wanted to share with him. Her feelings had rekindled as they climbed, and when he dangled from the rope, although she knew he wore safety lines, she had feared losing him from her life. Gillian realized that she should tell him what she felt; she wanted to discover if he still felt anything for her. "Have you seen Lucian?" she asked Dr. Stryent in the game room.

Distracted by the video game he played, he barely answered. "He said something about catching up on his emails."

Gillian nodded in reply and headed toward the communications room. Approaching the open door she could hear the soft murmur of his words. The sound of Lucian's voice caressed her throughout the rope climb; a shot of excitement ricocheted through her. As she stepped in the doorway, Gillian's eyes fell on the back of Lucian's head. He lounged lazily in one of the easy chairs, clutching a cell phone to his ear. She considered sneaking up on him until his words penetrated her conscious thoughts.

"I get it, Charlotte; you didn't like my helping Gillian during the show! You have to remember I'm under contract here."

Gillian froze; Lucian spoke to his lover about her. With a disillusioned shake of her head, Gillian slipped into the darkened passageway.

Lucian waited until Charlotte finished her rant before he responded. "Charlotte, we've had this discussion repeatedly. I'll see whom I want, and I want to see Gillian. Deal with it." He hit the "end call" button. Turning quickly, he stared at the door. Had he heard someone? No one was around, even in the hallway, but he'd a feeling things had just changed for the worse. Looking for the unknown, he made his way along the passageway. Unfortunately, he found it.

⌣⌒

Attempting to make her escape, Gillian turned the corner and, literally, ran into Daniel. "Hey, Gill, a good show," he offered to her startled face.

Stammering, Gillian took one last look toward the communication room before answering. "Oh...Oh, Daniel, I thought you had left already."

"I've got a late flight." Self-consciously, he took her hand. "Gillian, I've never properly thanked you for this opportunity."

"It's nothing, Daniel; I'm happy it worked out for you." She blushed, remembering how she had used him to make Lucian jealous.

"It's great!" He looked around nervously, checking for staff members who might overhear. "I'm really sorry you were put into that situation tonight. Gosh, I had no idea you were afraid of heights, but you handled it admirably. The women emulated your example."

Gillian's color rose again thinking of the intensity of Lucian's stare. "I couldn't have completed the course without Dr. Damron. Without Lucian's help."

Daniel searched her face for the truth. "Is he the one?"

"The one?" Gillian pretended she misunderstood the question.

"You know. The one you were trying to make jealous. Susan said you wanted me to pay attention to you because of some jerk of a guy."

Gillian actually reacted to his insinuation that Lucian was a *jerk;* even though his deceit had brought her pain, she had never thought of him that way. "What...what can I say?" She stumbled through the words. "I'm susceptible to the man. I'm sorry I brought you into this."

"At least, you didn't lead me on. Ours was a business arrangement, and I received more than what I'd hoped from it. However, I wouldn't want to see you hurt, Gillian."

Gillian dropped her eyes. "Well, I'm afraid if that's the truth, you'll have to look the other way. I seem to wear my heart on my sleeve."

"He doesn't deserve you," Daniel whispered. "I hope he discovers what he's missing before it's too late."

"A day late and a dollar short, as my dear mother used to say." He surrounded her in his embrace, permitting Gillian's head to rest on his chest while she allowed herself the comfort of his arms. "Thanks, Daniel."

From the shadows of the hallway, Lucian watched the scene unfold. His heart clutched in despair. He knew, instinctively, that Gillian felt what he felt when they were on the ropes course, but now she found solace in Daniel's arms. Slowly, heart bursting with disgust, he turned toward his rooms.

Cuttles sat in his office; with the assistance of a couple of tech men he had previewed the reviews for the show, along with blogs set up at the show's website. "Well, how does it look?" Hood called as he entered the room.

"You wouldn't believe it," Cuttles laughed. "People are already sizing up their favorites. And they are ecstatic about Cornell and Damron. The show's been over for two hours, and there are over two hundred thousand comments and tweets about them alone. Listen to this one. 'Lucian Damron is HOT! Gillian Cornell should thank her lucky stars. They are so obviously in love.'"

"The public thinks the docs are in love?" Hood laughed.

"Don't you? Didn't you see how he tried to cover for her before their climb? Did you see the expression on both their faces when he nearly fell? Those were real tears streaming down her cheeks." Cuttles strummed his fingers on the chair arm.

Hood slid into a nearby chair. "If you believe they're in love, maybe we should try to catch them."

"Screen the tape we have already shot, and add to it with some additional surveillance on the good psychologists." Cuttles steepled his fingers in thought. "God, I love it when things come together!"

Lucian had known that Gillian was an early riser; she liked to hit the gym or go for a run before breakfast. With that in mind, he *accidentally* met her in the hallway leading to their private quarters. "Good morning," he called as she emerged from her room. "Off to your morning workout?"

"Yeah, I'm a bit sore from yesterday's escapade. I used muscles I don't normally use; I thought a light jog might work them out."

"May I join you? I had similar thoughts this morning." His face kept an easy, mildly amused expression as he surveyed her. Gillian's presence sent his heart spinning out of control—wanting more of her—wanting her badly.

He noticed her indecision, but she, finally, said, "Sure. Are you ready?"

"Let's do it."

Their run took the trails behind the mountain retreat; little conversation occurred as they took turns with the lead along the narrow path. Gillian's long, loping stride accented the shape of her legs and the firmness of her hips; Lucian found following her a pleasurable experience. At the turn-around point of the trail, she stopped to catch her breath and to stretch. Bending over, hands propped on her knees, Gillian closed her eyes, as if to shut him out.

"Are you ready to head back?" Lucian stood so close that his stance paralleled hers: his right foot between her two. Gillian slowly stood; her body heat overspread his. Lucian sensed a change in her; minor it was, but it was still there. "Gillian?" After an elongated moment, she shook her head as if nothing had occurred. He wanted her physically; holding her in his arms yesterday was stunningly sensual, but she remained adamantly against their reconciliation; she had proven that by turning to Daniel Lewis. Frustrated, he forced himself to not react to her. "Do you want to walk back instead?"

She nodded and took her place beside him. "Barb said you're her hero for saving me last night."

The struggle to not react to her continued; finally, he allowed his fingertips to caress hers. "May I be your hero instead?" he whispered close to her ear.

Gillian paused briefly before shaking her head in denial. After another pregnant pause, she added, "Lucian, you shouldn't say things like that to me."

"I've no one else to whom I would want to give my attention." Lucian's gaze swept over her, amazingly sensual, while his tone became low and seductive.

Despite her objections to his words, Gillian flushed, and Lucian found the touch of color to her skin very sensual. Deep in such thoughts, he was unprepared for her saying, "You prove nothing with your words; your actions have hurt me more than you will ever know. And just because we lust after one another, that's no reason to continue our relationship."

Lucian caught her hand in his and clutched it to him. "You believe all we have is lust? Gillian, how can I prove you're an important part of my life?"

"I'm just desirable because you can't have me. We both know that. I admit to wanting to be with you, Lucian, but I can't. Please understand that I can't care about you halfway. I'm not that type of person."

"Who says I only want a *halfway* relationship?" Lucian couldn't believe he had said the words out loud; he had thought them for sometime, but saying them aloud made them real.

"God! Lucian, please don't do this to me," she pleaded.

"Gillian, tell me what I did, and I'll make it right. I swear I'll make it right."

Her gaze held her doubts. Doubts he couldn't seem to overcome. Without a word, Gillian darted away. Lucian watched her retreating form; he stood, eyes in supplication, wondering what to do next. He should let her go; he should move on with his life, but a life without Gillian would shatter all his hard-earned equanimity. After ten minutes he turned toward the mountain retreat. He still had six weeks to make her understand. Make her forgive him. With a renewed resolve, he moved to his future.

~

At breakfast, Gillian sat with four of the women contestants, her knees pulled up, and her chin resting on the arm encircling them. She held a toasted bagel, but she didn't eat. Lucian rested in the recesses of her mind. No matter what she did, she couldn't make it right with him; he betrayed her one minute and then rescued her the next. It made no sense.

The subject of her musings appeared; Lucian casually fixed himself a plate at the sideboard. "May I get anyone anything?" he called over his shoulder. The women all declined his offer.

Reluctantly, Gillian's eyes followed him, and she unfurled from the chair and readjusted her seat. She took a bite of the bagel, chewing without tasting. Lucian brought his plate to the table before seeking out the coffee urn.

However, when he returned from the beverage table, he carried a cup of hot tea. He walked straight to where she sat, leaned over her shoulder, and set the cup before her place setting. "You looked like you needed a cup of your favorite tea." His voice held no desire, just concern. Gillian's eyes shot to his; before the contestants and the television cameras, he had just declared that he knew some intimate detail about her life. "I put in two sweeteners—the way you like it." Then he turned back to fix his own coffee.

Joining the table, he knew immediately that the furtive looks between Gillian and him confirmed the women's suspicions. "How are you ladies doing after your first experience with television?" He addressed the group as a whole, but Gillian held his attention.

"The obstacle course was quite a surprise," Ada finally responded. She sipped her tea and nibbled on a piece of bacon. "You were quite adept at helping our Gillian, Dr. Damron," she teased.

"Gillian knows I'd never let anything happen to her." He didn't look at anyone except Gillian. "By the way, has our Miss Cornell told you about her sister Barb? Barb is phenomenal; I so enjoyed watching her participation in the Special Olympics. That girl knows how to run. Did you tell them the story about her falling down but finishing the race? I was never prouder of anyone in my life."

Gillian's mouth dropped open. Again he had blatantly professed his knowledge of her private life for what could be millions of Americans. "My sister is an amazing person." Gillian wanted to say more, but what retort could she give with the cameras rolling?

Unable to speak, the women sat and watched as Lucian sopped up the egg yolk with his toast. Finally finished, he sat back and relaxed against the back of the chair. "That smells delicious," Lucian turned his attention to Ada once again.

"It's vanilla chai tea. Would you like to try it?"

"Ah, that's what it is!" He smiled a wicked one. "Vanilla. I should have known. Your Miss Cornell prefers either vanilla or lavender." He stood immediately to take his leave, pleased with the look on each of the women's faces. "I'll see you in a bit, Ladies." He winked at Gillian's flushed countenance and strode from the room.

"My God, Gillian," Melinda gasped. "Your mystery man is Dr. Damron!"

Gillian's voice quivered. "Lucian is not the man," she protested.

"Oh, he is so the man!" Ada laughed lightly. "He knew about the vanilla and lavender, knew about your sister, and knew how you like your tea."

"Please," Gillian begged as she pointed to the camera.

The women followed her gaze to the voyeur observer mounted in each corner. "They're taping our lives, not yours," Nicole insisted.

"But you are discussing my life."

"Okay," Ada agreed reluctantly, "but this isn't finished. We want details."

～⌒

Lucian heard the tap on his bedroom door and knew immediately who stood without his room. "Come in, Gillian," he called.

She expected him to be at his room's desk or lounging in the chairs, watching TV. Instead, he lay across the bed, pillows propping up his head. His gaze immediately caressed her.

"What were you thinking?" she demanded. "The cameras were rolling when you opened up my private life."

"Come, Sweetheart," he said as he leisurely rolled out of the bed, "I said no more than what any friend might know about you. Everyone knows we're, at least, friends." Coming from anyone else, the explanation would sound foolish, but with Lucian's natural ease of persuasion, his declaration only sounded practical. "In fact, your coming to my bedroom probably is more damaging than what I said in the breakfast room."

Gillian, in hindsight, realized he spoke the truth. Flushing with color, she turned to him, "Please, don't continue this pursuit, Lucian."

"I wasn't pursuing you, Sweet One. I was just making conversation." He edged closer to her. Now, directly before her, he reached out to run the back of his knuckles lightly over the curve of her jaw. "However, if you would like for me to pursue you, I'll be happy to comply." He knew the extent of his masculine power over her so he leaned forward to kiss her right temple.

He could sense her need for flight, but a primitive part of her wanted what he offered. Lucian kissed the corner of her mouth before lowering his lips to hers; yet, he didn't kiss her at once. He drew out the moment, tantalizingly hovering over her mouth. Involuntarily, Gillian's frustration showed in her face, a grimace shooting across her countenance. Lucian smiled seductively. "I want this too, my Love," he whispered. The warmth of his breath tickled her sensibilities before he finally covered her mouth with his. Her lips parted as Lucian coaxed her with his tongue. He cupped her chin with one hand as the other slid around Gillian's waist, pulling her closeness to him; yet, he never released her mouth.

When he did withdraw, Gillian's breath came in short pants, while Lucian worked hard to control his breathing. "You're not going to stop this madness, are you?" She said the words, but she rested her head on his chest.

"I'm afraid not, Sweetling. I need you too much." He pulled her closer still, his hands resting on the fall of her hips. He ground his growing erection into her abdomen.

Pushing away from him, Gillian turned to leave. "They have me on tape coming in here; I must leave."

"Of course, you should," he chuckled softly. "Then again, I would have no problem if you decided to stay." His gaze skimmed her breasts before returning to her face.

Instinctively, she leaned toward him before catching herself. Frustrated, she nearly stomped her feet in place; growling with no fulfillment, she yanked open the door and escaped to the hallway's safety. With a great deal of pleasure, Lucian softly said, "Strike one, Miss Cornell."

Thus began Lucian's seduction. He never once said or did anything that could be misconstrued as more than friendship. However, he never passed up an opportunity to touch her–a brush of his shoulder as they passed each other, a steadying hand on her elbow, a rub of his knee against hers under the table.

When they conferenced with Dr. Stryent, Lucian passed her a scrap of paper, which said, "You are so very beautiful. You take my breath away." When no one watched them, he often whispered into her ear, but he never lingered, just a brush of his breath against the side of Gillian's cheek. With some satisfaction, he noted that each time he did so, she caught her breath in a quick intake. However, for the cameras she refused to respond.

Frustrated with her uncontrolled reactions to Lucian's continual assaults on her psyche, Gillian looked for unique ways to keep her thoughts from him. One late afternoon, she wandered into the communication room. Thinking she would check her work emails, she had just signed onto the computer, when Ted Morris, the same show staffer who approached her previously about Lucian, appeared in the doorway.

"Hey, Miss Cornell," he called as he entered the room. "Would it be a big problem if I checked my emails while you're in here?"

"Of course, not." She gestured to the bank of computers. "Help yourself."

"I wasn't certain," he said sheepishly, "if you were checking medical records or something like that. I know you must have to keep those things private and all."

"No, I'm just killing a little time before my next session." Gillian turned back to the computer screen.

Morris signed on and opened an email with a double click. "My wife and daughter email me each day." He began to explain although Gillian showed no signs of interest.

She turned toward him at last. "My sister's medical staffer does the same. It's quite comforting."

"I hear your sister is under constant medical care." He was definitely not a perceptive conversationalist.

A look of frustration crossed Gillian's face before she recovered. She found it annoying to always have to explain Barb's condition. Many people thought her sister institutionalized. "My sister is capable of the same skills as all of us," she finally corrected him. "It just takes her longer to complete many of them."

"I'm sorry. I didn't mean to offend you, Miss." Morris looked at her earnestly. "I already offended Dr. Damron; I don't want to tick you off too."

"When did you offend Dr. Damron?" Her curiosity caused Gillian to forget her annoyance at his remark.

"A couple of days ago. The doc sat at the dinner table beside me, along with some of the other technicians. You never told me whether he thought any more about the pictures I wanted to show him."

She interrupted, "I'm sorry, Ted; it slipped my mind."

"That's okay; I should mind my own business anyway," he assured her.

"So, what happened?"

"I tried to show the doctor the pictures. I went back to my room and got the book, but Dr. Damron got really upset. He warned me not to approach him with such a crazy idea again. Those were his words–*such a crazy idea*. I shut my mouth fast; I don't want to get fired because of something stupid. I got my wife and daughter to consider."

"Really?" Gillian's surprise crept into her voice.

"Yes, Ma'am. The doc was blood red in the face." He stood, having closed out the email box. "I thought he was going to burst a blood vessel or something."

"Wow! I'd never have suspected that Dr. Damron would react so adamantly." Gillian wondered what this meant.

"Well, I learned my lesson." The man headed toward the door. "I'm gonna keep my mouth shut and do my job." Then, he was gone as quickly as he came.

Gillian shook her head in disbelief. Lucian's getting angry over something so insignificant seemed out of character. With a nagging uncertainty, she turned back to the computer. In the Goggle search box, she typed *Marcus Chambers*.

Gillian searched all the normal sites for information on Marcus Chambers, but try as she may, nothing appeared. The fact that the man had no "history" bothered her: no address–no phone number–no collegiate records–nothing. "I wonder what's going on," she said aloud.

"Hey, Beautiful," Lucian said softly behind her.

Flustered at being caught looking for information on Lucian's *twin,* she quickly clicked the box closed on the latest search. Face flushed, she turned toward the sound of his voice. "Lucian!" she started.

"Did I catch you doing something naughty?" he teased.

Gillian stammered, "Of...of course, not. I was just trying to find information to help a client." She swallowed hard. "What are you up to?"

"Looking for the most beautiful woman I've ever known." Lucian leaned down to brush the side of her cheek with a kiss.

Instantaneously, her breath became raspy. Sometimes Gillian hated how her body betrayed her best efforts to resist him. "Lucian, please..."

He took the seat next to her and scooted in close. "Please what, Sweetheart? Please kiss me? Please touch me? Please, please me? Pick any of the above, and I would gladly oblige." He traced a finger up her arm.

"Lucian," she tried again. "Someone could walk in."

"This is the only place besides the bath and our private bedrooms where no cameras can see us." He leaned in to kiss the side of her neck while cupping the other side of her head, holding her in place. "So which will it be, Sweetling? A kiss? A touch? Pure pleasure?" He trailed a line of kisses along her neck and behind her ear.

"Why do you do this?" Gillian's voice came out in a bare whisper.

He continued to nibble on her ear lobe. "You know why. You don't want to admit it, but you know why."

For a few seconds, her body and her heart told her to succumb, but finally Gillian's mind took control. She bolted up and hurried from the room. Tormenting Gillian with the knowledge that he still held control over her, Lucian's soft laughter followed her down the hall.

Chapter Seven

FOR THE WOMEN DURING THE second week, Gillian concentrated on how to flirt and ways to make the relationship work. "Why must a wife flirt with her husband?" Ada asked as they lounged in the meeting room.

"Every woman should flirt on a daily basis. After all, if you really want to flirt well, you must remember that practice makes perfect," Gillian assured them as she made eye contact with each woman. "You don't have to give each man your name and phone number, but you can make seductive eye contact with someone in the local coffee shop or make casual conversation while waiting in line at the supermarket. Get your flirt on." The women all laughed lightly as they pictured themselves doing exactly what Gillian just described. "By flirting regularly, you learn all the right moves to please your man."

"Assuming you want to please your man," Mary grumbled.

"Well, some of us do want to learn how to fix our broken relationship," Melinda redirected the conversation. "Go on, Gillian."

"In reality, you know how to do these things already. Make eye contact and smile. Laugh at his jokes. Give him the occasional compliment. If you're talking and want to emphasize a point, squeeze his hand. The idea is we become so wrapped in the mundane, everyday life, we forget to foster the relationship that brought us to life." Gillian leaned forward as if she shared state secrets. Automatically, the other women in the room followed suit. "Of course, there's several things you should do, and others you shouldn't even consider," she continued.

Nicole asked, "Such as?"

"Well, like thinking about your appearance for one thing. Cute, comfortable clothing with a touch of makeup–no more sloppy clothes. No provocative, revealing, wrong message type clothing. There is a

117

difference between flirting and being easy. Make him work a little to earn your attention. You're the catch. Don't give away the cow when all he needs is a glass of milk. At least, that's what my mother used to say. Leave him wanting more."

"That simple?" Ada seemed disappointed.

"That simple," Gillian said softly. "Men thrive on our attentions. You don't have to reinvent the wheel; you just have to make sure not to let the wheel go flat. You need to reevaluate how you failed in that area, and then think how you can fix it."

"Is it acceptable to start now? I mean while we are on the show," Melinda asked.

"The idea behind the show is to see if you're really compatible with your ex-husband. How do you know that if you don't try?"

~

"May I join you?" Gillian looked up from her lunch to see Lucian standing by the table.

She gestured to the empty chair. "Sure."

"I saw your session with the women this morning," he said casually. "You amaze me; you could get them to drink the sand simply because you led them to the desert. They so trust you."

Gillian blushed with his words. "Thanks. It's going better than I expected."

"You've a special way of handling people; you engender confidence and trust. People want to share with you. Cuttles and Hood were right; you're perfect for this type of program."

"Is this a compliment or pure flattery?" she teased nervously.

"Maybe I took some of your advice; I'm giving you a genuine compliment. If it flatters you, then that's so much better for me." A devious grin turned up the corners of his mouth.

Gillian just shook her head; she knew she was susceptible to him and fighting it earned her nothing. Of late, she had decided to keep a friendly relationship for the camera and bide her time. It would not be easy, but time would absolve her heart of its pain. "When's your session with the men?"

"Later this afternoon."

Gillian looked around, making certain no one could hear. "I've been thinking about sensate sessions later on. The women would like some degree of intimacy. Right now the show's format does not allow such activities. Should I present the idea to Dr. Stryent or to Hood?"

"Actually, when we get down to the final three, that's probably a good idea. Such intimate activities need to be re-established. If I were you, I would seek Stryent's support before I would approach Hood. Cameras can't run in such a session."

Gillian nodded in affirmation, stealing around to look at the cameras. "I agree."

A wicked smile crept across his face. "Maybe Hood will insist that you and I participate in those challenges. They would certainly be preferable to climbing ropes."

A flicker of desire flashed across Gillian's face. "This isn't about us, Lucian. It's about our clients."

He leaned in to whisper, "When will it be about us?"

Exasperation filled her. "You're the most stubborn man!"

"I prefer to call it determined," he teased.

"You say that now, but what happens when we go home?" Hurt laced her voice. "I recall your former girl friend quite clearly."

"How does that change things?" he demanded. "The operative word in that sentence is *former.*"

"It changes because you have a history, which keeps us apart." Gillian forced a smile to her face in case others watched them.

"I was thinking more in terms of the present and of the future. Who doesn't have a history?" he insinuated sharply.

Anger grew quickly, and Gillian snapped. "I know one person with no history, but he's not you." She fought to keep her voice low and even.

"That makes no sense. Would you like to offer an explanation for such an asinine remark?" Lucian too struggled for control.

"Marcus Chambers has no history; I know because I looked. Although Ted Morris has pictures of the non-existent Mr. Chambers, who certainly resembles you; you, however, insist you know nothing about him!"

"Leave it, Gillian," he insisted.

"Why, Lucian? Do you have something else to hide?" she challenged.

Confrontation obviously wasn't what he had expected when Lucian had joined her for lunch. "I don't know Marcus Chambers! Neither do I have anything to hide! Jesus, Gillian, why are you doing this?"

"I don't know, but your insistence makes me wonder." In frustration, she stood to leave. "It seems he doth protest too much."

As she stepped away from the table, Lucian stood and blocked her passage; he grasped her arm, forcing her to look at him. The intensity between them made the pain in her arm radiate throughout her body. "Gillian, please. I beg you. Listen to me. You know me; when all is said and done, you know me–the real me. All you have to do is listen to your heart."

"My heart can't hear you any more, Lucian." She jerked her arm free and returned quickly to her room. Yet, thoughts of the anguish on Lucian's countenance haunted her.

—~—

"Did you notice the little tiff between the doc and Gillian?" Hood asked Cuttles as they sat in the production trailer.

"Yeah, he's been pursuing her for several days now. The small touches–whispering in her ear. We have her going into his room, don't we?"

Hood laughed, "We got her, but she wasn't there long enough for them to have some kind of tryst."

"I know that, but the American public doesn't," Cuttles smirked.

"You don't mean you want me to manipulate the images?"

Cuttles paused, watching the film from the past few days. "We manipulate the other images, don't we?"

—~—

During the first week, the show introduced the American people to Gary and Melinda, Yvonne and Sean, and Theo and Grace. The other three couples would be highlighted during this second week. The show dedicated an expose' to each couple. The segment showed wedding photos and contained interviews with family and friends. Dr. Stryent predicted the reliability of the sessions supervised by Lucian and Gillian. Technicians who screened hours of film daily orchestrated the final product. After the second week's show, one of the couples would be going home.

"Well, Ladies," Gillian announced as she came into the room, "I've this week's challenge." She held up an envelope.

"Read it," Ada called.

"We have to wait on the men," Gillian reminded them. As if on cue, Lucian entered, followed closely by the ex-husbands and Dr. Stryent.

"They're all here now," Ada insisted. "Read on."

Gillian broke the seal on the oversized envelope. Removing the card, she paused to clear her throat before reading.

> Contestants,
>
> There is no obstacle course this week. Instead, we will celebrate with music. You will each choose a song symbolic of your relationship with your former mate. We will have our own karaoke songfest. Each of you will sing the song of your choice. You will tell our staff member your choice by first thing tomorrow morning. The music will be secured for your use if you wish to practice. Enjoy yourself. Don't worry about your voices. That's what the reverb switch is for. Tell your story through the song. As we did last week, our three psychologists will join you, adding their vocal talents to the mix.

"I can't believe this," Mark Clayton spoke the words everyone was thinking.

Sean Griffin laughed, "I only sing in the shower."

"Well, tomorrow night, you'll sing on national TV." Michael Hood came into the room along with Daniel. "So, I guess you better get busy making your choices."

The group left the room immediately. Gillian led the women one way while Lucian, along with Dr. Stryent, escorted the men another. Once they were alone, Hood saddled up to Daniel. Placing an arm around Daniel's shoulder in false camaraderie, he asked, "What's the story with Gillian Cornell and Lucian Damron? Obviously, you know something; you went out with her a few times."

Always anxious to ingratiate himself to the media executives, Daniel held no qualms in sharing what he knew. "Oh, she's crazy about him. Actually, I think they're both really into each other. She wanted to make him jealous; that's why she was with me. Of course, I didn't know it was him at first, but it wasn't long before I figured it out."

"So, you think they're an item, huh?"

"Well, they were at one time," Daniel assured him. "Something happened. If I was guessing, I'd say it had something to do with that woman he brought to the show's kickoff parties."

"Really?" Hood feigned innocence as he further plotted to include Lucian and Gillian in the TV ratings. "Then maybe they'll get a second chance too."

"Hey, that's a good one." Daniel laughed softly. "A second chance."

The way the men and the women approached the challenge fell very much along stereotypical lines. The men took the list of songs provided by the show, perused the titles, looking for familiar ones, and made their choices. "Remember, if there's a song you want which is not on the list, just let a staffer know, and he'll secure it for you." Lucian reminded everyone as he searched the titles for something, which would speak to Gillian. He knew this could be an inroad, especially after their last argument.

"This is idiotic," Andrew bemoaned.

After picking several titles each, in mass, they retired to the communication room to search lyrics on the Internet. Once there, they reviewed several songs to see if it fit their relationship with their former mates. Occasionally, they rejected a song lyric for themselves and then suggested it to one of their fellow challengers. However, the male need to compete and win kept most of them from sharing "gems" with their fellow competitors.

In sharp contrast, Gillian and the women retired to their favorite meeting room. For them, this was a chance to commingle. They poured themselves drinks, found snacks, and instead of looking at lists of song titles, they popped in CDs, playing snippets of their most poignant "cry in your beer" songs. They talked over each other, calling out titles their fellow competitors could use. While the men were glued to the computer screen reviewing words and listening to melodies, the women cranked up the volume and sang together at the top of their lungs.

By the time Lucian had made his choice, he found Gillian engrossed in the music emanating from the room. With several show technicians, he watched her mingling with the female participants. They listened to Kelly Clarkson's *Breakaway*. Gillian, Ada, and Nicole pretended to have microphones, and they belted out "Since You've Been Gone." Lucian realized how therapeutic these sessions were for her. Having cared for Barb since her college years, Gillian had been deprived of bonding with other women. His heart went out to her; she had deserved so much more than what life had bestowed upon her. She deserved a family of her own and a successful career. She deserved a man who would cherish her. Lucian wanted to be that man, but he suspected he could never live up to her image of the perfect mate.

⌒

The second week's show featured segments on Mary and Bruce, Ada and Andrew, and Mark and Nicole. Excerpts from the sessions on flirting and on desire dominated. Daniel narrated each of the vignettes, adding insights into the private lives of each of the couples. Although no comments were made regarding Lucian and Gillian's relationship, the show's producers chose scenes, which highlighted their interactions. They showed images of Lucian lightly touching her arm, his whispering to Gillian and staring lovingly her way. Gillian was pictured blushing under his attentions and returning his stares. These images were mixed in with those of the contestants, but the show's producers definitely told their story.

The karaoke challenge was the last part of the second show. After the songfest, the American public would vote off the first couple. The half hour results show would air the next evening. Daniel stepped before the camera. The contestants and psychologists surrounded him. He set up the competition to the viewing audience's delight. "Our own Dr. Stryent will start. He'll be our warm up act so to speak. Then we'll have the couples choose numbers to see who goes next. We'll finish with our other two psychologists belting out their favorite relationship songs. Of course, you, the voting public, are only voting for the couples. Our show psychologists are just joining in the fun. Our telephone banks will be open for two hours following the conclusion of the show. You may text your votes to EXLOVE at Summertime Wireless or sign onto the show's website at www.secondchances.com. Now, let's bring up our own Dr. Stryent to start the show."

Stryent made his way to the microphone. "First, I would like to apologize to the viewing public for my voice, as well as the voices of some of our competitors. Trust me, I've heard them. Anyway, I first thought I would sing my wife's favorite song, which is 'Unchained Melody.' We've been together for twenty-five years, and I quickly realized that she would kill me for murdering such a beautiful song. So on a lark, I chose a Trace Adkins's song. It's not that Trace Adkins doesn't have some poignant love songs; it's just based on this very publicized experiment in love, I thought this was an appropriate one."

The music started, and he laughingly began to sing "(This Ain't) No Thinkin' Thing." The contestants began to laugh as the words flashed on the screen. On the second verse, they joined in and sang their own plea for "self help psychology." The cameras panned the contestants as they followed the words on the big screen, all of them nervous about their singing debuts.

By the time he finished, the group was in the perfect mood for continuing what the elderly psychologist had started. Daniel stepped forward again, adding his staged mirth to what the others genuinely felt. "Well, that was an excellent way to start. Now, we will get down to the real competition. Ada and Andrew drew number one so they will begin with their own song styling."

Ada took the microphone first. Laughing at herself, she began her introduction. "When I think of Andrew, I remember how sexy he is." Everyone in the group laughed nervously. "So, for my song, I have chosen one from the man who has been sexy for generations. I chose Tom Jones's *SexBombs*." The upbeat music allowed everyone to join in once again. When Ada sang the final verse, she gyrated her hips to the music and directed the chorus to Andrew, assuring her ex that he could "turn me on."

Laughter and high fives greeted Ada when she returned to her seat. "You were fabulous," Gillian gushed. "I cannot believe you danced that way before America."

"That just goes to show you how desperate I am to win this man's love again. I embarrassed him before everyone we knew–humiliated him with my own insecurity. I rightly deserve to suffer some humiliation if it levels the playing field."

Taking the microphone and still a bit embarrassed by Ada's display, Andrew confessed to the camera, "When Ada and I broke up, the ramifications were many. I want her to know that I miss her." The music began; it was a slow, plaintive song. Andrew lowered his head, refusing to look at the camera, but his voice was clear. He sang a song from Terry Knight and the Pack. "I Who Have Nothing" spoke what he could not.

By the end, the camera captured tears streaming down Ada's face. Placing an arm around Ada's shoulders, Gillian moved beside her. The woman collapsed against her; the teasing sexiness of a few minutes ago was gone with Andrew's words of love. When he finished, she rushed into his arms. He held her close, stroking the back of her head. Lucian encouraged them to return to their seats. Holding Ada's hand tightly in his, Andrew never released her.

"Well, that was a telling display," Daniel said as he recaptured the camera's focus. "If Andrew and Ada are your choice for receiving a dream wedding and a quarter million dollars, then place your vote at 1-866-395-6831. That's 1-866-EXLOVE1. Phone lines do not open until after the show. So stay tuned for our second couple after these messages."

Yvonne and Sean were the second couple to perform. They both chose songs from sound tracks. She chose "To Be with You" from *Chasing Liberty,* while he selected "When You Say Nothing at All" from *Notting Hill.* With rich, sensual lyrics from both songs, the group should've been near tears again, but the love demonstrated in the performances of Andrew and Ada didn't prove true through Yvonne's and Sean's renditions. They were fond of each other, but no deep-seated emotions played across the screen.

Daniel did his sales pitch once again, and then it was Theo and Grace's turn. Grace boldly took the microphone. "When Gillian asked us what we missed most about our ex-husbands, my immediate answer was I missed Theo's kiss. Therefore, I chose the song "Kiss." The pounding beat lifted the group's spirits once again, and a sing-a-long ensued. Most of the women stood and clapped to the music, like a sisterhood supporting Grace's performance. Reluctantly, a few men joined them. Of course, Theo and Lucian led the way. When she finished, she jumped from the platform and danced around.

Theo embraced her as he took the microphone and headed for the stage. "Hi, I'm Theo. When I started looking for a song, I couldn't think of any one song to express my relationship with Grace, and then on the list there was this one entitled 'Amazing Grace.' I looked at the lyrics, and many of them matched so that's what I'm doing."

His voice held clear innuendos when he looked upon Grace's countenance. Gillian realized why people considered him such a womanizer. Theo Jenkinson was a natural flirt; women would be susceptible to his charms. Then she looked at Lucian. Originally, she had thought he was a *ladies'* man to the n'th degree. Now, she realized he possessed natural charisma, but she never observed him purposely leading a woman on.

When the words to the final chorus came up on the screen, everyone supported Theo's efforts by lending their voices to his performance.

"That's exactly what you are Gracie. You're amazing!" Theo hugged Grace when he left the stage, handing the microphone back to Daniel. Daniel gave the audience the phone number for couple three; then he signaled for another commercial. The contestants gathered around one another during the break. Everyone came together in the middle except Gillian and Lucian. They remained seated staring, unable to remove their eyes from one another. Gillian cringed with the thoughts of the song she had chosen. It had seemed so appropriate at the time, but now she wondered if it would hurt Lucian. She had never wanted to hurt him, and she had never wanted him to think poorly of her.

"Our next couple is Mark and Nicole." Daniel smiled for the camera as it came in for a close up. "Let's bring them up to see what their choices are."

After the group's applause faded away, Nicole laughed nervously. "Like Dr. Stryent I want to apologize ahead of time for my voice. I am definitely not Faith Hill. If you want to join me, in fact, if you want to drown me out, go for it." Her comments were met with loud whoops and a pumping of arms. "Okay," she said at last, "Mark and I were not together long enough to develop the kind of history we should have after so many years of acquaintance. So, I often question what we should do. Here's my song, 'If I'm Not in Love with You.'"

The country song touched the hearts of many of the women. The lyrics spoke volumes. Nicole finished strong and then passed the microphone to her former husband. He caressed her cheek. "Thank you, Sweetheart," he whispered softly as he kissed the corner of her mouth. "Truthfully, the song I chose is not directly associated with my relationship to Nicole, but I love the chorus. Like Nicole, I beg you to drown me out."

Trace Adkins's popular, "You're Gonna Miss This," came tumbling across the airwaves. Mark actually mumbled his way through the verses, but he was loudest of all those who sang on the chorus.

"If Mark and Nicole are your favorites, please call 1-866-EXLOVE4. Phone lines are open after the show. Now we're moving on to our fifth couple. Welcome Gary and Melinda." Daniel smiled once more for the camera. Lucian wondered if his face was in a permanent smile. *How could Gillian even look at someone so fake?* Would the song he had chosen make a difference to Gillian? He was taking a chance, but he had few opportunities to speak his heart to her.

Gary chose to go first of the pair. "Melinda and I've been together for years. In fact, we've never really been apart. She's on my speed dial, and we know each other's likes and dislikes better than anyone else. Although we've both sought comfort in the arms of other people, we have always come back to each other. I purposely chose a seductive song that I know Melinda will like, and I hope it will make her laugh. I miss her laugh."

The music cranked up, and Gary started strutting around the stage as he sang the lyrics to Phil Vasser's "I'll Take That as a Yes." Making for good TV, the group followed the words as they flashed on the screen. They belted out the lyrics, swaying in their seats as they clapped their hands and shouted encouragement. By the end, Gary was doubled over in hysterics and barely able to finish the number.

Finally, Melinda took her turn as she stepped to the platform. "When Gary and I first met, one of the songs we considered to be our song was Lionel Richie's 'Hello.' That's what I've chosen to sing for my best friend."

The drastic change in mood swept over Gillian. She teetered on an emotional seesaw, expecting it to shift and throw her off into oblivion. She felt smothered by the sentiment of the song. How could she have believed that Lucian was untrue to her? She listened carefully as the song's words spoke of winning a person's heart.

When Daniel called for a commercial break, Gillian sat with her eyes down, hands in her lap. What could she do about the song choice? It was too late to change it; she needed to play it off somehow. Requiring a voice of reason, Gillian turned to Ada. She whispered, "I can't sing the song I chose; it will hurt Lucian."

"You've got no choice, Gillian." Ada pretended to straighten Gillian's collar, attempting not to draw attention to their conversation.

Gillian swallowed hard. "I've been foolish; I should've believed him."

"Do the song, and then go apologize to him." Ada looked quickly over to where Lucian sat. His eyes rested on their exchange. "Smile at him now; take your own advice; flirt with him, Gillian."

"It won't work," Gillian hissed.

Ada laughed lightly. "I've never seen a man so obsessed with a woman. Toss him a crumb; smile at him."

Gillian forced her eyes to where Lucian sat. She locked hers with his, holding his gaze; then she gifted him with a full smile. Suddenly, his body language changed. He leaned forward as if he planned to come to her–to take possession of her. Ada watched the interplay. "You got him, Gillian; he'll forgive whatever you do tonight." Ada took her hands and led Gillian to the group. "Now, let's play to the camera and join the others."

With the countdown from technicians, Daniel pushed away from the group and headed to the stage as the camera flashed on. "We are coming up on our last couple. Please welcome Mary and Bruce." Again, the other contestants whooped it up. Their time before the cameras was over. Of course, the cameras still watched them–watched their reactions. Mary was the only one of the group who hadn't shared her song choice with the others prior to the show. They all knew her animosity toward her ex-husband, and dread overspread their faces.

"Bruce and I've been apart for ten years, and my child has been raised without knowing his father." Mary's voice was strong and confident; she had come here to this show for this purpose. "My song choice was easy; it's a song I've sung at least once a day, every day, for the last ten years. It's called 'Men,' and it's by the Forester Sisters."

Mary belted out the lyrics as if they liberated her. Her anger and her disappointment seeped from her demeanor. She had used this national format to tell her ex-husband that she was an independent woman.

Bruce Nelson watched his ex-wife. His face clearly showed what he was thinking: Mary had deserved better than what he had given her. He had agreed to this format as his personal hell. Mary's song spoke of her hurt. Now it was his turn. "Mary, I'm sorry I wasn't the man you thought I would be. I tried to make it work, but I couldn't. I was too young–too immature–for all the responsibilities." The music started, but Bruce couldn't sing the words; he was too overcome with emotions. Finally, he said the words out loud. Elvis Costello's "She" haunted each of their hearts.

The camera panned each face of the other contestants as Bruce's song played out. The women cried for Mary, but they also shed tears for Bruce. Both had lost so much from their lives. They were out of practice when it came to love; Bruce had chosen a carefree life of a "bachelor"–no commitments, but guilt had overwhelmed him afterwards. He had failed everyone. Gillian watched as he fought to control his emotions; his jaw clenched and unclenched. Finally, the song finished; Bruce shrugged his shoulders and left the platform.

Daniel immediately hit the stage again. He gave out the obligatory call numbers and called for the final commercial break of the evening.

"Miss Cornell, you're on when we come back from the break," a show staffer told her. "Do you need anything?"

A dose of courage. Gillian glanced around nervously. "No, I'm fine." She looked to see another staffer doing the same thing for Lucian. He shook his head in response, but his eyes still rested on Gillian.

Too quickly the break came to an end. Daniel's ever-present smile filled the screen again. "Ours is a family; our contestants spend many hours each week in resolving the issues that has brought their marriages to an end. You see a smattering of what they go through. In the two weeks on the ranch, they have developed strong relationships with their three therapists. You heard Dr. Stryent earlier this evening. We will finish the evening with the two psychologists who spend their days in direct contact with the contestants. You saw them last week as they lead the couples through the obstacle course. Tonight we've asked them if they were in a relationship, what song might they sing? We will start with our own little cheerleader. There is no one like her. Please welcome Gillian Cornell."

Gillian reluctantly made her way to the platform. "Thanks, Daniel. Well, I don't know what to say. I'm not married so my point of reference is different from these lovely ladies about whom I've learned so much over the last two weeks. However, if I had a failed marriage, the following song would be one I might want to adopt as I moved on. The music started; Gillian refused to look at Lucian as she sang out the words that she had originally chosen to speak to him of her hurt, but she now wished she could avoid. She sang the words half-heartedly, knowing she no longer meant them–knowing she didn't want what she had with Lucian to end. Through a Clay Aiken song she spoke to Lucian of "survival."

She finished the song with tears streaming down her cheeks. A sob nearly choked out the final words, but the women spontaneously stormed the stage, joining her and supporting her through it. The camera focused on Lucian's face several times during the song, but he kept all emotions from his countenance; however, his chest had clutched at his heart. When the women surrounded Gillian, he had said a silent prayer, thanking them for their compassion when she had needed it most.

"Obviously, what you have just seen was proof of the family we have here." Daniel spoke off script and tried to interpret to what the American public had been privy. "We'll finish out the night with our resident *heart* doctor. Dr. Lucian Damron knows how to solve problems of the heart. Let's welcome him to the stage."

"Thank you, Daniel." Lucian blushed as the men cheered loudly for him. "I took a different approach to this task. First, I have chosen a song from the Broadway musical *Wicked*. Plus, I did have a particular person in mind when I made my song choice. In the play, the song is sung by two women and has spoken as well as singing parts, but the show's staff managed to find me just the music." The music played in the background as he picked up the melody Of "For Good." The song told Gillian of how people were changed "for good" by their experiences. Throughout Lucian never once removed his eyes from hers. He announced with his actions his intentions to love this woman.

Surprisingly, Lucian had a decent voice, and the song fit his vocal quality. Yet, those thoughts didn't enter Gillian's mind. She watched him, listening to the words. She knew the song was meant for her. Gillian fought to school her expression, knowing the camera's red light indicated that it focused on her. She smiled and responded to Ada's comment about Lucian's having a pleasant voice. She attempted not to listen to the remainder of the song, but that was impossible. The song spoke of "blame" and how insignificant that was in the scheme of things.

Swaying to the music, arms interlocked, the group stood and joined Lucian on the final chorus. He laughed at his own inadequacy but finished the song with enthusiasm. As Lucian sang the last strands of the lyrics, Daniel closed out the broadcast by recapping the competitors' performances and the voting phone numbers. Then the show wrapped; with exultations of joy, a simultaneous exclamation arose from everyone on the set. "Great show!" Hood shouted. Hugs and kisses spread quickly.

Daniel grabbed Gillian around the waist and lifted her to him. "You were very fetching tonight; I never expected you to be so adventurous." Without her permission, he kissed her.

"Put me down," Gillian insisted. "What are you doing, Daniel?"

"Don't worry, Gillian; the show's staff knows about us," he assured.

"There is no *us*. Where did you ever get the idea there was?" Gillian maneuvered him away from the cluster of people.

Daniel snaked his arm around her. "You're becoming very popular with the public. Did you know that, Gillian? The viewers are very interested in you." He rested a hand on each side of her waist and pulled her to him.

Gillian shoved against his chest. "So, you assumed that because the viewers have some interest in me, however perverted that may be, that's a reason for us to hook up?" Confusion reigned.

"You should read the blogs," he confided. "I read them to gauge how I'm doing as the host, but you're very popular among the bloggers too. I thought if we joined forces, we could take our careers to the next level."

"Daniel, I assisted you in landing this job. You helped me, but I paid you well for your services. That is the extent of our relationship." Gillian removed his hands from her body, but she favored him with an affectionate smile. "I guess I should be flattered."

"You're passing up a great opportunity for both of us." He caught her hands in his and gazed into her eyes.

Gillian took a deep breath. "It was great speaking to you again, Daniel." Her insistence became evident.

He laughed lightly. "You can't blame a guy for trying. It was worth the shot. If I made you uncomfortable, Gillian, I'm sorry." He released her hands and joined other show staffers as they exited the area.

Chapter Eight

LUCIAN WATCHED IN HORROR AS Daniel first lifted her to him and then kissed Gillian. The woman lingered in Lucian's mind every moment of the day, whether awake or asleep. He had never felt what he supposed to be love before; yet, now he questioned whether his obsession with Gillian Cornell was of what the poets spoke. The acknowledgment of love, if indeed what he felt now was love, shook him to the core. He had resisted the urge to knock Daniel's head off and then demand that Gillian return his love. Jealousy had invaded his blood; he hated this guy–hated his audacity–hated his familiarity. *Damn it!* He was jealous of Daniel's long-standing relationship with Gillian.

Deep in thought, Lucian took no note when Ada Colton appeared beside him. "Hurts like hell, doesn't it?" she whispered softly.

Lucian jerked around, caught in reflection's intimate moment. "Ex...excuse me?" he stammered.

"I said seeing her with someone else hurts." Ada's eyes never left Daniel and Gillian.

"I should say I don't know what you mean, but I have watched you share private moments with Gillian." He turned his attention to the scene again, unable not to look at the interaction between Daniel and Gillian. "I assume you're aware of my feelings for Gillian."

"And aware of her feelings for you," she added.

"Take a look." Lucian closed his eyes to the sight. "It appears her feelings for me are not that strong. If you'll excuse me, I think I'll retire for the evening." He made his feet leave the scene.

Some twenty minutes later, leaving the bathroom after having attempted to scrub the pain away, Lucian came face-to-face with Daniel. "I thought you left." Lucian fisted his hands at his side.

Daniel offered half a laugh. "No, I'm afraid you're stuck with me tonight. I must be here for the results show tomorrow night."

"Great!" Lucian purposely pushed past him.

Nearly to his room, Daniel's words froze him in place. "Have you ever told Gillian that you love her?"

"My private life is none of your business!" Lucian barked out. Charging toward Daniel, he grabbed the man by his shirt and shoved him against the wall. "Yet, allow me to give you a personal warning: If you ever hurt Gillian Cornell..."

"Lucian!" Gillian's voice brought him to his senses. He released Daniel slowly, turning to her.

Dead silence followed, and he felt some satisfaction in how his intimidation of the show's pretty boy caused her to shiver. He wanted her to know his fury. "Don't worry, Miss Cornell, I won't mess up his finely chiseled face," he sneered. Giving Daniel one final shove, Lucian strode away, slamming his room's door to punctuate his remarks.

"Lucian," Gillian opened the door to his room when he didn't respond to her knock. He stood with his back to her, refusing to turn around. "Lucian, we must talk." The light from the hall streamed through the open doorway; otherwise, the room remained awashed in darkness.

"There's nothing to discuss." Lucian's cold voice spoke of his jealousy. Blatant male aggressiveness still coursed through his veins. Somehow, it made him even more attractive. Still waters run deep she thought. In her very naïve mind, Lucian was the consummate playboy. Gillian had never considered how he would respond if provoked, and Daniel's earlier actions had certainly been provoking. To her, as well. It stirred some feminine strings to know that Lucian would, literally, fight for her.

"Tell me why you attacked Daniel, and I'll leave you alone." Lucian could hear the trembling inherent in her words.

He turned slowly toward her. "A misunderstanding." The words came from a banked fire of fury, and unable to help herself, Gillian retreated a step.

"A misunderstanding? Do you expect me to believe that?" The mere idea of what she had witnessed outside being nothing more than a misunderstand was obscene.

Lucian laughed ironically. "You've never believed anything I said."

Gillian bit her bottom lip. "You're right; I am stubborn. That's what Daniel said when I just left him. He says I should allow you an explanation."

"Daniel actually said that?" Disbelief played across his countenance.

Gillian edged closer. "Yeah, he says I owe you that much."

Lucian offered half a smile, but the shadows kept his eyes draped in darkness. "I could learn to like him."

"Somehow I doubt that." She now stood directly before him. Lucian was naked to the waist, and she reached to touch his chest before pulling her hand away.

"You're probably right; I would have to go some to like the man. At most, I can hope for tolerance." Lucian walked to the door and casually closed it; he turned on the lights, but lowered the dimmer switch to keep the room soft. Gillian didn't move during this; she didn't even turn her head. Finally, he stood before her again. "Did you have a purpose for being here, Gillian?"

She stared for the longest time into his eyes. Eventually, she found her voice. "I would like to call a truce."

"A truce?" A smile turned up his lips' corners.

"I propose a solution. We'll be honest with each other. We'll each be allowed three questions per day in which we'll demand the other be completely honest. No half-truths. No lies. We'll be honest, and we'll trust each other," she said tentatively.

"A game? I thought you didn't play games," he taunted.

Gillian caressed his jaw line, her thumb stroking his cheek. "It's not a game. It's a way to start over if you still would like to do so."

Lucian's breath caught. "You know I want nothing more."

His reaction gave her courage. "Then this is my proposal. We'll take it slow–really slow–because we didn't do that before. We'll learn about each other, and each day we'll be allowed our three questions, which demand honesty. Do you agree, Lucian?"

"Is that one of your questions?" he teased.

"No, but it could be if you wish it to be so." Gillian's eyes lit with playfulness in her tone.

Lucian caught her hands and brought her knuckles to his lips. "I'll allow you to keep your three questions, if you'll allow me to amend your proposal."

His lips did magical things to her insides. "I'll probably regret this, but what's your amendment?" she said on a rasp.

Lucian surveyed her, allowing his gaze to move up and down her body. His gaze smoldered with memories of which neither of them spoke. "I would ask that you allow me at least one hour each day to win you. I want exclusive time with you."

Gillian's eyes grew wide. "Exclusive time?"

"Yes, Sweetling, exclusive time. We cannot learn about each other if there are throngs surrounding us," he reasoned.

Gillian pursed her lips. "We're not talking one hour immersed in desire." The statement became a question. She swallowed convulsively—her throat suddenly very dry.

Lucian's smile grew in size. "Of course, I wouldn't mind that, but, no, I'll not seduce you. I will, however, allow you to seduce me if you're so inclined," he teased.

She paused to consider the wisdom of her acquiescing to his request. "Then I agree." Gillian unconsciously allowed her eyes to drift to the bed. "We'll start the exclusive time tomorrow, but we may begin the questions tonight if you like."

Lucian's brows shot up in surprise at her forwardness. "Then may I start?" Gillian nodded in affirmation. "Have I ever done anything to make you think my affection for you was false? I mean, me—not some lie you heard."

Gillian took a deep breath. She had repeatedly replayed her time with Lucian in her mind. "In all honesty, no, you didn't; I believed we had something special."

Lucian let out the breath he held. "Was your reaction to what you heard based on jealousy?"

"Honestly, I'd like to say that that is a foolish idea; yet..." Gillian paused, recouping her nerve. "Yet, although I sincerely hate to admit it, I was jealous. I despised your betrayal."

His fingertips grazed the back of Gillian's hand. Her brain stumbled through a gamut of emotions. Lucian's gaze moved from their intertwined fingers to her face "I'll ask you truthfully, do you wish to renew our relationship and take it to a new level?"

"I didn't expect that one," Gillian murmured. "Well, I suppose I would like to, at least, eventually, return to where we were; anything beyond that I've not totally thought through."

He blew out an exasperated breath while staring intensely at her. "I suppose I'll have to be satisfied with that for the moment."

"It's my turn." Gillian walked past him, but she let her hand drift over his chest, lingering on his abdomen. "Tell me what first attracted you to me."

Anticipation tightened her chest as Gillian waited for his answer. "You made me feel I was the most important man you'd ever met. You made every fiber of my being stand up and pay attention. However, the thing I noticed first was your eyes; it's as if I see them wherever I go. They are the deepest blue I've ever known; there's an acknowledgment of curiosity and delight and excitement and anticipation. You mesmerized me."

Gillian leaned into him. Instinctively, she wanted to hear more of his desire. Lucian gathered her to him as she rested her head on his chest. "You do realize my being here, compounded by your attack on Daniel, puts us in a different situation as far as the show is concerned?"

Lucian's hands rested on the curvature of her hips, and Gillian had never wanted to kiss someone so badly as she did him. "Obviously, we both should've been more discreet." He laughed lightly. "Now, what's your last question?" Her heart pounded so hard she could barely think. Surely he must hear it too.

Gillian paused, debating what else she should ask him. She wanted to know if his heart ever skipped a beat when she came in a room. Or did he ever feel like he would die of loneliness if he didn't see her each day? She felt those things about him. Could Lucian feel something similar for her? Instead, she returned to her earlier question. "Why did you attack Daniel?"

"How do I answer that question honestly?" Lucian wrapped his arms tighter around her. "I don't like to admit this, but I was envious. I thought of throttling him to an inch of his life when he kissed you. I hate that you have a history with him; I hate that you have a history with anyone but me. God, I'm even jealous sometimes of how much time you spend with Barb or with your patients. I know that's awful; I'm a terrible person."

Gillian wrapped her arms around his neck. "We're a destructive pair, are we not?"

Lucian brushed his lips across hers and then lightly stroked her cheek with his knuckles. "That's an extra question. It'll have to wait until tomorrow." His lips met hers, and desire rose quickly. "God, I've missed you." His mouth lingered above hers, tantalizingly driving them both mad.

Her voice came out in breathless pants. "I've missed you, too."

Lucian kissed the corner of her mouth and then trailed kisses along her jaw line and down the hollow of her throat. Gillian's head lolled backwards, allowing him easier access. Lucian's lips returned to her mouth, and he deepened the desire.

Gillian collapsed against him. Lucian pulled her hard to him and gazed into her blue eyes. Her body's heat molded to his, and she could feel his growing arousal. She twined her fingers in his thick hair and pulled his mouth to hers. His tongue parted her lips; Gillian met his ardor with a desire of her own.

Finally, he wrenched his mouth from hers. "I can't believe I'm saying this, but we can't do this right now." His breathing came in gasps. "We've caused enough controversy tonight, but you and I will continue this and very soon. I want you to feel comfortable with me again—to know that I do cherish you above all things. Plus, I want to find Hood and make certain none of our footage ends up on the show."

Gillian continued to kiss the underside of his jaw line. "You're right—obviously right." Her raspy voice held seductive tones. "*Soon* is for the best." But she didn't believe the words; her body wanted this man.

Reluctantly, he released his hold, and Gillian felt bereft of his closeness. "Gillian, I must get you out of here; you are a minx and a definite temptation." His eyes caressed her face, and she wanted nothing more than to return to his embrace. She had starved for his touch.

"I should go," she said finally, but a sigh escaped her lips before she could turn.

As she reached for the door, Lucian was behind her, his hands on Gillian's arms and his lips inches from her ear. "Thank you, Sweetling, for giving us a second chance," he whispered to her. Gillian forced herself to turn the door handle but before opening it to the prying eyes of the cameras in the hallway, she turned to him. Pulling his head to her, she pressed herself to him, devouring his mouth with hers. Then she bolted from the room and turned toward her quarters. Mischievously, she stopped, posed, and then waved at the camera, leaving no mistake that she knew the technicians watched her.

⌒

"Hood, I see you're still here," Lucian called as he entered the screening room.

"It seems I'm always here," Hood chuckled. "What brings you to this side of the camera, Doc?"

"A personal matter."

"Actually, I thought so." Hood took a swig of the soft drink perched precariously on the control board. "It seems you had a confrontation with Daniel Lewis. Is that what you mean?" With a long, slender finger, Hood touched one of the buttons.

Lucian swallowed hard as he watched images of his and Daniel's argument play on the viewing screen. "I would appreciate it," he said slowly, "if you'd omit that incident from any broadcast of show segments."

"It makes for good TV," Hood insisted.

"It's my life." Lucian sank down in the chair beside Hood. "What can I say to convince you that this is not the best thing for the show?"

Hood sat back and took in Lucian's demeanor. "I won't lie to you, Doc. You and Miss Cornell are a hot item. Your relationship is of *interest* to our viewers; there's as many, if not more, bloggers discussing you two as those discussing our competitors. People want to see you together. Watching you threatening to throttle the show's host for kissing her will thrill all those romantic middle aged housewives who are our show's demographics."

"I lost my temper," Lucian admitted. He sat quietly for a few minutes contemplating what he would say next. "Look, Michael, I'll be honest with you; I'm crazy about this woman, but if you sensationalize our relationship, I'll lose her. She offered me a second chance tonight; that's the name of the show; give me a second chance to win her affection and her trust. If I'm successful, we'll announce our love on the finale. Won't a little tease be better than an out and out shocker for the ratings?"

Hood steepled his fingers and then brought them to his mouth, tapping his lower lip while in deep thought. "Would Miss Cornell agree to such an announcement?"

"Even if she doesn't, you'll have plenty of footage of the two of us together to play to the public's interest. It's my intention to do all I can to bring us back together," Lucian confessed.

Hood turned questioningly to Lucian. "Are you going to tell her your plans?"

"Gillian consented to a return of my attentions; she just asks that I not rush her, so you see I don't need to tell her my plans. She and I have agreed to continue our relationship; we've settled on our intentions. Like the competitors, we just require time to learn to trust each other."

Hood laughed lightly. "Okay, Doc, you've sold me. I'll give you time to win Gillian Cornell. It ought to be amusing to watch."

Lucian breathed relief's sigh. "Thanks, Michael." He stood to leave. "By the way, I was thinking of our competitors. What do you think of a lie detector test as one of the challenges?" Lucian liked how Gillian's idea of the three honesty questions had brought them light years forward in their once floundering relationship.

Hood's head snapped up to take in interest. "A lie detector test? I like it! What did you have in mind?"

"Maybe the ex-mates could design the questions to be asked of each other–something like that." A wicked smile overspread Lucian's face. "They should answer questions with all honesty–hence the lie detector."

"Would you like to ask Miss Cornell a *yes* or *no* question?" Hood teased.

A flash of hope played in Lucian's eyes. "I don't think I'm ready to propose on national TV, but I wouldn't mind Gillian openly admitting her feelings. However, we should probably control the type of questions that are asked. Give the competitors parameters."

"Okay, I'll mull it over," Hood conceded. "A lie detector test? Why didn't I think of that? You're a devious man, Dr. Damron. I bet you could deceive the Pope."

Lucian felt a twinge of recrimination. "I'm no more deceitful than the average American male, I assure you."

"Sure, Doc." Hood's attention was lost to the film footage before him. "We'll talk more later," he said distractedly. "Hey, Charlie, run that last segment again. I need a better look at it," he called. Having been decisively dismissed by the show's director and his staff, Lucian shrugged his shoulders and headed for the door. He had more important things to consider: What his next questions of Gillian should be and how soon he could convince her to return his love.

Gillian returned to her room, her mouth still tingling from the pressure of Lucian's lips on hers. A light knock at the door increased her hopes of Lucian being on the other side, but opening it brought only a tearful Mary Nelson. "May I come in?" Mary whispered softly.

"Certainly," Gillian said as she ushered the woman into the room and closed the door. Standing all alone, Mary immediately began to sob, and Gillian pulled her into an embrace. "Come and sit down." For infinite minutes, all Gillian could do was comfort the woman. She stroked Mary's head and rubbed her back. Gillian assumed this had something to do with Bruce Nelson's musical performance. "Do you wish to talk?" she encouraged.

Finally, Mary raised her head, staring off in space, not really seeing Gillian. "Would you mind?"

"Of course not, that's what I do. If you need to talk, or you just need to sit here in companionable silence, this is the place to be." Gillian's sincere tones eased the tension Mary carried.

"I must tell someone before it's too late," Mary started.

Gillian adjusted her position: Holding both of Mary's hands within hers, she moved to sit before her. "Go on," she encouraged.

"I know," Mary stammered, "I must seem like a cold hearted, Lady B----, but I'm not. I am a woman who loves her child more than life. I would do anything to protect my son–even bring Bruce Nelson back into our lives."

Gillian looked away, unable to sustain the intensity found in Mary's gaze. "Bruce seemed sincere tonight." Gillian spoke softly, keeping her own emotional response from her voice.

"He did, didn't he?" Mary said, wistfully; then she turned to Gillian with a businesslike resolve. A shift in her shoulders served as a preamble to the strength in her words. "Look, I want someone to know the true story behind my appearance on the show. I came because I couldn't find my ex-husband on my own; the show's clout located him easily, and it was important for me to find Bruce. You see, Gillian, I am going to die–very soon." Despite her best efforts, a gasp escaped Gillian's lips. "I've an inoperable tumor; I needed to find Bruce to take care of our son; I can't leave my child alone in the world. I'm smart enough to know I'll be the first to be voted off the show; in fact, I'm banking on it, but I required assistance in bringing Bruce on board. Do you think you and Dr. Damron can do that?"

"We will do what is necessary," Gillian assured her. "We can start first thing in the morning. I'll see to it; don't you worry about anything." After a long awkward pause, she added, "Are you certain about the tumor?"

An ironic laugh echoed through the room. "Do you think I haven't asked myself that question a thousand times? I am certain–less than six months, most likely sooner if what the doctor says proves true."

Gillian couldn't hold back the tears. "I swear, Mary, we'll assist you through this. You've nothing to fear."

⁓

By the time the results show came on the air the next evening, Gillian and Lucian had counseled Mary and Bruce throughout the day. The Nelsons had agreed to move back in together, not as husband and wife, but as the parents of a child who needed them both. The counseling began the process, but Lucian made arrangements for continued sessions with a therapist from their hometown, whom he knew well from the lecture circuit.

As Mary expected, they were the first couple to go home. Bruce and Mary sat together on the sofa; he clasped her hand in his. Bruce turned to the camera when Daniel prompted a response to their departure. "Thanks to this show, Mary and I have a chance to rebuild a life together for our child's sake, and although we are the first to go home, that just means we get to start our lives over sooner than the other competitors." With that, he brought the back of Mary's hand to his lips and kissed it lightly; her smile indicated she was happy with the show's outcome.

Daniel turned to the camera, offering up his custom-made smile. "Tune in next week for round two of *Second Chances: The Courtship Wars* to see who will be our ultimate champion."

Lucian and Gillian snuggled together in the privacy of his room. He lounged against the arm of the sofa, one leg stretched out the length of the furniture and the other dangling from the edge. Gillian lay between his legs, her head resting on his chest where she could hear the regular rhythm of his heartbeat. This was Lucian's *exclusive* hour with her; he stroked the side of her arm and periodically kissed the tip of her head. "You were so helpful with Bruce Nelson today," she congratulated him.

"Who would have thought Mary and Bruce could come together for any reason?" Lucian's voice still held the astonishment he felt upon hearing Gillian's story of Mary's health problems.

"I know," she whispered. "It just shows a person cannot predict the future!"

Lucian pulled her to him and kissed her lips tenderly. "Have you ever thought about what could be?"

"Is that one of your questions for this evening?" she teased.

"I'll use one of my allotment if you'll attend to it." She gazed up at him; in the soft light, Lucian's eyes glowed with passion.

Gillian waited for several elongated seconds before she answered. "I assume your question is not speaking of generalities." He nodded ever so slightly so as not to break their connection. "My dreams are simple, as well as impossible. I dream of Barb living to an old age, but in counterpoint to that, I dream of my own family with a man who truly loves me and the typical two point two children." She made light of the seriousness of her thoughts, not certain how he would react to her dreams of marriage. "Considering you're now privy to some of my dreams, please tell me yours."

Lucian shifted his weight uncomfortably, and she wondered if he would preface his thoughts. Finally, he said, "This is a difficult question for me. As a child, I simply wanted a loving family." Gillian remembered he had once spoken of never being allowed a normal childhood. "I abandoned those dreams as I moved into adulthood; I made the assumption that a family lifestyle wasn't for me; I didn't need nor did I deserve such touches of the ordinary."

Gillian caressed his chin line. "And now?" she said quietly.

"Now...now, I want that family once again. I don't believe I have ever stopped wanting it." Lucian's voice betrayed his loneliness. He pulled Gillian closer to him, holding her tightly in his embrace, neither of them wanting to abandon the moment.

Tears pricked her eyes' corners; she didn't know how to tell him how much she cared for him. "Lucian," she began, but couldn't find the words.

"I know, Sweetling," he whispered. "Me too." Then he kissed her forehead. Finally, he spoke again. "Let me change the mood. Did you mean the lyrics of your chosen song?"

"When I chose it, all I could think of was I wanted to put distance between us. Then the competitors told their stories, and I realized how minimal my objections were in comparison to theirs. My Goodness, look at the drama just in the case of Bruce and Mary, and then I thought about how much the song might hurt you. I didn't want to sing it, but with the cameras rolling, I didn't have a choice. I felt awful!"

"I suppose you believed I deserved it." His simple words tore her heart to shreds.

"You didn't deserve it," she protested. "I was stupid to listen to Charlotte Blakeley."

"Charlotte? What does she have to do with this?" He pushed Gillian to a seated position as he bolted forward.

Gillian's bottom lip trembled as she relived that awful confrontation with Lucian's former lover. "Are you asking me honestly what I meant? You don't truly know?"

"Gillian, as God is my witness, I never knew what actually turned you against me. Are you telling me Charlotte was involved somehow?"

She stood and walked away from him, pacing the floor in agitation. Eventually, she turned to where he still sat watching her. "The day you returned from Tahoe, I ran into Charlotte while I was out shopping. She was with several of her friends." Lucian rolled his eyes in disgust. "Being Charlotte, she attacked my relationship with you. Thinking we were solid as a couple, I answered her insults; I know I should be above all that, but she stood there and talked about me as if I was invisible. It infuriated me!" He simply nodded in encouragement. With a deep steadying breath, she continued, "I nearly escaped unscathed until she said that she had been with you in Tahoe. She said you made love to her, and while she slept, you called me."

Lucian was on his feet immediately. He encircled her in his arms, letting Gillian's head rest against his shoulder while her tears cascaded down her cheeks. "Gillian, since the night we contested each other at the San Francisco conference, I've seen no one else but you. You consume me, Sweetling; I participate in life around me because it hurries my time until I can return to you. Before we ever went on our first date, I had ended it with Charlotte."

"Then how did she know where you were?" Sobs threatened to take over her thoughts.

"At one time, Charlotte assisted me with my presentation bookings. She probably remembered where I was and called your bluff." He kissed the side of her face. "Gillian, I wouldn't betray what we have; I have never known such contentment in my life. Please believe me. I can't erase my past mistakes, but my present and my future depend on you."

Gillian refused to abandon all her fears. "But she announced to the world that you two slept together. Why would she say it if it wasn't true?"

"Sweetling, you know how Charlotte is; you've experienced her barbs first hand. I cannot explain her motivations. She once told me that we're both users; we used each other, as well as other people." Her hands gripped his shoulders. "To my shame, there was a time her assessment was accurate. I pray I'm not that person any more."

Gillian snaked her arms around his neck while feathering kisses across his face. "I'm so sorry," she nearly wailed. "I let you down. How could I be so stupid? I put us through pure hell. Can you forgive me?" By then, she cupped his face in her hands.

Lucian took both of her hands in his, kissing the inside of each of her wrists. "You and I aren't going to permit these things to come between us any longer."

Gillian succumbed to her desires. She wrapped her legs around Lucian's waist as he lifted her to him. He turned to look at her, smiling wickedly. "Kiss me!" he demanded.

Before she could respond, he pushed her against the wall and smothered her mouth with his. Gillian's arms clung to his neck and shoulders, as he devoured her essence. She desperately needed to be in his arms; with him, everything felt so right. She relaxed against him, arching her back. His tongue slid into her warm, willing mouth as Lucian deepened the kiss. All reasonable thought disappeared with the strength of their mutual need. His hand slid down her shoulder and arm, cupping her breast, testing its weight; Gillian's fingers knotted in his thick hair.

The intensity of their passion rose quickly, and before long Gillian clung to him unable to stand, unable to know anything but him. "Lucian," she pleaded.

"Gillian, my sweet Gillian," Lucian whispered while he feathered kisses across her face and neck. He steadied his composure, forcing his hands still and his breathing back to normal. "You are my nemesis," he teased. "I've lived all these years in ignorance of what ecstasy I find in one of your kisses."

Letting her ardor wan, Gillian snuggled into the bend of his neck. "You taste delicious." She let her lips slide over his neck and into his shoulder's indentation. "Maybe my next research should be on taste, not scent."

"Maybe I should sit you down?" he chuckled lightly as he allowed Gillian to disengage her legs from around his waist, but he scooped her into his arms, strode to the chair, and settled her on his lap. "As much as I desire you, Sweetling, I want you to know it's you I want. All of you, not simply the feel of your body beneath mine." His mouth rested only inches from hers.

Gillian nibbled on his bottom lip. "You don't want my body underneath yours?" She feigned innocence.

A low growl escaped Lucian's lips. "Are you trying to drive me absolutely insane?" He purposely ground his arousal against her hips. "Does it feel as if I'm not prepared to make love to you until you scream out my name?"

Gillian caressed his hardness through his clothing; his breath caught in his chest, and she watched as Lucian's eyes glazed over with desire. "Lucian, allow me to touch you." Her lips rested just above his.

A slight nod was all he could manage as he closed his eyes to the hunger. Her heart pounded uncontrollably as she shifted from kissing his lips to where she could unbutton his slacks and release his tumescence. Feeling the length of him swell, Gillian cradled him in her palm. She drew in a sharp breath as her fingers closed around his hardness. She fondled him, cupping the heavy sacs and letting her thumb touch the velvety head. Desire-laden drops showed themselves as she curled her fingers around his solid shaft. The feel of him inflamed her passion. She increased the pace of her strokes. Within minutes, Lucian's jaw locked, his face became taut, and his eyes closed in primal need. His harsh, uneven breath filled the room as her own shallow ones reduced her to speechlessness. Swiftly moving up and down him, Gillian watched as his fingers clenched around hers. Seconds before his release, he jerked her hand away and cupped the head as his seed pulsed into his palm, driving his hips upward. He shuddered and stilled, a satisfied smile turning up his mouth's corners.

Gillian stood and walked to the vanity in the room. When he finally opened his eyes to her, she handed him a small hand towel. He wiped his hand and his body dry with it and tossed it to the floor. Adjusting his clothing, he welcomed her back into the safety of his embrace. Lucian kissed the top of her head as she rested underneath his chin. "A sensate lesson?" His breath finally returned to normal.

"Of course, not," she murmured, "I never encourage people to touch each other intimately, at least, not at first. That was especially for you."

Lucian kissed her tenderly, and Gillian whimpered. "Exclusivity has its benefits." He laughed lightly as he stroked the side of her face with his knuckles.

"I guess I should go; I've been here too long now." She shifted her weight to stand.

Lucian followed her to her feet. He took her in embrace. "When this show's over, we need not separate again."

"Slow," she cautioned, but Gillian went up on her tiptoes to kiss him.

"Okay, slow," Lucian grumbled, "but I'll speak my piece when we've finished here. I'm not giving you up again."

"No, Lucian. Don't give me up." Gillian's smile regarded his surprise. "Come, Love, it's time for my nightly talk with Barb; she'll be so excited to see us together."

Chapter Nine

THE PRODUCERS HAD DESIGNED the third week's challenge to reinvent romance in the relationships. All the sessions for the week focused on bringing romance into the lives of the couples. Gillian focused on what initially brought them together–those beginning moments when a man and a woman realize the attraction, which they cannot deny. Lucian's sessions dealt with the times prior to the marriage and the early days when the participants became "couples," while Stryent's rehashed the complaints, which led to the divorce.

The atmosphere at the retreat aided Lucian and Gillian too. Although they kept it in check when others were around, the changes in their situation became evident to anyone with eyes. Lucian touched her shoulder or squeezed her hand as they passed each other in the hallways. Others noted how he held the door so she had to scoot past him, bodies nearly touching and eyes engaged in seductive ways. He seated himself beside her at dinner, allowing his arm to drape over the back of Gillian's chair while they sipped coffee and enjoyed conversation with the others. Long, lingering gazes from across the room predominated their interactions.

"I think Dr. Damron had his hand on our Gillian's knee during dinner last night," Ada told Nicole as they enjoyed a glass of wine in the room they shared at the retreat.

"Well, something changed for them after last week's show; that's for certain. There is definitely an electrical charge between them. At least, someone is finding love here."

The third challenge followed the rekindling love theme for the physical part too. Hood brought all the contestants together. "We have a real treat this week; well, it'll be a treat for the ladies. You men may not be in your comfort zone." A light buzz ran around the room. "All the women in their show interviews spoke of wishing their husbands would take them dancing. So, for this week we've brought in Matthew Plum and Lauren Bateman; they are U. S. ballroom dance champions. Each of the couples will learn to mambo." The women all began to laugh excitedly, but the men looked around in bewilderment.

"I ain't wearing no tights and sequins," Theo stated adamantly.

"Don't panic, Men," Hood chuckled. "Previously, we put the women on the hot seat with the ropes course. This time it's you gents who must pay the piper. None of you know how to dance, but with our instructor's assistance, that will change. We've arranged an intimate dinner for each couple, along with a makeover and a new wardrobe. You'll dance on national TV next Monday night."

Sean grumbled, "I've two left feet."

"Our instructors know how to fix that." Hood took amusement in their reactions. "So, let's get started. You have your first lesson in ten minutes in the rec room."

Matthew Plum led the show's participants, along with Gillian and Lucian to the converted dance area before he addressed the group. "Obviously, the mambo is a Latin-based dance; it is written in 4/4 time. That converts into there being four beats to a bar of music, which translates further to mean that there are four dance steps to a bar of music. Luckily, for you non-dancers, you don't move on the first beat, but we have to remember to still count it." The men chuckled nervously, all of them looking around to evaluate how their fellow contestants fared.

"As we learn the basic steps you'll hear me use the commands: step-rock-close-pause. That will be how we proceed. So let us begin; please join me on the dance floor." The men and women spread out evenly across the space provided. "Okay, now, let's get started. This is a couples' dance and a very sensual dance, but the tempo is slow enough that all of you should master it quickly.

There are two basic mambo movements: the forward and the backward basic. Women will do a complementary move to the man's. So, if the man steps forward on the left, the woman will step back on her right. You ladies will save your toes if we all do this together. Therefore, face your partner." The couples moved across from each other.

Lucian winked at Gillian. When she blushed, he laughed lightly. Then uncharacteristically, Gillian seductively licked her lips, ending with a slight pursing of hers as she mimicked a kiss. Lucian's eyes intensified with a flash of desire, and Gillian watched as he gulped for air. "That's not fair," he whispered as he took her hand and led her to a place on the floor. "And you, my Sweetling, will pay for such impudence."

"Lucian, you wouldn't," she nearly pleaded.

He locked eyes with her again before finally responding. "I'll have to thank Hood for this challenge," he teased. "I get to publicly hold you in my arms all day." When he saw her blush again, he added, "Our bodies joined in a dance of love. Delicious!" The redness crept up her neck as he feigned innocence with a roll of his eyes heavenward.

After almost an hour filled with laughter and self-deprecation, the couples mastered the basic steps and were ready to put them together in close proximity. Up until this point, they simply stood opposite each other an arms length apart. Plum encouraged them to step into their partner's arms. "Remember, this is a Latin dance and as such there's a certain romantic sensuality about it. The man holds the woman lightly to him but in a possessive way. Let me show you." Plum took his partner in his arms and began to demonstrate the two movements, as they would look in the dance. "Now, it's your turn."

Gillian easily slid into Lucian's arms, their bodies joined by a close intimacy, with his gaze settled on her mouth. Breathing shallowly, Gillian attempted to give the impression that they weren't both thinking about the intimacy of the bedroom instead.

Lucian half listened to Plum's instructions. He had learned a good deal about dancing years ago. In high school, he had learned that holding a girl during a dance was a legitimate excuse for taking her in his arms. Plus, he had also discovered that girls loved guys who knew how to dance, so he had applied himself to being a passable partner. Yet, watching Gillian's hips sway during all those practice moments had piqued his interest beyond reason. If Gillian only knew how turned on he was, she would be embarrassed. Now, Lucian fixed his gaze on her slender waist and the curve of her hips and tried not to fantasize about her legs wrapped around his waist in the throes of passion.

The slow tempo of the music wafted over them. The torture of touch, a brush of the other's body and a shivered awareness, consumed them both. Gillian's fingers rested in his warmth while Lucian lightly possessed her waist and held her to him. He danced with the supple grace of a natural athlete. "You are a very good dancer, Dr. Damron," she mused.

Lucian blessed her with one of those lazy smiles he so rarely shared. "I'm impressed, Miss Cornell, with your lightness of foot."

"I'm not just another pretty face," she taunted. "I've other talents."

"I beg your pardon, Sweetling, but I'm all too aware of your many talents, as well as your beautiful face." Her smile disarmed him as it always did, and Lucian felt a lurch deep in the pit of his stomach.

"You're a shameless flirt, you know."

His wicked grin slowly turned up his mouth's corners. "I'm just taking advantage of all my opportunities."

"Think of the dance as foreplay," Plum coaxed from the other side of the floor.

Lucian already recognized her as a temptation. Considering the dance as foreplay could be his undoing. He was barely aware of the music coming to an end. Gillian instinctively drew closer to him, lodged next to his hardness. Hearts pounding and pulses racing, they stood riveted in each other's embraces. Lucian's stare was hot and loaded with passion. However, a throat being cleared brought them from their trance and forced them to recall their surroundings. Even so, Lucian elongated the moment before he released her, finally allowing Gillian to avert her gaze.

"Well, everyone seems to have the basic steps," Plum continued. "Now it is up to you to perfect them. Add your own little touches; practice together; use the time to rediscover your relationship with your ex. Lauren and I will be here until this time tomorrow. If you need extra practice or want some suggestions, we are at your disposal."

The couples left the area discussing when they would get together again. "At least, they're now in a position to spend time together," Lucian noted. "Up until today, the show's not encouraged their being alone together."

"That means we have to practice too," Gillian whispered as they watched everyone disperse.

Lucian felt a flash of desire shoot through his body. "May we return to our rooms to practice?" he murmured.

"I'll meet you in thirty minutes. Come to my room." Gillian squeezed his hand and headed out of the area with Ada and Nicole.

<hr>

At dinner, Lucian and Gillian shared a table with Gary and Melinda. "Were there costumes in your rooms when you returned from practice?" Melinda asked excitedly.

Lucian noted Gillian smiling from ear-to-ear. "Yes. My costume is red. Can you imagine? I don't believe I have ever worn red in my entire life."

Lucian said casually, "It's a power color. With your hair, I imagine some shades of red would not be readily acceptable, but certain shades could highlight the color and make it more pronounced." He was certainly interested in seeing her in this new color. Strong and independent and perfectly sexy. The thoughts of Gillian in a satiny, tight-fitting costume made him shift uncomfortably to hide his growing erection. Of late, it seemed he remained constantly stiff. It wasn't a bad feeling–just one he had never experienced prior. Gillian Cornell had certainly turned his world upside down.

Gary's grumbling brought Lucian from his reflections. "I can't believe I'm going to have to dance on national TV."

"Well, if you hadn't been so stubborn when we were married, you might not have so many qualms now," Melinda asserted.

"I just hate dancing, Mel."

Lucian looked knowingly at Gary. "When was the last time you took Melinda dancing?"

"Gosh, I don't know." Gary looked a bit bewildered by the question.

Melinda added quickly, "I can tell you."

"So, when?" Gillian asked out of curiosity.

"In the twenty years, I've known Gary he has taken me dancing once. We went to Florida on vacation, but I was pregnant, and I couldn't take the hundred plus degree heat. We left and came up the coastline to South Carolina. One of the nights we went out to a club. He danced with me then–three dances–two slow and one fast. That's it."

Everything got quiet at the table. Finally, Gary said, "I didn't realize it mattered."

"It did," Melinda whispered.

"But I'm a terrible dancer," Gary protested.

Tears formed in the corners of Melinda's eyes. "I didn't care about that. Dance was so much a part of my life before we met, but you didn't allow me to share it with you. I felt cheated, Gary. I know it sounds bitter, but I resented the fact that you couldn't go out of your way to take me dancing. Would it have been such a big deal to do something for me once every six months–once a year even?" Gillian reached across the table to take Melinda's hand in hers.

Feeling attacked, Gary turned indignant. "When did you go out of your way for me?" he accused.

Lucian blocked the growing resentment. "Gary, that's the problem in most marriages; people don't want to do something simply to give their mate pleasure. If you admitted it, you didn't take Melinda dancing because it made you uncomfortable. You weren't an expert so you avoided it. And, Melinda, I'd bet you quit doing things for Gary because he didn't reciprocate. Unfortunately, both of you quit working at the marriage."

After a few moments, Gary let out a deep sigh, as if he had expelled the devil from his back. "When we get out of here, you and I are setting up a regular date to go dancing or to a musical downtown or something like that."

"That would be wonderful." Melinda slid her arm through Gary's. "Thank you for listening to me."

"You're welcome, Sweetheart." Gary kissed her forehead. "I want you to be happy, Mel. I truly want you to be happy."

⌣‿⌢

"You look like the cat licking the cream." Gillian teased as Lucian led her onto the dance floor.

"Why not?" He spun her around before he took her into his arms. "I get to dance with the prettiest woman in America. It's just you and I and fifteen million of our closest friends."

They were to dance the group dance with all the contestants and then cheer on the individual couples as they danced for the cameras. Lucian and Gillian watched *Mad About Mambo* the previous evening. Gillian insisted it would get them in the mood. Of course, with a demonstration, Lucian assured her he was always in the mood.

"This has been an enjoyable week." Gillian moved easily into Lucian's embrace. "Do you suppose Barb is watching tonight?"

Lucian laughed softly. "She'll be jealous."

"Barb will be so excited; I'd hate to be her caregiver tonight." Gillian began the backward basic as Lucian stepped into the forward one.

The elimination sent Yvonne and Sean home, leaving only four couples to compete for the grand prize. The ratings skyrocketed for this second elimination thanks very much to the instant popularity of Lucian and Gillian. Cuttles nearly drooled over the numbers, pleased with how well his prediction had played out. Hood strutted around like a peacock, while the staff seemed relaxed at last. Things had come together.

"So when do you think it will happen?" a show staffer mumbled.

"What do you mean?" Dr. Stryent inquired.

"There's always another shoe to fall so to speak," the man continued. "Every show has its glitch when things fall apart. I've seen it happen time and time again."

Stryent looked surprised and a bit amused. "Surely you don't believe in such superstitious gobblygook?"

"Just bide my words. I'm rarely wrong." The man shook his head as he left the area.

The sessions for the new week centered on foods and eating. "As we all know, much of life revolves around the dinner table," Stryent's voice rang clear as the couples gathered in the ranch's kitchen. "Most families these days have abandoned eating together, but a lack of that bonding affects the family dynamics. Therefore, part of our focus this week will be on cooking and eating together. You'll be given cooking lessons by famed chef Raoul Sebastian. Therefore, let's gather around and see what he can teach each of us."

They found five workstations set up—one for each couple and one for the three psychologists. Sebastian showed them new techniques and new foods. Lucian and Gillian found the "domestic" scene stimulating even though Stryent shared their work area, and the cameras recorded their every move. "I'll have to remember how handy you are in the kitchen," Gillian said as she cut up the vegetables for the stir-fry.

"For the nights you have to work late, and I don't?" he whispered as he leaned over her to drop in the zucchini.

Gillian blushed and resisted the urge to caress his cheek. "I could get used to this," she said softly as she stirred the mixture and added the soy sauce.

"I sincerely hope so." Lucian added the rest of the ingredients. "Twenty-four/seven." Their eyes locked, and Lucian's breath caught in his throat. They stood transfixed, chests heaving as images of such intimacy danced through their minds. Finally, Lucian forced his eyes from hers, gifting her with one of his wicked smiles.

It was thrilling to know he wanted her as much as she wanted him. Gillian shook her head and returned to the dish at hand. "How is the salmon, Jonathon?" she addressed Dr. Stryent as he checked on his creation.

"Be ready in minutes," he called.

"Lucian, you take over here, and I'll set the table." She handed Lucian the wooden spoon, while squeezing past him in the tightly fitted space.

"These close spaces should make it romantic for our competitors," Jonathon laughed as he maneuvered between Lucian and Gillian to set the salmon on the table.

Lucian winked at Gillian. "Yeah, the remaining couples should find the closeness very desirable." He knew by accepting Gillian's offer for a renewal of their relationship that the truth of his past would eventually become public knowledge. But, he always assumed it would be he who told Gillian and the world of his transgressions. When he looked at her now as she skirted around the table happily taking care of the place settings, Lucian smiled, quite genuinely, before taking his seat. This could

155

be his life: Gillian, along with Barb, and their children and their careers. Sitting back, he met her gaze and melted into the all businesslike smirk on her lips.

"Your dinner is served, Sir," Gillian teased as she placed a plate before Lucian.

"Moments like this make me miss my family more than I can say. My wife and I have dinner together every night. I think that's one of our secrets for keeping our marriage strong," Stryent mused as he took his seat. "You'll realize that too, Lucian, when you finally decide to settle down."

Lucian couldn't remove his eyes from Gillian's form; she stood at the stove filling her plate. "I'll keep it in mind, Jonathon. I do believe it is about time to be thinking of getting married." His words penetrated Gillian's consciousness; Lucian watched as she stiffened momentarily; but when she turned to look at him, he saw the glow for which he searched. His smile changed tenor when he met her eyes. "Yes, Jonathon, I agree; I should be considering taking a more serious tone to my life."

Gillian flushed, but she managed to keep her composure. "What are we talking about?" she asked as she slid into her seat.

"I'm trying to convince Lucian that being married has its advantages." Stryent laughed as he dug into his meal.

"Really?" Gillian laughed as Lucian squirmed, being under the microscope.

"Don't you think our Lucian should get married soon?" Stryent continued. "He needs a woman to straighten out his life."

Gillian giggled as she dropped her eyes. "Maybe *our Lucian* isn't ready for a wife, Jonathon."

Jonathon finally looked up from his plate. The electricity between his colleagues very evident. Lucian watched her, quietly demanding that Gillian return his gaze. When she raised her eyes to his, Lucian's scrutiny called to her. The rising heat between them couldn't be hidden. Stryent's clearing his throat, brought their attention to the current situation. "Well...well, I believe in marriage; it's a fine institution," Stryent stammered.

"I believe you're right," Lucian agreed as he turned his notice toward the food. "This smells delicious, Gillian." He took a bite before saying,

"Jonathon, why don't you tell Gillian and me about your wife? Was it love at first sight?"

They all settled in to congenial conversation with Stryent leading the way. Neither Lucian nor Gillian added much to the discourse, but the intimacy increased nevertheless. The only indication anything changed between them was the narrowing of Gillian's eyes as she studied him. His countenance gave away little of what he thought, but his eyes were unusually stormy.

⌇

"Gillian and I thought we would tease you a little with the concept of food and sex." Lucian walked around the room where the four couples met.

"Chocolate sauces and whipped cream? Is that what you had in mind, Doc? Or were you thinking about edible underwear?" Theo continued to joke, but the man failed miserably. Lucian found he had less and less respect for Theo Jenkinson.

"Truthfully, Theo, I was thinking of the kind of food we all have every day in our refrigerators. Research shows that certain foods can improve a person's sex drive."

"Well, I don't know about you, Doc, but my sex drive doesn't need any help." Lucian thought, *Me thinks the man doth protest too much.* Likely, Jenkinson had a bit of a Napoleon complex. Always having to prove himself a man. Real men didn't require all the glitz and glamour. The thought brought him to a clear realization of how often he had used similar techniques to hide the misery he had known as a child. Suddenly, regrets rested on his shoulders.

"Just for once, would you please keep your mouth shut," Grace chastised him. "We're not here for laughs."

"Excuse me, your Highness," Theo barked. "The Doc knows I'm just joking."

"It's okay, Theo, but Grace is right; we have a lot of things to discuss. So, let's begin." Lucian redirected the group. "We eat with our senses: smell, taste, and sight. Some ancient cultures, for example, think there's a direct link between certain foods and evoking sexual drives. I'm certain you've heard about raw oysters and the like. Some people believe because the phallic shape of carrots, bananas, and asparagus, that those foods increase sex drive. Likewise, oysters and figs represent the female genitalia. That's where many of those stories began." He held up each of the foods he mentioned to emphasize his point.

Gillian took over from there. "I am doing extensive research into attraction and the sense of smell. We have found certain scents affect our sexual desires. Three very potent smells are almond, vanilla, and truffles." She passed around scent strips very much like those found at expensive perfume counters, only these held the extracts of common flavorings. "Of course, chocolate is a powerful aphrodisiac," she continued. "It's actually a caffeine-like stimulate found in chocolate which increases one's blood flow. Ginger, lesser known, has the same effect."

Lucian picked up the lecture; since that day he had visited her college course and answered questions, he had realized that they worked together very well as a couple. Both gave support and acknowledgement. "Spicy foods, garlic, and a little wine also affect blood flow, which, obviously, has something to do with our sexual performance. Now, I will turn the floor over to Miss Cornell. Her research on scents is phenomenal." Lucian quickly took a seat behind the contestants, leaving Gillian the opportunity to highlight her work and, therefore, her future book sales. He was certain that Gillian would recognize and would approve of how he had manipulated the contestants, as well as the camera time.

"Thank you, Dr. Damron," she began. "Our emotional brain is directly attached to our sense of smell. I'm sure each of you has a childhood memory triggered by a particular smell or food. For me, it's the greasy smell of funnel cakes at a county fair. My parents loved the atmosphere of a fair. Young 4H students showing their prized animals. Homemade pies and jams. That sort of thing. As certain scents bringing on pleasant memories, a particular scent can trigger memories of sexual encounters. Our research shows that a woman's sense of smell is more sensitive than a man's. All of us have what is known as a major histocompatibility complex or MHC. If we can root out a mate with dissimilar MHC, we find a compatible one."

An hour later, Gillian finished answering questions about her research project. "Gosh, Gillian, I had no idea," Nicole gushed. "It sure explains why we're drawn to certain people even when we resist the temptation."

"It's only theory," Gillian cautioned, "but it is a fascinating concept."

~

The fourth show included the food sessions, as well as many of Gillian's research concepts. The producers clearly displayed the resurgence of Lucian's feelings for Gillian.

Prior to the broadcast, he had accepted a call from Charlotte Blakeley. She had called at least once daily since his karaoke performance, but he had refused to speak to her. The only reason he had tolerated her call this evening was he wanted to confront her for her part in Gillian's withdrawal.

"It's about time, Lucian," she protested.

His disgust laced his voice. "I really have nothing to say to you, Charlotte. I want nothing more to do with you."

"I assume your love song won your insipid miss. Is that the way it is?" Charlotte mocked.

"I told you a long time ago, Charlotte, that you don't control me, but you have insisted on inserting yourself into my life." Lucian lost control quickly. "You're lucky that you're not here right now. I could easily inflict you with bodily harm and enjoy every minute."

Her voice dripped with sarcasm. "I always liked it a little bit rough; you're turning me on."

Lucian warned, "What I'm offering won't be pleasant."

"So, I told your girl friend a little lie about Tahoe and sharing your bed. It's not my fault she's so gullible. Can't you see she's not worth your time?" Charlotte insisted.

"I'm sorry, Charlotte–really sorry. I've made you into a pathetic beggar–a woman with no scruples and no potential lovers," he said coldly.

Lucian's words had the desired effect. "Who do you think you are?" she stormed. "My father could buy and sell you ten times over."

"Then have him buy you a new man! This one is looking for genuine love, and no one will deny me the opportunity to finally find happiness."

"You're a fool, Lucian," she screeched.

"Good-bye, Charlotte." He terminated the conversation with a flourish. With a deep sigh of regret for time wasted, he sought out Gillian and his future.

Chapter Ten

DANIEL LEWIS STOOD IN THE CENTER of the platform waiting for the camera cue. As the red light began blinking, he pasted on his usual smile and started his spill. "Our four contestant couples will face a new challenge tonight. They will each be strapped to our lie detector and will be asked questions designed by our staff. In fact, all our contestants will be asked the same five questions so you'll be able to compare apples to apples, so to speak. In addition, we have allowed each contestant to ask three *honesty* questions exclusive to their ex mates. To demonstrate the effectiveness of our device, we are putting our own psychologists to the test once again. Now, because they are not in a relationship, they will not be asking each other questions. However, our show staff chose the questions for our medical resources. We have told our therapists they may answer the questions truthfully or purposely tell a lie. Either way, it proves the accuracy of our evaluations."

Lucian was to go first; Gillian, meanwhile, watched with interest. The technician began Lucian's evaluation with obvious questions such as *Is your name Lucian Damron?* and *Do you currently live in New York City?* to set a base line. Eventually, the man asked the more personal questions.

"Do you have secrets you wish no one else knew?"

Lucian thought of his past and grimaced. He would like to offer an explanation to accompany his response, but the machine only recorded *yes* or *no* answers. "Yes," he finally said.

"That answer is truthful," the man responded as he marked the tape. "Did you sleep alone on your most recent visit to Tahoe?"

Lucian flushed with anger. *How in the hell did they know about Tahoe?* Of course, the show monitored the phone calls coming into the communications room. He and Charlotte had argued about what she had told Gillian, and a show technician heard every word. Well, at least, it would give him a chance to prove to Gillian he had not lied to her. "Yes."

The man smiled. "Again, that answer is truthful."

"Do you hope this show leads to your own TV show?" The questions continued.

Lucian laughed lightly; he thought he would lie this time. "No."

The test evaluator marked the tape once again. "Dr. Damron is not telling the truth on that one."

"Have you ever heard of Marcus Chambers?"

Lucian felt the sweat run down his body. How could he answer that? Did someone on the set know the truth about Marcus Chambers? He took a deep breath and said, "No."

"That response is not truthful."

Gillian's head snapped up with the question. Over the past two weeks, she had nearly forgotten about her curiosity over Lucian's resemblance to the unknown Marcus Chambers. A flutter of butterflies hit her stomach, and a mask fell over her countenance. She now regretted the moment she had succumbed to her perverted interest and had ordered a background check on Marcus Chambers. She had, truthfully, not expected anything to come of it; yet, now she felt she had betrayed Lucian. *He purposely lied for the machine*, she reasoned. *Ted Morris asked Lucian about Marcus Chambers, so, of course, he's heard of the man. Plus, the machine indicated he had told the truth when he said his name was Lucian Damron.*

Little did Gillian know that Michael Hood watched her response to Damron and made mental notes as to her demeanor and her reactions. She had become so accustomed to the show's staff observing her every move–to the point where she no longer guarded her emotions before the all-knowing lens.

The technician adjusted the dials and the connections before asking his last question. "Are you in love?"

Lucian couldn't believe this challenge essentially was his idea. He had never expected the show's executives to ask such intimate questions. Was he in love with Gillian? Did he even know what love was? He knew that he didn't want to spend the rest of his life without her. He knew that if he didn't see her or talk to her or hold her, he was miserable. "Yes."

The word hung in the air. The technician grinned. "That answer is truthful."

"Told you," Ada whispered in Gillian's ear as the show's staffers released Lucian from the machine's monitors.

Gillian turned quickly. "Do you really think so?"

"Well, at least, you didn't deny it this time." Ada half smirked.

"He is so gorgeous," Gillian gushed. "I know what I look like. How could a man who looks like that want anything to do with me, as well as to be in love with me?"

"Call it fate. Call it destiny, but above all, call it love. The man is besotted with you, Gillian. If you don't take advantage of this admission, you're a fool." Ada loosely draped an arm around Gillian's shoulder as they stepped out of the way of prying ears.

Gillian, murmured, "Dare I?"

"You're the relationship expert. What advice would you give to a client in the same situation?"

Gillian took a deep breath. Her eyes drifted to where Lucian now straightening his clothes stood beside the lie detector chair. "I would tell my client to jump into that man's arms and never let him go."

"I think you just answered your own question." Ada moved away, leaving Gillian with her fully verbalized realization of her feelings for Lucian.

"You're next, Miss Cornell," a show staffer called to her.

With a deep sigh, she took her place. She knew without a doubt that if the man asked Lucian about being in love, he would certainly ask her the same question. Hood, as well as Daniel Lewis, had indicated that the American public had taken an interest in her relationship with Lucian. Now, on national TV she would admit that she loved this man. They would make a commitment, taking them to a new level. Ironically, she half wondered if they should not have done this in private, but nothing about their courtship was normal. Normally, one whispers words of love in intimate moments, but she and Lucian would declare their love while hooked up to a lie detector and on national television.

"Are you ready?" the man asked after starting the tape.

A smile of acceptance flitted across her countenance. "Fire away."

The man inquired about Gillian's feelings on her parents' deaths, asked about her winning money at the Derby, asked had she had learned hard lessons on trust, and asked if she wanted a book deal from the show. Like Lucian, Gillian's final question demanded that she acknowledge her growing affection. She had attempted to lie on a couple of the questions, but Gillian knew she would answer the final one truthfully–give Lucian an honest response. "Yes, I am in love."

"That answer is truthful," the man declared as he marked the tape.

Lucian watched her with satisfaction. He had told Hood he would not mind if Gillian admitted her feelings for him on national TV. Of course, he had never expected that Hood would be so devious. After all, if things developed as he had hoped, Lucian had agreed to announce their relationship on the final show. He told Hood to offer the public a *tease*. Well, he had gotten his wish: Gillian had shared her feelings; she loved him. Lucian held no doubts when she admitted to being in love that he was the recipient of that love. Part of him shouted for joy; Gillian Cornell, the most extraordinary woman he had ever met, loved him. Part of him dreaded the change in the dynamics of their relationship. How could he keep his feelings a secret while the cameras rolled? Sharing their love with the American public couldn't be a solid basis for a lasting commitment. They had three weeks at the ranch before they could return home to something he couldn't define.

Late in the night, Lucian paused outside Gillian's door; he took a deep breath and stared at the barrier between them. How could he be this nervous? She had already admitted that she loved him. He raised his hand to knock, but he couldn't do it. Heaving a resigned sigh, he sank to his knees before the portal. What would he say to her? Lucian had never found himself in such a position. Everything he had wanted in life lay on the other side of her stupid door, but he feared screwing up what he most needed.

Dejected, he turned to lean against the frame. "What can I really offer Gillian Cornell?" he had asked himself. Before answering his need to be near her, he had practiced what he would say to Gillian. Would she be pleased to see him? Without thinking, and nearly to the point where he considered it best to wait until tomorrow, he let his full weight rest against her door, and it gave way behind him as he tumbled into her room. The door swung wide as he scrambled to his feet. He waited for his eyes to adjust to the light, and realized he had no idea what to do now. What a fool! He stood in her room's middle. Uninvited! Lucian certainly didn't want to startle her. Was she asleep?

He cleared his throat. "Gillian?" he whispered her name.

"I was wondering when you would get here." Gillian's voice rang clear as she sat up in the bed. She didn't sound at all as if she had slept any better than he had. She touched the lamp on the bed stand, and the room glowed with soft amber.

"You were expecting me?" Hope sprang to his voice.

She slid from the bed. Unfortunately, for Lucian, the nightie she wore clung to her every curve, and he felt the blood surge to his groin. "We do have something about which to speak, wouldn't you say?" She stroked his neck and ran her fingers teasingly over his shoulders.

He took a step toward where she stood. "May I tell you how beautiful you are right now?" His eyes drifted down her body.

"Although I am flattered, Lucian, those aren't the words I wish to hear coming from your lips." She crossed her arms over her chest.

He knew what Gillian wanted, but Lucian had never said the words to anyone. Not a parent, not a sibling, and never to a woman. "I'm not very good with this sort of thing." A nervous chuckle escaped his lips.

"The great Lucian Damron having trouble with words? The man who has charmed woman after woman with his silver-tongued barbs? Not good with words? I'm amused," Gillian teased.

"So I'm good with words. I'm just not good with words when there's this much at stake." Honesty was obviously a good choice; Gillian smiled at him.

"Give it a try, Lucian; you've got a chance. I'm inclined to be receptive to your glibness." She walked slowly toward him.

"Gillian," he stammered, "I...I find myself completely overwhelmed by my feelings for you." He began slowly to build confidence. "I've been terrified because I've no control over how consumed I am with you." A tiny hint of amusement sparkled in her eyes, encouraging him to continue. "When the technician asked me tonight if I was in love, my first thought was of you. I'm in love with you, Gillian." He moved closer and stared into her eyes.

"Did you say you love me?" She shook her head, giving a soft toss of her curls.

Realizing the words didn't strike him dead, his eyes lit up. "Is there something wrong with your hearing, Sweetling?" He pulled her into his arms.

"No, I just like seeing the infamous Dr. Lucian Damron fazed by three simple words." One arm wrapped around his neck while the other hand rested on his chest.

"You do love me; don't you?" Lucian buried his head into her hair.

"Of course, I love you, Lucian. Didn't you hear my response to the same question? We danced before fifteen million people; now we've declared our love before a like number. I must admit, this isn't what I imagined would happen when I fell in love." She caught his hand walked backward toward the bed, tugging him along with her.

Husky with renewed passion, he answered, "It's a surprise to me also." Lowering his head to hers, Lucian captured her lips with his, drinking in the pleasure of holding her in his arms. When he withdrew, his gaze skimmed over her, creating a warmth they both recognized.

His hands played over her back. Then, Lucian slipped the nightgown from her shoulders. He bent to kiss the hollow of her throat, before dropping lower to kiss between her breasts and to run his tongue along the sensitive flesh surrounding the nipple.

"Lucian?" she offered a mild protest.

"Shush, Sweetling." His mouth returned to hers. Lucian pulled her closer to him. Her mouth opened to his–hard and demanding. Her arms snaked about his neck, fingers intertwining in his thick hair; Gillian pushed her body tighter against his. Lucian's hands cupped her hips, pulling her against his quickly growing arousal while Gillian moaned with need.

Lucian released her slowly. "Gillian?" he gasped, waiting for her response.

They both knew the commitment he demanded when he called her name. Her eyes drifted to the bed. Gillian reached out to take his hand. "Come, Love," she whispered.

He followed a few steps, and then Lucian picked her up and carried her to the bed. He caught Gillian's hands, trapping her wrists above her head. "I've never felt this way, Gillian," he murmured as he nuzzled her ear. "It'll be the first time I have actually made love."

Gillian half giggled. "Then I'm more experienced than you. I made love to you the last time we were together." She pressed her lips to his, softly lingering with need.

Any vestiges of reservations or false hopes or indecision disappeared as he thrust into her sweet dampness. "Then love me again. Love me always," he whispered.

———

The third elimination had sent Theo and Grace home. All the contestants answered the same five questions: Do you love your ex-mate? If you could choose anyone to marry, would your ex-mate be in the top three choices? Do you regret the end of your marriage? Would you be willing to continue couples' therapy after the show? Did you cheat on your ex?

No new realizations came from these questions. Both Ada and Theo had admitted their extramarital affairs. The thing, which turned the tide against Theo, was Grace's question about whether he would cheat again. He couldn't honestly say he would not. "I don't intend to betray Grace ever again," he explained, "but no one can ever say never."

Andrew asked Ada about her fling. "Were you with him more than once?"

"No, I swear it, Andrew. Only the one time. I was terrified of losing my independence so I latched onto a stupid idea that if you found out you'd leave me, and I'd be free again. Except when you left, I realized you had allowed me to be free. I wish I hadn't hurt you." When they released Ada from the machine, Andrew drew her into his embrace, holding her close as tears streamed down her cheeks.

The test had showed that both Theo and Ada answered truthfully. Obviously, the viewers saw Ada's indiscretion as a mistake, but Theo's many forays as a way of life. And then there were three couples leading to the season finale.

———

Cuttles congratulated Hood as he entered the service trailer. "Great show!" he praised. "I love the way that you manipulated Damron and Cornell last evening. It was pure genius."

"I'd say it was," Hood handed his boss a drink. "He spent the night with her."

"Did he really?" Cuttles smiled in complete satisfaction.

Hood assured, "At least, several hours in the middle of it."

"I assume that we have some tape showing just that?"

Hood joined in with the amusement. "Can you find a bear in the woods?"

"Oh, yes," Cuttles laughed. "People are so predictable."

Once Lucian and Gillian had admitted their love, a calm came over their interactions. He often caught her hand or touched her back for a few minutes. Gillian touched his arm or massaged his upper shoulder. They didn't openly hug or kiss, but a new intimacy obviously remained.

"May we take a walk?" Lucian asked after dinner.

"I'd like that. Allow me to retrieve a jacket; I'll meet you out front."

Lucian's eyes sparkled with anticipation. "Ten minutes?"

"Make it five," she said as she hurried away.

When she reappeared on the lodge's front porch, Lucian fell into step beside her as they headed toward the wilderness trail. "Thank you for joining me." As they cleared the area where the cameras could see them, he took Gillian's hand in his. "I thought we should talk about us."

"About us?" Gillian moved closer to him.

"Needless to say, the show's producers have planned on playing up our interest in each other."

Gillian looked at him as if seeing Lucian for the first time. "They promised us a certain degree of anonymity."

"Gillian, the bottom line is Hood will do what he has to do to maintain the show's ratings."

"I suppose I knew that on some level; it's just that I'm a very private person," she protested.

Lucian led her to a carved out bench along the trail. "I realize that, Sweetling, but I don't think Hood cares about your privacy."

"Then what do we do?" Gillian rested her head on his shoulder.

"I believe that we beat him at his own game. We quit avoiding only minimal contact; we let everyone know the natural progression of our involvement. Hood has indicated that he wants to tease the viewers with our relationship. I don't want to ravish you before the cameras."

Gillian laughed seductively. "Don't you?"

Lucian followed her laughter. "Ravishing you is one of my favorite things." He kissed the top of her head before continuing, "However, ravishing aside, I would prefer not to hide everything. If I feel like sliding my arm around you, then I want to do it without wondering who's watching."

"I believe that's acceptable. Needless to say, we can't be overtly all over each other, but I really don't want to hide how I feel about you."

"I will demand that Hood stop taping the hallway outside our bedrooms," Lucian added.

"They wouldn't use that, would they?"

"I wouldn't put anything past Hood." Lucian declared. "At least, if we don't seem to be hiding anything, then he won't be able to twist the images to create his version of our story."

Gillian weighed his words. "It makes sense. We'll be professional as staff members, but personal as partners."

"Now, Sweetling," he cupped her chin in his palm, "I move we get personal."

"Mmh," she groaned. "Personal would be an excellent way to go." Lucian kissed her, his mouth lingering over hers. "I love you," she whispered.

"Say it again," he pleaded as he kissed her.

Gillian taunted, "You'll tire of my saying it."

"A man starving for you affections would never tire of hearing you say those words." His lips brushed her several times.

"Lucian Damron, I love you," she gasped as his hand reached her breast.

Holding her gaze as he manipulated her nipple, Lucian smiled wickedly. "I love you, too. More than you'll ever know."

Gillian pressed herself into his hands. "You'll come to me tonight?" she sighed as she kissed along his chin line. "I need to sleep in your arms."

Lucian pulled her to him. "I'll come to you tonight and every night. Now that we're finally together, I'll let nothing separate us again."

⌒

Ada and Andrew, Mark and Nicole, and Melinda and Gary gathered with Lucian and Gillian in the meeting room. Gillian cleared her throat. "We have determined a new focus to our counseling. In order to do so, we have asked that the cameras be turned off for these sessions." The couples all looked around, noting the camera angles and the lack of filming. "Please understand that none of you are required to participate in these sessions. Because they are of an intimate nature, you may withdraw without it affecting your success in this competition."

Lucian picked up the angle. "These are highly structured sensate focus exercises; they are designed to increase your comfort with physical intimacy. We are sensitive to the fact that as couples you're no longer married, and you may be reluctant to participate. You're all consenting adults. No one will check on you; no one will question you on whether you chose to participate."

"These sessions are designed to eliminate anxiety in your sexual performance and allow you to relate to each other in new and intriguing ways," Gillian explained. "An hour will be blocked from your time each day for the next four days. During that time all cameras will be turned off. You may choose to use the hour for the sensate sessions or spend them how you wish."

"How does this work?" Ada asked.

"I will provide you with individual scenarios for each of the sessions, which will increase your intimacy through several stages."

"The idea," Lucian assured the couples, "is to concentrate on the sensations and your reaction to them. If what we suggest bothers you, you may substitute simply holding hands. A good back rub or a foot massage is effective also."

"You've got our attention, Doc," Gary added. "We understand we don't have to participate. Just tell us and let us decide."

"Okay, then," Gillian laughed nervously. "Today's focus session will emphasize touching. You will touch each other–caress your partner without touching the breasts or the genitals. Touch head to toe and front to back. Each person will be the giver, and each will be the receiver.

However, today how the giver touches his partner is tantamount. You may touch as you wish, barring being openly cruel or unpleasant."

The couples eyed each other, all very self-conscious. "Tomorrow," Lucian continued, "the receiver will communicate to his partner the kind of touch he wants. Still one may not touch the breasts or the genitals."

"The third session," Gillian inserted, "may include touching of the breasts and genitals, but one may not concentrate purely on those areas. Communicating with one's partner must take precedence. Orgasm is not the purpose; intimacy is."

Lucian finished the session's explanation. "If you choose to be involved in the fourth session, you are free to enjoy the pleasure of your partner."

"Could we enjoy our partner's pleasure today?" Mark snickered.

"No one will ask; no one will check on you," Gillian reiterated. "However, we hope that you choose to participate as we have outlined the sessions. These behavioral techniques have proven effective in assisting couples heal intimacy problems."

"No one will ask you to commit or not commit," Lucian stepped beside Gillian, resting an arm around her waist. "We will see you in one hour. The cameras are turned off until then."

The couples left the area, heading off to decide whether to take advantage of the sessions. "It's hard for me as a sexologist not to ask them if they'll be involved," Gillian sounded frustrated.

"It's the only way we can do this, Gillian," Lucian cautioned. "We can't mandate that they exert control or even consider the idea."

She circled her arms around his waist and rested her head on his chest. "May we find some quiet time together?" she invited.

"Ah, Sweetling, you are my tempting minx." Lucian brushed his lips across hers as she tilted her head upward.

"We're going straight to Session Four." She kissed his cheek and behind his ear.

"Come, my Love, we're wasting our hour." They left, arms laced about each other's waists.

Chapter Eleven

LUCIAN HAD KNOWN FROM THE beginning that if what rested between them was to last, then he must tell her the truth.

He and Gillian lounged on the sofa in his room after sending the couples off to their second sensate session. Yesterday, they devoured each other; today, something more sedate–more connecting–prevailed. Reclining against the pillows, they lay limbs intertwined, in silence, lost in thoughts of each other.

Gillian's eyes drifted closed. "When I'm with you," she whispered, "I cannot tell where I stop, and you begin." She lightly stroked Lucian's jaw line.

He caught her hand in his and kissed her fingertips. "When we leave here," his voice caressed the side of her face, "we must make some big decisions."

"Do things have to change? Why can't there just be this?" Her delicate ministrations continued along his hairline.

Lucian wondered about the sensibility of sharing his secrets and risking the chance of driving Gillian from his life. Truth was he didn't think he had the strength to recover if that was her decision. But he had chosen his path, and Lucian would see it through. "Gillian, we must move to the next level, or this thing we hold dear suffocates. *This* will never die as long as it's only one step in our lives together." Lucian raised her lips to his and lingered there. "We both have things in our past that we should share, and then from those, we will plan a future."

His words frightened her. "Is the past likely to hurt our future?" She rose up to where they could make eye contact.

"If you're asking me if I have done something vile, the answer is *no;* yet, what you think you know about my past is not totally accurate." His thumbs made small circles at her temples. "I must explain things to you; I must be honest."

"Lucian, if this is about Charlotte Blakeley or any other woman from before we met, I don't care. It doesn't matter to me. I knew you were more experienced than I." Her words came out in a rush.

"Sweetling," he interrupted, "I would not pretend to think that you don't already know my previous stupidity nor my chagrin at having to subject you to my history. Yet, that particular *history* is not of what I speak, and I won't test your intelligence by perpetrating such a sham on you."

She cupped his face in her palms and showered him with kisses. "No matter what, I won't stop loving you," Gillian declared.

Cater kissed her fully, his tongue pushing its way to the soft roof of her mouth. Gillian pulled herself as close as possible. When he raised his head, Lucian sighed before closing his eyes. "Gillian, I must say this; I can't hide it from you any longer." She froze, holding her breath. "I lied when I said I didn't know Mar . . .'"

An abrupt pounding on the door cut the moment short. "Miss Cornell! Miss Cornell, are you in there?" The pounding continued as before.

"What the hell?" Lucian swore as he strode to the door. Gillian scrambled to her feet, following close behind him. When Lucian jerked open the door, the man was preparing to resume his knocking.

"Oh, Dr. Damron," he gulped, "have you seen Miss Cornell? It's important!"

Gillian pushed ahead of Lucian. "What is it?" she demanded.

"You have an emergency call in the communications room."

Panic hit her, and Gillian took off at a run. She already held the waiting phone to her ear when Lucian entered the room. He waited to take his cue from her. "This is Gillian Cornell," her voice trembled. In the brief seconds before she spoke her next words, Lucian watched her go pale. She swayed in place, and his arms came around her. "I'm on my way," he heard her say before she clicked off the phone.

"What is it?" He pulled her to him, and she leaned a cheek against his chest for comfort.

"It's...it's Barb," she stammered. "They've taken her to the ER; she collapsed." Her words sank in, and she pulled away from him. "I have to go," she faltered. "I've got to go now."

He clutched at her hand. "You pack what you need," he spoke reassuringly, "and I'll see Hood about getting you out of here immediately." Gillian shook her head, pulled away from him, turned, and ran from the room.

Less than a half hour later, Lucian led her to the teleport established close to the show site. Although Lucian knew she only heard part of what he said, he explained, "The helicopter will take you to the airport; there's a private jet waiting to take you home." The blades whipped up leaves and grass, swirling about their feet. "She'll be fine," he yelled over the noise. "Call me when you know something." Gillian swallowed hard, forcing back the tears bubbling at the corners of her eyes. Lucian watched her fight for composure. This woman was one in a million. "Do you want me to go with you?"

Gillian blinked at him in obvious confusion, and she shook her head in the negative. "I'll call tonight." Gillian kissed him hard on the mouth. It was a brief need for his support–a way of taking him with her. Then ducking her head, she ran toward the waiting copter. With a swish, the machine lifted off, and she was gone. Lucian stood for a long time looking at the spot where Gillian had been only moments before while he fought the foreboding shiver working its way up his spine. "Please God," he murmured. A twinge of guilt followed his return to the ranch. He hadn't told Gillian *his truths*, and now it could be too late.

⌒

Near midnight, Lucian sat alone in the communications room waiting for Gillian's call. He had wandered in there hours prior, oblivious to everything around him. Dr. Stryent had taken on the role of show therapist, directly in charge of the three remaining couples. Lucian totally withdrew from the group; he sat head in his hands offering prayers for the innocence of Barbara Cornell. *I am thankful,* he whispered, *that the Cornells opened their hearts years ago to a child who knew only love. Even if it cost me...*

"Dr. Damron," a voice came over the PA system, "you have a call on line one."

Lucian's head snapped up. With shaking hands, he grabbed the receiver. "Gillian?" His voice shook with anticipation.

The line appeared dead, but as he strained to hear her voice, sobs of anguish filled the space. Tears leapt to his eyes, and he could no longer breathe without forcing gulps of air into his lungs. "Gillian?" he coaxed. "Tell me." Silence remained. "Tell me what happened. I'm here with you."

The minutes ticked by as he clamped down on the dread pitied in his stomach. "Lucian?" Gillian's voice cracked sharply. "She's dead."

The words sucked the air from his body. What could he say to Gillian now? It all seemed so easy when he offered grief therapy to his many patients. Now, he realized how meaningless people in the midst of grief must find his advice. "Do you wish to talk, Sweetling?" He felt powerless in all his former pomposity. "Do you want to tell me what happened?"

"She was pregnant! Pregnant! How could that be, Lucian?" He knew Gillian didn't really expect an answer; she asked rhetorically. The words came quickly now, like the bursting of a dam. "She had a stomach ache; that's what they said, but it kept getting worse so they transported her to the hospital. When they called me, they were doing tests for flu, for food poisoning, for E coli, for meningitis–the works. Of course, no one thought to see if my sweet, innocent Baby Girl was pregnant." Lucian closed his eyes to shut out the pain. "Right before I arrived, Barb's tube burst; it was an ectopic pregnancy. No one knew. I saw her for a few brief moments as they rushed her to surgery. She was so scared, Lucian. She told me she loved me; she said she loved you, and she was glad you and I were together. Then she said Mommy and Poppy had been in her room taking care. She knew, Lucian; Barb knew she was going to die. She'd lost too much blood before anyone knew what was going on. They couldn't save her. If Barb hadn't been Downs Syndrome, someone might have thought about her being sexually active, and they might have looked at her before it was too late to save her." Sobs burst from the other end of the line, and Lucian let his own tears join hers.

"Where are you, Sweetheart?"

"I'm with my great Aunt Hilda. She and Uncle Joe came after me. I couldn't go home tonight. Not without Barb." She sounded so vulnerable it hurt Lucian to listen.

Lucian knew where he needed to be. "I'll be there in the morning."

"You can't, Lucian," she protested. "They'll fire you. You'll not get the talk show."

"Jesus, Gillian, do you think I care? You can't do this alone; I won't have it. If I could get a flight out tonight, I would. As it is, I'll be there tomorrow. Will you be all right tonight?" His words answered her prayers.

"Thank you," her voice sounded so small. So vulnerable. "I need you here."

"Did the doctor give you something to help you rest?"

"Yeah, but I wanted to call you first."

"Listen to me, Sweetling," he began, "I must speak to Hood about a flight out of here. I want you to take the medicine, thank your aunt and uncle, crawl into bed, and then call me back. I'll hold you with me and stay with you while you sleep."

"Would you?"

"Of course," Lucian reassured her.

"I didn't want to sleep without you; you know, just in case I can't put it out of my mind."

"I'll be on the other end of the line until I can stand beside you tomorrow. Now do what I told you, Sweetheart. I'll take care of everything else."

"I'll call you in a few minutes." A large sigh escaped before she could hold it back. "What would I do without you?"

"You never have to find out. I love you, Gillian."

Two days later, Lucian sat in the small church beside Gillian, offering comfort, during Barb's funeral. She clung to him, barely allowing him from her sight. He had a major row with the show's producers about his leaving, but Lucian insisted. Eventually, Cuttles decided to send a camera crew to film them together and play up their budding relationship as part of the program's appeal. The commercialism of the act appalled Lucian, but he soon found out how popular he and Gillian were with the viewing public. Having been in relative seclusion for the past several weeks, he held no idea of their instant celebrity. Not only did *Second Chances* send a crew, but also similar media coverage by several of the national tabloid television outlets followed, as well as some independent sources.

He had originally agreed to return to the show for the next broadcast, but now that he was with her, Lucian no longer considered that idea possible. Gillian had withdrawn from life. She had not cried even once since Lucian's arrival. She stayed in his arms; yet, Gillian didn't talk beyond the occasional comment on the weather or on the beauty of the service. He had assisted her with decisions regarding the funeral and the burial. He had taken her home with him because she had insisted that she couldn't return to the townhouse "just yet." She went about her business on autopilot. However, Lucian understood that if Gillian did not allow the grieving to begin soon, he would not be able to return to the set. She had no close family; Lucian had discovered that her aunt and uncle lived a couple hundred miles away. She had no one else, and he would not desert her.

The day after the funeral, Gillian agreed finally to return to her home. "Come, Sweetheart," Lucian encouraged, "I'll go with you."

"It must be done," Gillian said robotically, "but I'm not looking forward to it."

"Hood wants me back for the next show," he told her as he assisted Gillian into his car.

"Must you?" A look of fright lodged in her eyes.

Lucian touched her hand, bringing the back of it to his lips. "I won't leave you; I've told Hood that. Until you're ready, I'm here with you."

She looked at him closely and caressed his cheek. "How could I have survived this without you?" Tears formed in her eyes, but Gillian fought them away once again. Lucian wanted her to cry–to finally face the truth of Barb's passing.

"You never have to find out." Lucian caught her hand, turning his face to kiss her palm, but he hoped today would be the beginning of Gillian's return to her own independence.

Her hand shook as she inserted the key into the lock of the townhouse she owned. Gillian swallowed hard as she stepped inside. It had been five weeks—a lifetime ago—since she'd been there. The last time, she had taken Barb to the extended care facility—the last time she'd seen her sister alive and well. Gillian was pale and distraught, her appearance hollow and expressionless.

Lucian moved up behind her, placing a hand on her lower back. Her eyes locked on his. Cobalt blue streams. "We don't have to stay if you don't want to." His voice softly caressed her sensibilities.

She nodded and then took a step forward, propelling herself into the room. "I must do this," she whispered.

Lucian took her icy cold hand and silently walked with her into the house's interior. They passed through the living room, entering the kitchen. Lucian hit the switch, flooding the room with light. "Would you like for me to fix you a cup of tea?" he asked as he stepped toward the stove.

Gillian froze, looking at the breakfast nook. "We ate there every morning together." Her voice sounded miles away. Lucian stilled and waited for reality's impact. "She's really dead, Lucian."

Lucian knew she still clung to the hope that somehow there was a mistake, but today she would face her demons; the grim truth would arrive at last. Gillian had chosen him to assist her through this; their relationship had taken on a whole new level of understanding. "Yes, Sweetling, she is."

Lucian nudged her into his embrace. Gillian leaned against him. She wept silently. "May we see Barb's room?" Her voice shook with fear.

Respectfully, he turned her toward her sister's room. Pausing on the threshold before opening the door, he asked, "Are you certain?" When she nodded her head in the affirmative, he pushed the door wide. His arm came around her shoulders immediately; he felt Gillian tremble, and he watched the tears streaming down her cheeks. When had she become so vital to his life? When had he developed this relationship—one to surpass any he had ever known?

Gillian drifted away from his embrace. He watched her as she moved gingerly about the room, picking up and touching Barb's personal "treasures," the things, which meant the most to her beloved sister. She held a stuffed animal to her chest, closing her eyes and inhaling the essence of her sister. Tears flowed freely now—the dam breached. Finally, on sensual overload, she collapsed to her knees in the middle of the room.

Her shoulders shook with violent sobs, and Lucian, at first, allowed her to cry.

He waited patiently by the door. Finally exhausted by the effort, Gillian curled into a protective ball. Quietly Lucian lifted her from the floor and carried Gillian toward the sofa. He sat heavily, cradling her as if she were a child that he must protect. Gillian turned one cheek against his shoulder. Her tears left damp trails down his neck and shirt, but still Lucian held her, allowing the woman he loved to grieve.

She required this protective comfort so Lucian tightened his hold. Accepting the "door" he had opened for them, Gillian snuggled further into him, and Lucian held her tightly. She wept. Gillian's heart had been ripped open, and only he could heal it. They were lovers, but they were also friends.

How long he held her, Lucian knew not, but when her gaze locked with his, his onyx-colored eyes darkened. Instinctively, Lucian lovingly lowered his mouth to hers. The passion flashed, his mouth covering hers— her tongue plunging into his depths. Their arms closed around each other. A hot, insistent embrace. Clinging heat. Despite the pain. Despite the absurdity, Gillian demanded that life go on even in the face of death, and Lucian would assist her hold on it. "Sweetling?" he gasped as their mouths moved apart.

But all Gillian did was pull his mouth to hers again. He recognized her grief, then her desire. Whatever Gillian required of him, Lucian would answer. So, although his intellect told him this was a nonsensical act, Lucian allowed Gillian the response she demanded. She needed him on a primal level; therefore, he folded her to him and deepened the kiss.

Gillian unbuttoned the blouse she wore, and Lucian watched intently as she removed it and followed with the bra. Then she unbuttoned his shirt and pressed herself to him. Lucian took it from there, hands splayed across her back and on her breast; he returned to the assault of her mouth with his tongue. She clawed herself closer to him. He surrounded her, allowing her to burrow into his heart and to find love and life there. He cupped her buttocks, lifting her to him, pressing her flesh to his. Lucian would swallow her pain; he would protect her from the anguish. *Punish me,* he silently begged. *Don't let her suffer anymore.*

He kissed her lips and her breasts while Gillian moved against him, increasing his arousal. "Please," her raspy voice escaped from her swollen lips. She pushed him back on the sofa and straddled him, moaning with his ministrations–the center of her desire moving against his erection.

Gillian demanded the passion–demanded the life. He couldn't fill her quickly enough. Lucian refused to take his time; she required instant completion. She unhooked his slacks, freeing him, and then lowered herself onto him. Lucian grasped her hips, holding her to him, impaling her with his fullness. She did not stop until he was embedded to the hilt in her, pulsing with life. Then she bent over him, returning to his mouth, kissing Lucian with a passion he had never known. She brought him along with her, pounding their bodies together in a frenzy designed only to forget her loss in a consummation of their love. Finishing with cries of joy, at last, they clung damply together waiting for focused reality.

Gillian lay on top of him breathing evenly, dozing in a sleep that she hadn't found in the previous week. A deep sleep hadn't yet come, but peace had found her. "I love you more than life." Her words, spoken dreamily, held a new resolve.

Lucian stroked her cheek with the back of his hand. "When the show's over, we must find a place of our own," he whispered.

She nodded, but then she raised herself up on him. "Could we stay here?" Her eyes pleaded for his agreement.

"Are you certain, Sweetling?"

"I'm certain, Lucian." She looked so innocent, like a child swearing a truth she may not be able to keep.

"If you still feel that way when the show is over, then we'll stay," he told her as she shifted her weight to lie in the crook of his arm.

"Thank you, Lucian." She kissed the underside of his chin line. "You're everything to me."

He kissed the top of her head as he pulled her to him. "Let's rest." He picked her up and carried Gillian to her own bedroom. "I must have you safe in my arms where I can love and protect you."

~

They sat across from each other in the breakfast nook. Lucian had prepared a meal from the staples Gillian had in the pantry. It certainly wasn't fancy, but it held symbolic significance. It was their first as a fully committed couple.

"Why didn't I see Barb as a woman, as well as a child?" Gillian still struggled with the knowledge of how her sister died. "They said she was over two months pregnant so I can't even blame the care facility for not watching her. My God, she was here with me when it happened. Why didn't I recognize the changes in her? I don't even know with whom she shared herself."

Lucian joined her on the bench. "Barb told me she had a boyfriend. I didn't think anything of it; she always called me her boyfriend too."

"When did she tell you this?" Gillian looked surprised.

"That first night at the ranch. Remember you were called away, and I asked if I could talk to Barb until you returned." He took her hand in his. "I made her promise she'd tell you about him. His name is Thad."

"I've never heard of Thad." She shook her head to clear away the confusion. "Barb loved you so much that she shared a secret with you, even when she wouldn't tell me." Gillian looked around the room, which held so many memories.

Lucian offered his own reprimand. "I should've told you."

"Don't," Gillian insisted. "Don't blame yourself. It wouldn't have mattered. She was already pregnant at the time." She paused before adding, "It's not as if I never anticipated Barb's passing. After all, she had Downs Syndrome. The fact that she lived over thirty years is saying something. I just always assumed the disease would kill her. Her youthful innocence disguised the fact that she possessed the desires any woman feels."

"In reality, Barb's desires were probably more like adolescent curiosity. Yet, if anyone exuded love, it was Barb. She so loved life; she taught me so much in such a short span. Your sister believed in us."

Gillian laughed, "That she did. I remember sitting here with her as I fumed over the society picture of you and Charlotte." Lucian flinched with the memory. "But Barb knew. She said you wore your fake smile; then she proceeded to demonstrate your real smile. I should've listened to my sister; she was smarter than I was."

"Let's return to my place," he said as he assisted her to her feet. "This is enough for today."

"I think you're right. Barb will be here when I return." She laced her arms around his waist. "In retrospect, this was a good day," she whispered solemnly. "A good day, indeed."

Lucian returned to the show at week's end, but Gillian, still in grief, didn't. The couples completed a scavenger hunt for the fifth week's challenge. They searched the ranch and the surrounding area for five clue pieces, which spelled out *Second Chances* when linked together. Mark and Nicole won the challenge, earning them a luxury cruise, but they lost the popular vote and were the next couple to be sent packing.

Along with Cuttles, who represented Starline and the show, Lucian, looking both haggard and distraught, made a statement to the public at the end of the results show.

"Last week, our show family suffered a loss. Our Gillian Cornell's sister Barbara passed from complications of surgery. Barbara was thirty-three years old.

"What can I say about Barbara Cornell? The Cornell family adopted her when she was three years old. The Cornells were exceptional people; they opened their home over the years to a hundred different foster children, but they chose to adopt a special needs child because Barbara would have floundered in what can sometimes be an overwhelmed foster care system.

"Yet, the Cornells received so much more: They spent their lives loving Barbara. I am honored to have had Barb as a part of my life. I spent the last Special Olympics event with Barbara and Gillian. Barb ran two track events; one she won, and the other she placed third. The magnificence of that day, however, was the triumph found in each of the athletes competing. Barb, or Baby Girl, as Gillian called her, gave each of us pure, untainted love.

"Many of you have contacted the show and would like to express your sympathies somehow to Gillian. Your emails and words of condolences will be forwarded to her. Others of you have offered monetary support. In that vein, this is Sam Cuttles; he will speak this evening to a memorial fund established in the name of Barbara Cornell, to be used for medical research and to support the Special Olympics. Starline has set aside $100,000 to honor the Cornell name. If you would like to make a contribution, an address will be displayed at the beginning of the closing credits, as well as being posted on our show's website, along with an explanation of how you might be part of this remembrance.

"On a personal note, we would like Gillian to know that the show staffers and the contestants miss you. We love you and are awaiting your return."

Lucian paused before the last line; he had wanted to tell Gillian of his love while the cameras still rolled, but he left the remarks as a generalized outpouring of love rather than the personal one perched on his lips. As the image of Lucian faded from the screen, a montage of pictures of Barbara Cornell flashed on the monitor, followed by the information on the memorial fund.

As he walked away from the cameras, both Melinda and Ada caught up with him. "How is she really?" Ada caught his arm.

"I...I wish I could tell you for certain," he stammered. "She's lost everyone else in her life; I'm afraid Gillian may suffer for some time."

"She has you, Lucian," Melinda assured him. "Just give Gillian time."

"I hate being here when I should be with her right now." He blew a resigned breath.

Melinda led him toward a table in the dining area while Ada poured him a cup of coffee. "Isn't one of the stages of grief being alone with oneself and coming to grips with the loss?"

"It is." Acceptance didn't make it easier, however.

They sipped their coffee in silence for a few minutes. Ada broke the quiet. "Gillian is strong. You've chosen very well; you will be very happy with her."

"Do you think so?" Lucian seemed dismayed.

"We think so," Melinda added. "You found your great love. I know we sound overly romantic, and for a woman who has seen the backside of marriage, I for one believe you have a chance to have that happily ever after of which we all dream." Lucian squeezed her hand in companionship. "Make Gillian's nightmare into a fairytale. Neither of you seem to have much other family. Maybe that's because God plans for you to create your own bonds and complete each other."

Tears misted Ada's eyes, and Lucian fought the emotions choking out his breath. In a raspy voice, he said, "Maybe you should be the therapist." He smiled away the pain he felt at being separated from Gillian. "I'll just be glad when this is over; I will be on the first plane east."

Unable to remain over night in her own home, Gillian stayed in Lucian's apartment. Yet, she returned there each day to visit with her memories. She had forced herself to go through her sister's belongings. She kept only two outfits from Barb's wardrobe. Just as carefully, Gillian limited the personal effects she would store. Each item held a special memory associated with her sister. She donated the remainder of the clothing and usable items to a local charity.

"Then you cleaned it all out?" Lucian asked as they spoke during their nightly call.

"I kept things to cherish Barb's memory, just as I did with my parents, but I cannot build a shrine to her. My parents didn't teach me to wallow in my grief; they believed life must survive the worst the world has to offer. That's why they devoted themselves to helping children survive when things seemed in total chaos."

Lucian sighed, "I wish my life had such completeness."

"I thought initially that we could use Barb's room as an office. What do you think?" Gillian's voice held traces of uncertainty.

"We could use the office space." Lucian wanted to know what else she thought. "You said *initially*?"

Gillian laughed nervously. "I was...I just..." She fought to put into words what she wanted to say. Lucian waited patiently. "I...I thought the room might make a good nursery some day."

Lucian couldn't hide the surprise. "You've thought about that?"

"I want a family some day, Lucian. Don't you?" Gillian sounded a bit defensive.

Lucian stammered, "Yeah...yeah, I want kids. I don't have any family so I often wondered what it would be like; I just never allowed the dream to become a reality."

"I'm real, Lucian," she whispered softly.

He laughed self-consciously. "Let's set a date first," he teased. "Then we'll see if can put Barb's room to a better use than office space."

"Lucian, do you mean it?"

"I love you, Gillian," he assured her. "I want us to spend the rest of our lives together."

Lucian conducted the sessions for the last week of competition. Counseling both couples at the same time, he worked on what characteristics made relationships work. "Besides the initial physical attraction and the need for that intimate release, some qualities–some mannerisms–must be evident. For example, a sense of humor is essential. So much of life is absurd; one has to be able to laugh at it. Of course, the person must be kind, as well. Yet, the most important quality is flexibility. Because conflict is potentially a relationship killer, life requires us to make compromises. Sometimes, you have to give even when your first instinct is to win your point. Both, I stress *both*, people in the relationship must give a bit so they can come together in a new way. If one person does all the giving and one all the taking, the relationship is doomed for failure."

The final week's challenge sent the couples off to write their own marriage vows to be shared on the show with the nation. Ada and Andrew took the more traditional route. Andrew began, "Ada, I will devote my life to loving you. I will protect you and cherish you with my every fiber. We will grow old together."

Later, Ada answered, "Andrew, you are so remarkable; I am blessed to be loved by you. Your strength makes me stronger; your love completes me, and my heart imagines only you when I say the word *husband*."

Gary took the microphone next. He laughed when he looked down at his notes. "Well, Dr. Damron said in this week's session that we should develop a sense of humor. Melinda and I've known each other for twenty years. That time taught us that it's the little things, which can destroy a marriage. So, here goes. Melinda, I promise you the following: I will put the toilet seat down and make sure the toilet tissue roll dispenses over and not under." Melinda began to laugh. "I will put my dirty clothes in the hamper. I will not eat over the sink. I will take out the garbage without your prompting me, and, finally, I promise to take you out for a date on a regular basis."

Melinda kissed his cheek when he finished. Now it was her turn. "Gary, I promise to watch NFL games with you, to encourage you to join a golf league because I know you enjoy the game and need time with your male friends, and to stock beer in the fridge, although I insist that you switch to lite beer." He patted his stomach in mock surprise. "Finally, I will joyously entertain the prospects of seeing numerous action movies, as long as I am with you."

The end shots returned to Daniel. "You have seen our two finalists for the past seven weeks. Now, it's time to make your final vote. The phone lines will be open for two hours after the show. If you want to vote for Andrew and Ada, call 1-866-EXLOVE1 or 1-866-395-6831. If you prefer Gary and Melinda, dial 1-866-EXLOVE5; that's 1-866-395-6835. Next week, we bring back all our couples for a reunion before we name our first champion. Join us then for our results show." The credits began to roll, and the show wrapped for the night.

Lucian made his way to his room to wait for Gillian's call. "One more week," he mumbled as he shoved the door open. Finding Sam Cuttles sitting on the sofa surprised him, but noting his packed bags brought him a true feeling of uneasiness. "Hey, what goes on here?" he demanded.

"Come in and have a seat," Cuttles insisted. Lucian shrugged and started forward. "Close the door." The words hung in the air.

"Do you want to explain what this is all about?" Lucian slid in the chair across from Cuttles.

"Maybe you should see this." Cuttles extended a large manila envelope to him.

Lucian took it tentatively. "This is addressed to Gillian." The statement came out as a question.

"We have an agreement where we monitor all the mail and communication coming in and out of the ranch." Cuttles rested his elbow on the upholstered arm while steepling his fingers together. "You should be interested in this packet. It appears Miss Cornell was curious about Marcus Chambers."

Lucian reached for the envelope, while fighting to maintain his composure. "Why would she do that?" Lucian's voice broke with fear.

"Don't you want to know what the file says?" Sarcasm laced the words. The producer paused triumphantly. "I suspect you already know what it says."

"Why don't you tell me and save me the time of reading it?" Lucian could barely hear his voice over his heartbeat.

"It says you are a fake. Lucian Damron died nearly ten years ago, and you've been using his name every since. We're going to ask you to leave the show with Daniel tonight, and you're not to come back. We'll think of some way to explain your sudden departure. We could face real problems if the word escaped that you were administering to our patients under an assumed name."

Lucian bolted to his feet. "I am a doctor of psychology!" he insisted loudly.

"If you say so." Cuttles dismissed him with his tone.

Although Lucian attempted to mask it, his voice held desperation. "I am!"

"But you're not Lucian Damron." Cuttles rose too, refusing to give Lucian a point of dominance.

Lucian's eyes went wild. "My name is Lucian Damron," he assured.

Cuttles tapped the envelope Lucian now clutched to his chest. "That's not what the evidence says." He strode from the room. "I want you gone within the hour!"

The room felt devoid of air. How could Gillian check on him? Did she not love him enough to trust him? "I wanted to tell her before Barb died," he mumbled. "Now, what do I do? She'll never understand." Lucian buried his face in his hands. Where would he go? He couldn't go home; Gillian was there.

A light tap on the door brought his attention to his immediate dilemma. "Excuse me, Doc," the staffer said. "Mr. Cuttles says your flight leaves in an hour. The helicopter will be ready in ten."

Lucian snapped his attention back to the room. "I'll be ready."

Chapter Twelve

WHEN GILLIAN RESPONDED TO THE doorbell, she had prayed that she would find Lucian on the other side. Four days had passed since she had last heard from him. For two of those days, she had stayed at his apartment, but when he didn't return her messages, she decided reluctantly to return to her own townhouse. Misery filled her home; with no Barb and no Lucian, the place seemed too large, too empty, and too lonely.

She had convinced Lucian's doorman to contact her immediately if Lucian returned home. "I don't care if it is the night's middle, you're to call me when Dr. Damron reappears," she had insisted.

"Of course, Miss Cornell," the man reassured her. "Dr. Damron has never allowed anyone else to stay here; I'm certain he would expect me to keep you informed."

Gillian wasn't so convinced; she couldn't understand why Lucian had simply disappeared. She had called the show, but Hood had told her that Lucian had departed shortly after the last broadcast. She had sent him numerous text messages and had probably filled his voice mail twice over with her pleas. After Barb's death, they had spoken words of love and words of their future. Had it been too soon for him? Could Lucian not make a commitment after all? Had she rushed him? Why would he not speak to her?

"Lucian," she instinctively said his name aloud when the doorbell rang a second time. Rushing to the door, she impulsively pulled it open without checking the security peephole, fully expecting Lucian to be standing on the other side. When she found Sam Cuttles there instead, Gillian staggered back in defeat. Cuttles grabbed her elbow to steady her as she let the disappointment drain her energies.

"Miss Cornell," he said as he supported her to the nearest chair. "Have I come at a bad time?"

"No," she forced the regret from her speech. "I was simply expecting someone else." She took the seat and motioned him to the one across from her. "What brings you to my home, Mr. Cuttles?"

"Obviously, you were expecting Dr. Damron." Cuttles eyed her sympathetically. Any fool could see that she had been crying.

"I was," she corrected. "I mean, I had hoped."

"So, you've heard nothing from him?" Cuttles's eyes next took in the disarray of the room.

Gillian's gaze followed his. "I've been trying to go through my sister's belongings," she apologized.

He nodded, obviously, a bit uneasy.

"What can you tell me about Lucian?"

Cuttles cleared his voice. "Unfortunately, we have dismissed the man after the last show."

Gillian bolted to her feet. "Why for God's sake?"

With the control of a man who daily negotiated big media contracts, Cuttles simply waited patiently for Gillian to return to her place. "Actually, Miss Cornell, our decision was based on something you provided us."

Gillian's eyes focused on the envelope he held. "I'm afraid I don't understand." However, dread quickly spread down her spine.

"As I explained to your Dr. Damron, our agreement for the show included our previewing all communications coming and going from the ranch. This past week this envelope arrived addressed to you." He handed Gillian the manila covered package.

Gillian looked at the return address, and she knew without examining the contents what was inside. "For the sake of my sanity, why don't you summarize what's I'll find inside." Tears began to stream down her cheeks.

"Damron has jeopardized the entire season. I won't ask why you chose to have Damron investigated, but we are thankful that you did. If you had not done so, we could be looking at several lawsuits for allowing a bogus physician to administer to our contestants. At least, you and Stryent were there. Luckily, we had the foresight to have more than one licensed physician working with the groups." Cuttles looked please, but his satisfied stare ripped at Gillian's heart.

She whispered, "How was Lucian a fake?"

"Surely you know," Cuttles began. "The real Lucian Damron has been dead for ten years. The man you knew was Marcus Chambers."

Gillian's breath caught in her chest; choking out the words. Through the blackness, she made herself respond. "What did Lucian say when you confronted him with this?"

"Of course, he denied it!" Cuttles said incredulously.

"He said he wasn't Marcus Chambers?" Gillian looked confused.

"The man insisted he was a doctor of psychology, and that he was Lucian Damron. However, your report proves otherwise." Cuttles gestured toward the packet.

"Lucian wouldn't lie," she protested.

Cuttles caught her hand in an act of comfort. "I know you have developed an affection for the man. In fact, we even encouraged it, and for that, I must apologize to you. You do not deserve to find heartbreak so close to your family loss. However, the proof is in your investigation. He did lie. To you. To me. He is Marcus Chambers."

Although she fought them bravely, sobs escaped. "Do you know where he has gone?" Gillian still believed there must be some sort of mistake.

"He flew out on the same flight as Daniel Lewis, but he bought his own ticket out of Chicago. We offered him only a flight that far."

Gillian swallowed hard. Having not totally digested the information, she said lamely, "So, no one knows where he is?"

"I'm just thankful he's gone." Cuttles dropped her hand. "That's the reason why I'm here, Miss Cornell. We need for you to return to the ranch for the final show."

"You're kidding," she gasped.

"With Damron's dismissal, we need you for the reunion show. You and Damron were fan favorites; I cannot have both of you missing from the final show," he asserted. "I don't want to be the bad guy in this situation, but you have a contract, and I will insist if you don't return voluntarily."

"Forcing me to *volunteer*?" The irony played through her reply.

Cuttles actually chuckled. "I do what is necessary for the show's success. You can fly in the day of the show, but you will be there, Miss Cornell. Too much depends on this for me to demonstrate leniency." His tone demanded she acquiesce.

"I see I've no choice," she said at last.

"You will also accompany the winners for their appearance on the morning news shows on Wednesday." He outlined her duties. "Then your obligations to the show will be at an end."

"You will send a car for me?" Acceptance appeared in her voice.

Cuttles stood to make his exit. "Of course, I'll make the arrangements. I'll send you an email later today with the details."

Gillian followed him to the door, clutching the envelope in her fisted hands. "Would you tell me if you hear from Lucian?"

"I don't expect to, but if I do, I'll let you know." Cuttles reached for the doorknob. "We'll come up with a logical scenario as to why Damron's not there. I must insist that you keep up the pretense. You cannot refer to Damron other than in relation to the show; we will downplay your personal relationship with the man. You will make no private plea for his return; no one is to know of his deception. Do I make myself clear?"

Although her heart told her that she should defend Lucian, Gillian compelled herself to answer in the positive. "I'll see you on Tuesday," she murmured.

Trying to clarify whether this she had dreamed this nightmare, she stared at the door for infinitely long seconds. Finally looking at the crumpled envelope, Gillian made her way to the chair she recently vacated.

Opening the flap, she withdrew the papers to stare at the report. "Oh, God," she moaned. Cuttles was right; the report stated that the man she knew as Lucian Damron was really Marcus Chambers. No doubt existed in its accuracy. "God, I did this to him," she cried. Why? He had made her angry because she didn't understand the kind of man he really was. Now, she had ruined him. He would never forgive her. Why couldn't she have just trusted him? Who cared what he called himself? The man behind the name was what was important. Lucian, or Marcus, or to whatever he answered, was still one of the finest men she had ever known. "What am I going to do about it?" she thought aloud. With a deep breath, she declared, "I love him, and somehow I shall have to find him again and make this right. I have no other choice. I can't allow Lucian to suffer because of me."

⌒

Sleep didn't arrive that night. Instead, Gillian had paced the entire length of the townhouse, in an attempt to reconstruct the truths of the last few weeks. She had first believed Lucian to be disloyal, his having been with Charlotte Blakeley. Then step-by-step, he had won her back, showing her the love that he felt–the depth of his regard. Just as they had acknowledged their feelings, Gillian had lost Barb, but Lucian had brought her hope. Now because of her stupid pride he was gone. She replayed every scene–every word, trying futilely to discover some answer to right her own ship. She had failed him in, oh, so many ways. He had not varied throughout their relationship. He was the constant: she had been the wild card. "Damn!" The realization hurt as much as the pain of losing him. All along, she had thought herself the superior one in their relationship. Thought herself without censure. "Until this moment, I never knew myself," she mumbled, remembering that moment in *Pride and Prejudice* when Elizabeth Bennet finally recognizes her own prejudices.

Gillian sadly discovered that she had missed him more than she should admit. The feel of him inside her made her ache for him; the memory of him obsessed her–turned her inside out.

"The answer must be in here." Gillian morosely stared at the report she had ordered on Lucian. "Nothing else makes sense. Somehow discovering the secret that Lucian hid must be turned for his good and mine. That is the only way that he might forgive me...might come back to me." Subtly, Lucian had become vital to her existence.

Hugging herself tightly, Gillian took up residence in her favorite chair to think. Pulling her knees up under her chin and bracing her feet on the cushion, she rubbed her brow in frustration. *What had Cuttles said? Even after he confronted him, Lucian had insisted his real name was Damron, and that he was a doctor of psychology.* Of course, Lucian could have hoped he could change Cuttles's mind, but she didn't think that sounded like him. He had always spoken the truth; he would not claim to be Dr. Lucian Damron if he wasn't. Such a denial would have served no purpose. If Lucian said he was a renowned psychologist, then he was exactly that. She searched the report again for a clue.

At the bottom of the file, Gillian noticed a promo for additional information. "Why not?" she thought out loud. "Could things get any worse?" She went online and filled out the account profile, ordering a full investigation, not just the overview that she currently held in her hand. Maybe the answer was asking for the complete truth: Something had to be missing from the report. Things didn't add up.

⁓

"We're happy to see you," Ada hugged Gillian tightly. "We're all so sorry to hear about your sister."

"Thanks," Gillian gave a slight smile. "Things are settling down, but it will take some time before the hurt lessens."

"Is Lucian assisting you?" Melinda asked innocently.

Gillian started, but quickly recovered. "Lucian is dealing with some personal issues of his own." It wasn't a lie, but Gillian hated not confiding in these women. When she had returned home for Barb's funeral, she had missed their camaraderie. "I can't divulge more than that."

"How's your relationship?" Ada inquired.

"We've backed off for now. We both have some key issues to iron out." Gillian bit her bottom lip and hoped that they couldn't see her deceit.

Placing her arm about Gillian's shoulders, Melinda sat beside her. "Take your time if you need it, but don't let that man go. You'll regret it. Look at us, and you'll see what happens when you turn away from love. Second chances are limited."

"I don't plan to let him go." Gillian fought the tears forming in her eyes' corners.

"Good for you," Ada added. "Now, let's hit the makeup chairs for the last time."

⁓

The reunion show highlighted the key moments associated with the six couples, showing some scenes not seen previously. Decisively, Cuttles had made a point of displaying film only of Gillian and Lucian interacting with the couples, with no emphasis on their budding romance. The execs also minimized the number of scenes involving Lucian, only using those not showing his therapy sessions. The staff made certain that the American audience was not reminded of Lucian Damron as a member of the medical staff.

At the show's conclusion, Daniel announced Melinda and Gary to be the champions. "By less than one percent of the popular vote we have a winner," Daniel read the teleprompter. "Because of the overwhelming popularity of Andrew and Ada, our producers are going to do something quite unprecedented. They have opted to give Andrew and Ada fifty thousand dollars to use as they see fit on a dream wedding or something more practical." Gillian knew immediately that the show's producers wanted to turn the popularity meter in their direction. It would be impossible to hide Lucian's lies forever. Starline wished to be portrayed as "benevolent parents."

Immediately upon hearing the announcement, with tears streaming down their cheeks, Melinda and Ada were in each other's arms. The cameras came in, capturing their joy. Shrieks filled the air as Daniel took over once again. The confetti streamed from the rafters, and balloons peppered the floor. "Season two auditions begin the end of next month. We'll be coming to eight U.S. cities to interview hopefuls so get your tapes into us by the fifteenth of next month. Tell us why you and your ex deserve a second chance. Check out our winners and runners-up on Top of the Morning tomorrow in the eight o'clock hour. See you next season America."

⁓

They all had left her alone on the flight to New York. Gillian had attempted to sleep, but all she could think about was Lucian. Both TV couples snuggled in their seats on the other side of the aisle. She could hear heavy breathing and the occasional gasp; their intimacies had reignited in the darkness. In reality, she was a bit envious. She and Lucian could be together right now. She felt so alone with only her dreams of him. Closing her eyes, she could see his playful open expression–feel his hot kisses making her writhe beneath him. If she kept her eyes closed, she could remember touching his skin, warm fingers trailing down to his stomach, caressing him, knowing she would never have enough of him. The image was so real, Gillian had to shake herself to clear it away; she wanted desperately to arch against him and call out his name. A sense of pure loss engulfed her. "Lucian," she whispered. "Come home."

⌒

Laura Simpson, the morning show host, greeted the two couples and Gillian. "How does it feel to be the winners of *Second Chances*?" she asked Melinda and Gary.

"It's fabulous!" Gary beamed. "Melinda deserves all this."

"What will you do with the two hundred-fifty thousand dollars?" Laura continued.

"We've talked about it," Melinda added quickly. "We'll put some down on a new home, and then we'll invest the rest. We'll need something for our child and hopefully some day for our grandchildren."

"And what about your prize?" Laura turned to Andrew and Ada.

"Like Gary and Melinda, we've had our own conversation," Andrew responded. "We've decided to keep our wedding simple. After all, we had a big one the last time. We're just thankful the producers decided to reward our efforts. I think a sizeable down payment on a home is in order for us too."

Simpson smiled at each couple. "So, you've become friends?"

Ada nodded. "Gary and Melinda are older than Andrew and I, but we have come to respect one another."

"The American public also became caught up in your story, Gillian," Simpson's remark had surprised her.

"Thank you. It was a compelling time; I was blessed to be a part of their lives–all the couples brought something unusual to the table; from Mary and Bruce's reuniting for their child to Melinda and Gary's life-long devotion to each other, the show offered everything."

"What of your own love life?" Simpson probed.

Gillian tried unsuccessfully to feign innocence. "What do you mean, Laura?"

"Come now, Gillian; it wouldn't take a rocket scientist or a relationship therapist to see the sparks flying between you and Lucian Damron."

Gillian flushed with color. For a moment she thought about what Cuttles had said, but she shoved those warnings aside. When she spoke, it was with a determined resolve only a few realized that she possessed. "At the moment, Lucian is dealing with some personal issues, but I want him to know I trust him, and I am looking forward to this trouble finding a resolution and his quick return."

"Sounds like you're serious," Simpson implied.

Gillian cleared her voice. She hoped Lucian listened with his whole heart. "I care very deeply for Lucian Damron."

"Well, you heard it here first. Maybe the next dream wedding will be the best one yet." Laura Simpson smiled for the camera. "We'll return after these messages."

Gillian returned home; for the first three days, she didn't even get out of bed, change clothes, or eat more than a few crackers or a piece of toast. Her world had imploded, and she required time to wallow in her own grief and misery before she could take on life's challenges once again. She barely slept–images of Lucian and of Barb and of her parents flooded her hours. Everyone she loved no longer touched her life. Ripping her chest open and removing her heart would have hurt less than knowing she was alone.

"I can't go on like this!" So, on the fourth day, she forced herself from bed. "First, a shower and then breakfast." Gillian had to tell herself what to do. Nothing came naturally any longer. "I need food, and I need to participate in life."

Sitting at her desk, she paid her bills before responding to an offer from Jackson Ryder for her book contract. Impulsively, she included a private note to Ryder to let her know if heard anything from Lucian. It was a long shot, but Gillian took it just the same. Much of her other mail went into the shredder. The hospital made insurance inquiries, and the funeral home sent over the last of the official paperwork. Online, she had the usual emails from clients, students requesting references, and personal notes from Ada, Melinda, Nicole, and Mary. She spent time responding in some detail to each of their inquiries, assuring them that she would be well soon. Then she spied one from an unknown address. The subject line simply said "Sweetling." Her heart caught at seeing the word. If she hadn't looked at the subject line, she would have deleted the message as being junk mail. Hand shaking with anticipation, she moved the mouse to rest on the hypertext and then double clicked the line. The cursor spun, and the message appeared on the screen.

Sweetling,

I'm using a public library server so you'll not be able to reply to this message. I suppose by now you've seen the report, and that you think that you know the worst of me. There is an explanation, but it is too complicated to include here. I belatedly realized how much you didn't trust me; if you had, you wouldn't have ordered the search report in the first place. I suppose I deserved that; I haven't always done the right thing, but I will ask you to keep in mind that I never purposely hurt anyone. And you know in your heart that I would never deliberately hurt you, Gillian; when I promised you my love, I meant every word.

I am staying away from you because this situation will become worse before it takes a turn for the better, and I hope that my absence will protect you from the fall out. This grieves me because I realize with Barb's passing that you need me with you. Please forgive me for I've no choice. Until I can prove my identity, I cannot involve you. What I did, was done for self-preservation; it seemed so logical at the time–a way to survive what life had dealt me. It was a selfish act, but not a mean one and not an illegal one. It is all so much more complicated than that. Eventually, the truth will be known, and although it seems a scrambled mess at the moment, the explanation will make some sense.

Even with that hope, there is still one more secret I fear will keep us apart. I've known it since right before we went to Louisville. I don't know how to make an explanation, but I will offer my version of the truth when it is time and then pray that it is not so bizarre as to affect your feelings for me.

I love you, Gillian. I've been in love with you since the time that we exchanged barbs at the San Francisco conference. You were my salvation, my lifeline. When you discover the truth, please believe me when I say that I never knew our connection–how our lives were entwined–until much later on. Please remember that as the details from this "sham" become known.

Gillian, you make me want to be the kind of man who a woman like you could love unconditionally. I want to spend every minute of every day with you. Even now, I find myself saving up ideas and experiences to share with you when we're together. I want to hold you close, to kiss your sweet mouth, and to smell the lavender as it engulfs me. You make me want to be Lucian Damron, but as you now know, I was born Marcus Chambers. Please forgive me. I attempted to tell you right before we heard about Barb. By putting this off, I have created a quagmire. Yet, I beg you to please not give up on me. Things will work out if you will only give us a second chance.

I will return, Gillian. Maybe by then, you will learn to love me again.

L. D.

Tears streamed down her cheeks, but she made no effort to brush them away. Gillian swallowed hard, fighting the urge to retch up the small breakfast she had consumed earlier. She wasn't ready to face all the chaos surrounding Lucian Damron, but she couldn't simply turn her back on him either. She loved the man. She didn't understand why Lucian had passed himself off as a psychologist. She didn't know all his secrets, but she did know the man; she knew him intimately, and Gillian knew only he could make her happy.

Nearly two weeks passed before someone leaked information to the media. Cameras and reporters greeted her as Gillian left for a therapy session on a Wednesday afternoon. Microphones and flashes of light bombarded her as she descended the steps. "Where is Lucian Damron?" A reporter jammed a microphone into her face.

Refusing to respond to their entreaties, Gillian clamped down on her jaw. However, they followed her to her cab, even blocking her exit until some of her neighbors cleared the way. "What do you know about Marcus Chambers?" "Do you still love the man?" "How do you feel about his deceiving you and the TV audience?" "Why did you order the identity search in the first place?" The questions continued as she took each step, as she entered the cab, and as she left the scene.

"Now what?" she murmured. Gillian rushed to her office and signed onto the local news. Headlines loomed, calling Lucian a "Shock Doc" and a "Fake Rake." Someone on the show had leaked information on Lucian's dismissal and on Ted Morris's belief that Lucian was really Marcus Chambers. An excerpt from the identity report also appeared among the story's lines. She even found an interview where Charlotte Blakeley decried how foully Lucian had treated her and how she had known all along that he wasn't what he claimed. "Poor Lucian," she moaned. "How can I stop this?"

⌒

"At last," he whispered to the TV screen. In a dingy apartment outside of Vancouver, Lucian had monitored the news continually. He had waited for the leak to occur; word of it hadn't surprised him. Actually, he had hoped for it for several days. Maybe when the truth came out, he could get on with his life. According to the agreement he had signed a decade ago, he couldn't speak of what he had done–how he had sold his soul for a better way of life. He couldn't speak of how he had hungered to be someone he wasn't–to be judged as a person of merit rather than a nonentity. He couldn't speak of how he had wanted to be identified with a name, which could be his.

Images of Gillian being besieged by reporters flashed on the screen. He could tell she wasn't angry with him; instead, Gillian recognized his troubles and had agonized over her part in them. Her face betrayed her concern for him; her eyes had kept his secrets. She had faced contempt because of him, and the chaos would grow around her. If he could stay out of sight–to disappear, maybe they would leave her alone. He had expected this pandemonium for years; this madness was why he had never made commitments. Even though he hadn't broken the law, most people wouldn't understand how he had come to be where he was–who he was—now his deeds would catch up with him. If he hadn't desired the glory, the spotlight, everything would be different. If he had lived an ordinary, mundane life, no one would have cared how he had become Lucian Damron. He chastised himself for his vanity and his pride. Foolishly, he had involved someone for whom he genuinely cared in his personal turmoil. Gillian certainly didn't deserve to be mixed up in all this. Lucian had hoped that she would feign being shocked by his actions and would distance herself from him. Instinctively, he held no doubts that she would defend him rather than preserve her own reputation. Part of him reveled in the idea that Gillian Cornell loved him that much, while part of him prayed that she would act otherwise.

~

"At last," she said, snatching the enveloped from her unlocked mailbox. Lucian had been missing a little over a month before Gillian finally received the report she had requested. Reading it thoroughly, she allowed that she had expected something worse when she ordered the investigation. Admittedly, Lucian treaded on the edges of propriety, but he hadn't committed any crime, at least from a legal standpoint.

"Now, what do I do?" she thought aloud. "I need assistance." Her first instinct was to contact a professional, someone like Dr. Stryent, but upon reflection, she knew she required common sense, a practical touch. Picking up the phone, Gillian dialed the number of someone she now considered to be one of her closest friends.

"Hi, Gillian." She heard the familiar lilt of the woman's voice.

"Hi, Ada. Am I disturbing you?"

The woman laughed. "I always have time to talk to the person who taught Andrew to finally forgive me." There was an awkward pause. "Have you heard from Lucian?"

"Not exactly. But I do have news. That's why I called. I need a sounding board. If I fly out to Denver, could you help talk me through this? I don't trust my own instincts at this point."

"Melinda is coming on Friday. She and I have decided to do a double wedding. She only lives a hundred miles from here. Would you believe it? Why don't you join us for the weekend?" Happiness danced through her words.

Gillian thought to back out of the offer. "I don't want to bring my problems into your mix."

"Don't be silly. Andrew and Gary are going camping. Melinda and I are off shopping. Obviously, you can join us two. We'll have late night gossip sessions just like we did at the ranch. Please, Gillian," she continued. "Take your own advice. You can't do this alone."

Gillian stifled the sobs. "I cannot believe how I fought not to do this show and how I now realize I am blessed to have found you and Melinda."

"Then you'll come?" Ada added brightly.

"I'll be there late tomorrow afternoon." Gillian sighed, "Thanks, Ada."

"You're here! I can't believe it!" Melinda squealed.

"Neither can I," Gillian laughed lightly. She curled up in the oversized lounge chair stuffed in the corner of Ada's condo. "Tell me about the wedding plans."

Melinda sipped on the strawberry wine cooler. "After we left the show, Sam Cuttles wanted Gary and me to get married right away to ride the show's publicity, but we decided to wait a few months. Then Ada and Andrew decided they wanted to wait too. Cuttles went ballistic when we approached them about sharing our wedding day. At first, he absolutely refused, but I sent my Gary into see him. The man's a used car salesman; he could sell sand to a camel. So now we're getting married on the same day a few weeks before the new season starts. What do you think?"

"It's romantic," Gillian gushed. "I can't believe it's happening; it's all coming together. I'm so happy for the two of you." She raised her glass in a mock toast.

Ada joined them at last. She pulled a blanket over her legs. "We want to hear about you and Lucian."

"What's with the blanket?" Gillian teased.

Melinda took another swig of her drink. "She thinks if she covers everything up that no one will notice that she's pregnant."

"You're pregnant?" Gillian gasped.

"Are you disappointed in me?"

For the first time in several months, Gillian laughed easily. "Disappointed? God, no, I'm delighted. Is Andrew happy?"

"The man waits on her hand and foot," Melinda taunted. All three of them burst into rapturous laughter.

"Okay," Ada forced composure into her voice. "We want to hear about Lucian."

"I don't know," Gillian started. "I don't want to dampen the mood."

"Gillian," Ada's voice took on a maturity not noticeable moments before, "we want to hear it all. Please don't hide it from us."

Melinda leaned forward to indicate her interest. "Come on, Gillian; we're your friends. You can tell us."

Gillian's eyes filled with tears. Taking a deep breath, she stumbled through a retelling of her relationship with Lucian up through his dismissal from the show. Of course, they knew parts of her story, but they hung on every word.

"And you haven't heard anything from him?" Ada whispered, mesmerized by the narration.

"I received an email four days after the show ended." Sadness crept into the conversation. "I don't know how to find him. He apologized for putting me through this, but it was I who destroyed his life." A tear slid down her cheek before she could push it away.

Melinda cleared her throat to fight back her own tears. "Where do you go from here? You're not giving up?"

Gillian let out a deep sigh. "As I said awhile ago, I ordered a full report. Could I share it with you? I need your insights."

"Heck, yeah," Ada encouraged.

"This will take a few minutes so bear with me. Lucian Damron was born Marcus Chambers. He was a foster child, moving from family to family. The longest he spent with any family was the four years when he attended high school. That's probably why Ted Morris remembers him so clearly. This next fact is really creepy, but at one time Marcus lived with my parents."

"You're kidding?" Melinda cried out.

Gillian shrugged her shoulders as if she didn't know what to say. "He lived in my home for eighteen months, right before my parents adopted Barb. I wasn't even born."

Ada turned to Melinda. "How weird! Like déjà vu!"

201

"Did he know?" Melinda looked confused.

"I don't think so. At least, not at first. In his email he said he had fallen in love with me months before he knew our connection. I assume that's what he meant, and I believe him." Gillian rolled her eyes in exasperation. "Am I being foolish?"

"I saw the way the man looked at you. He loves you, Gillian," Ada assured her.

"I just wish that he'd come home and clear all this up." A shiver ran down her spine. "I feel such a profound emptiness."

Melinda whispered, "Like part of you is missing?"

Gillian gulped for air. "Exactly."

"Okay, tell us the rest," Ada insisted.

"Marcus Chambers enrolled in a medical assistance program shortly out of high school. According to the records, he had wanted to be a nurse or a doctor. When he finished the program, the school placed him in the employment of Lucian Damron. Not a whole lot is known about the man; Damron was a recluse–quite eccentric–very intelligent–owned multiple patents and copyrights–and quite wealthy. Although he refused to take regular classes, the man also held multiple college degrees. He earned all his degrees through correspondence courses or online. By the end of his life, the real Lucian Damron no longer ventured outside of his New York penthouse. Reportedly, he took a liking to Marcus, who became Lucian Damron's constant companion. Damron was a germophob. Marcus tended to his every need. In return, Damron paid for Marcus's schooling. He really does have his doctorial degree in psychology."

Melinda laughed. "At least, Cuttles will have to eat his words on that one."

"He'll need to eat more than that phrase," Gillian declared. "When Lucian Damron passed away from pneumonia nearly ten years ago, Marcus Chambers legally changed his name to Lucian Damron, Ph.D. Cuttles got that part wrong too."

"So why did Lucian run away and not fight Cuttles's accusations?" Ada appeared perplexed with Gillian's facts.

"That's the part I don't understand either. I mean what he did was unusual, but it wasn't illegal. Why run away?"

"Come on, Gillian. What aren't you telling us?" Melinda asked after remaining silent for several minutes.

"The real Lucian Damron had a fetish for male prostitutes. Could my Lucian have been involved somehow?" Saying the words brought her fears to the forefront.

Melinda moved to kneel before her. "Gillian, listen to me. Your Lucian was never part of that lifestyle. Think about it; you were intimate with the man, weren't you?"

Gillian's eyes grew large with the realization. "Yes," she murmured. "He was my first; I wanted him to be my last. He couldn't have been involved; I know him like no one else knows him. He would not delve in such debase activities. If you asked me was he a womanizer, I would have at one time agreed. I mean, I know he's more worldly than I, but I still don't think he had as many women as his reputation declares."

"Then put that out of your mind." Melinda patted her hand and moved back to her own chair. "Is that all you know?"

"That's all the report says." Gillian shifted her weight nervously. "I just don't know what to do with the information. "I could go to the media and explain how he's really a doctor, and his legal name is really Lucian Damron."

"But then the media might dig into the life of the real Lucian Damron. Plus, why did Marcus take Damron's name in the first place?" Ada thought aloud. "Some people could jump to conclusions about our Lucian having been in love with his employer and make it into something vile and depraved."

"Those were my thoughts too." Gillian seemed frightened by the news. "I can't ruin Lucian's reputation further."

Melinda hesitated. "Then I guess you need to keep quiet until Lucian reappears on his own."

"What if he doesn't come back?" Gillian whispered.

Ada sniffed, trying to hold back the tears. "Then you'll have to get on without him."

"I can't, Ada." Gillian shivered. Attempting to compose her words before she said them, Gillian took a deep steadying breath. "I am pregnant with Lucian's baby. What am I going to do? Every day for the rest of my life I will see Lucian staring back at me. He'll never know his own child."

"We'll work it out, Gillian." Ada moved to where she could embrace her friend. "He'll be back; Lucian can't stay away from you."

The news of Mary Nelson's death shook Gillian's composure. The show had ended two months earlier. Other than the one email, she had heard nothing from Lucian. The life growing within her had become more evident each day. She had agreed to be in the show's wedding as a bride's maid. She and Ada had laughed about the increase in their breast size and looked for dress styles, which would disguise their conditions. They would dress for the cameras.

"I'll meet you at the airport," Gillian told Ada. "I am leaving a few days early to make certain Bruce and his son have proper medical assistance to deal with the loss."

"Poor Mary," Ada sympathized. "Only a woman would postpone her own death to make certain her child was safe. Since I've become pregnant, I really understand her motivation. Mary Nelson put herself in a place where she would receive the public's censure in order to find her ex and make certain someone assumed the care of her child."

"Maybe we should say just that at her memorial service?" Gillian mused.

Ada sounded amused. "Are you saying that we should admit our pregnancies?"

Gillian smiled. "My child kicked the living day lights out of me last night. I want Lucian to be here and experience it all with me. Maybe if I let my condition be known, it will force him to play a different hand. I'm desperate, Ada. If you want to keep your pregnancy a secret, I'll respect your wishes, but if the cameras show for Mary's funeral, I plan to make mine known."

"Andrew has been wanting to shout it from the rooftops; I'm certain he'll be relieved he doesn't have to hide it any more. Besides, the wedding is only three weeks away. I don't see where it would hurt."

Sam Cuttles controlled the media circus surrounding Mary Nelson's funeral. Only affiliate stations received permission to report Mary's passing. Four of the couples from the show, along with Gillian and Dr. Stryent had attended. Gillian also noted Michael Hood and several show staffers making an appearance. She found it ironic that so many people made appearances to pay their respects to a woman they barely knew, especially considering Mary's act of desperation was her only claim to fame. Otherwise, Mary Nelson led a common, ordinary life, but her cry for "help" painted a heroic portrait of the woman.

"Those who first met Mary thought her to be hard, but I call her resilient. She survived when others would have failed. She raised a fine young man...taught her child about responsibility and love and honor. And she taught me about the power of love." As planned, Gillian spoke at the service, offering an intimate picture of a valiant woman. Her words brought comfort to Bruce and to Mary's child. They struggled with a relationship, which had been thrust upon them. Yet, knowing it was Mary's last wish that they become a family had paved the way to their success. Cameras captured Bruce's honest grief at Mary's passing, as well as their son's placing of roses on his mother's casket.

After the service, several media outlets approached Gillian for a comment on the rites. Having resolved to use the format for a personal plea for Lucian's return, she squared her shoulders and prepared to make her response. Before the words escaped her mouth, Melinda and Ada appeared at her side for support. She gave them a quick nod of gratitude.

"Mary Nelson," Gillian began in a quiet tone, "sacrificed everything for her child. A mother's love knows no bounds. Mary made the grand gesture for her son Matthew. She knew she couldn't be here to protect him, so she opened her heart to a man who had once broken it. I don't blame Bruce Nelson; in fact, I admire his resolve to be a positive influence in his child's life. A parent would do anything for his child."

A microphone appeared from nowhere. "What is the status of the other couples on the show?"

"Yvonne and Sean, as well as Theo and Grace, have not moved forward with their relationships. Mark and Nicole remarried a month after the show's completion." Gillian caught the hand of both Ada and Melinda. "These two ladies," she smiled at each of them, "have agreed to a double wedding, which will take place in three weeks."

A reporter turned to Melinda. "What about the dream wedding you won on the show's finale?"

Melinda laughed lightly. "I'm still getting that. The only difference is I'm sharing my dream with Ada."

"So, you're really friends?" Someone else called out.

"Yes, we're friends." Melinda paused for dramatic effect. "In fact, Gary and I will serve as godparents for the Beldens' child."

The cameras quickly spun around to focus on Ada. "I guess Melinda let the cat out of the bag," she teased good-heartedly. "Andrew and I are thrilled to be welcoming our first child. We debated on marrying immediately, but because *Second Chances* brought us together again, we thought it only fair to share our life with the fans, who supported us throughout the show. Gillian will be our maid of honor. We've been busy buying dresses and baby clothes together."

Gillian cringed internally, knowing the spotlight would now turn on her. The cameras spanned the closeness between the women. "Miss Cornell, did we hear Ada correctly? Are you also buying baby clothes?"

She shrugged in embarrassment. "Ada and I are only a few weeks apart."

A buzz ran through the crowd surrounding the three women. "Dare we ask," came another voice, "about your relationship with the man formerly known as Lucian Damron."

"Before I answer the question about my pregnancy, I want to clear up a few misconceptions about Lucian Damron." Gillian bit her bottom lip wondering how far to take this; she wanted to protect Lucian from further censure. "I know for a fact the man you call Lucian Damron earned a Ph.D. in psychology. I also know his original name was Marcus Chambers, but he legally changed it nearly ten years ago."

"Then why was he dismissed from the show?" The crowd pressed forward, demanding an answer.

"It was a misunderstanding. The show wished to protect the couples against possible malpractice, but they only possessed part of the information. They rushed to protect the show's integrity, and no one here is faulting their actions. It was the responsible thing to do. Yet, the reputation of Lucian Damron should be restored." Gillian's voice broke with anticipation, praying she hadn't caused Lucian additional pain.

"Then you're in touch with Lucian Damron?" a reporter beside her asked.

Gillian wouldn't lie, but she wouldn't allow them to know that she held no idea of Lucian's whereabouts. It would make him look guiltier. "Lucian is dealing with the last of the fallout from this show."

"How does he feel about the baby?" A petite woman on her left asked, pushing a videophone at Gillian.

Ada answered before Gillian could respond. "Lucian Damron is an honorable man. Like my Andrew, honorable men love the women in their lives and love the children from that union." Gillian gave Ada's hand a quick squeeze.

"Then you'll also be getting married soon?" The same woman probed.

"Lucian and I haven't discussed the particulars. I've been dealing with the passing of my sister, and Lucian has had more than a little chaos in his own life. When this madness clears, we will deal responsibly with the birth of our child." Gillian looked directly in the camera, trying to convey her need to the elusive Lucian Damron. "Our task today is to remember Mary Nelson, not to celebrate weddings or births. Mary's cancer should be a red flag to every woman to seek regular medical screenings. Please support cancer organizations with contributions so hopefully a cure can be found." With that, Gillian terminated the conference. As she walked away, with Ada and Melinda in tow, she let out a gigantic sigh. "I hope I didn't just put Lucian in a more tenuous situation."

"Only time will tell," Ada whispered. "We must wait for Lucian to make the next move."

Cuttles cornered Gillian shortly after the news conference. "I don't like being played, Miss Cornell," he threatened in a low tone.

"No one is playing you, Mr. Cuttles. My contract with the show is at an end," Gillian hissed.

He looked around at the dispersing crowd. "We have offered you a continuing contract. Is that what this is about? Do you want more money?"

"It's not about the money or the book contract. It's about the man I love. The father of my child. He requires vindication. Someone from the show, probably with your blessings, leaked damaging information about Lucian." Gillian moved in to let him know he hadn't intimidated her.

His eyes darkened under her accusation. "So, you think I did this to Dr. Damron on purpose?"

"I believe, Mr. Cuttles, that you'd sell your own mother's secrets if it meant higher ratings for the show." Gillian's voice held pure contempt.

Cuttles's eyes drifted to where Ada and Melinda stood. "Isn't that a pretty picture you paint? How long have you known about our misunderstanding?"

"For a few weeks."

"Then why if you so love this man have you made no move to clear his name?" Cuttles demanded.

Gillian flinched but recovered quickly. "I can't fight Lucian's battles for him."

Cuttles smiled. "Then what were you doing today?"

Gillian stepped back, picking up her sweater and purse and preparing to leave. "I offered my condolences to Mary's family and made an announcement about my blessed event. Good-bye, Mr. Cuttles." She walked away briskly to catch up with her two friends.

Gillian returned to her home to wait for Lucian's response. Meanwhile, she developed plans for a more thorough search. "I suppose I could hire someone to trace his steps out of Chicago after he left the show," she spoke to herself as she went through another box of her parents' belongings. Clearing away the clutter in her life had become an all-consuming obsession. Without eliminating all the memories of her sister in the process, she would convert Barb's room to a nursery for her child. Gillian had decided after seven years that she no longer required paper copies of all her parents' legal papers. She scanned many of the documents before shredding them, eliminating multiple boxes of applications for foster children and for Barb's adoption.

"Try to keep busy and not think of Lucian." That was her task again this particular afternoon as she went through file after file of information. And so it was that surrounded by papers from the year her parents had adopted her sister that she had found Marcus Chambers' file.

With shaking hands, she opened the manila folder to read about the boy who had become her lover. "His mother was a morphine addict." She read parts of the folder aloud. Marcus's mother had abandoned him to the system when he was age four. Up until that time he bounced around from distant relative to distant relative while his mother attempted to beat her addiction. When the woman had overdosed, Marcus became a ward of the State. "Looks like he fought the system by being a terror to deal with." The thoughts of a defiant young Marcus Chambers didn't surprise Gillian.

"At age six, when he came to stay with my parents, he had already been in five different homes." Evidently, Marcus had liked to play with matches, creating havoc and fear in most who had agreed to take him in. As he had done with all the children who had lived with them over the years, her father had made notations about the lives of their wards. Gillian automatically picked up the book containing her father's "truths." She flipped to the dates corresponding to Marcus's file to read, "I have never seen a child so frightened as young Marcus. He desperately requires someone to accept him as a person of worth. I'm certain Mama's chocolate chip cookies and a few fishing trips will make a difference."

Gillian smiled; her father's words brought tears to her eyes. Her own father had seen the man Lucian would become when he knew love. She realized how twenty-nine years later the same thing could be said about Marcus Chambers. He was still frightened and still required someone to accept him as a person of worth. In many ways, she had failed Lucian in that matter. She should have trusted him from the beginning. He would have told her the truth. Deep inside, Gillian had known him to be a man of honor, but she had allowed her own insecurities to cloud their relationship. If she were given another opportunity to prove herself to Lucian Damron or Marcus Chambers or whatever else he might want to call himself, she would not fail him again. She continued to read her father's notations on the boy. Evidently, her parents were quite taken with Marcus. "Mama and I are thinking of making young Marcus a permanent member of our family."

Gillian froze. The words rebounded through her mind. Her parents had considered adopting Marcus. He would have been her brother! Completely involved, she searched for why they had allowed Marcus to leave. Reading quickly through the other journal entries, she came to the last one. Her fingers traced her father's handwriting, channeling his voice in her head as she read. "Mama and I have discussed it repeatedly. We cannot take both children. Barbara will not survive in the foster care system; no one else is likely to adopt a child with special needs. Young Marcus will never understand. How could he? I don't understand it myself. He called me 'Papa' the other day, and now I must break his heart. Yet, he is a fine boy, and I'm certain someone will recognize what a jewel he can be. I will tell him why we must keep Barbara and let him go. I hope he will find the ability to forgive us some day."

Tears flowed freely now. Her father had always wanted a son—someone he could teach to fish and someone with whom to watch football games. Gillian wondered how her father had felt, knowing that his prediction for Marcus had never come true. Did her father regret letting Marcus go, especially with the realization that no one else bothered to see how much Marcus needed to be loved unconditionally? She knew her father had kept track of what happened to the boy that he had wanted as part of her family. He had kept in touch with nearly every child who had passed through their home, whether the child had spent years with them or had been with them for only a week or two. Her father had always said, "We never know when it is our turn to make a difference in another person's life. God, as always, works in mysterious ways." Had her father known Marcus's fate? Had he grieved over his decision and over Marcus's loss?

A twist of fate had changed every thing! Had her parents brought Marcus into her life and into their home? She realized it was a "silly" concept, but Gillian felt contentment with the idea that her parents still wanted Marcus as part of their family. "What do you think, Papa?" Her eyes went up in supplication. "Help me, Papa. I love Marcus, too. Help me bring him home."

~

The fact she had heard nothing from Lucian disappointed Gillian. She sat with Ada and Melinda. "I just have to accept that I will raise this child alone."

"I am so sorry, Gillian," Melinda empathized. "I was so certain that once Lucian heard about the baby that he would return."

"I guess he doesn't love me after all." Gillian stared out the window of her hotel room. She would be glad to have this situation over with; then she could resume her life. If Lucian cared for her, where was he? No. He had his chance; he, evidently, wanted no part of her now that she needed him to step up and take responsibility. A tear slid down her cheek, and she turned away so her friends couldn't see her heartbreak.

"What if he didn't see the news conference?" Ada wondered out loud.

Gillian spun around. "How could he not? It played over and over again for a week. Was he out of this world?"

"What if he was? I don't mean out of the world, but what about out of the country? It's possible. If I faced what he did, I would be tempted to lie low in some little hacienda in Mexico."

"It doesn't matter," Gillian lied. "I've prayed and cajoled enough. If Lucian loved me, he wouldn't leave me here alone to face Barb's death and the public outcry against him."

Melinda played with the ribbons on a floral arrangement. "Maybe he thought staying away was the only way to protect you."

"Don't give up, Gillian; Lucian will be back." Ada rose to depart. "We've a busy day tomorrow. Let's go, Melinda; the cameras will be rolling, and we can't have black circles under our eyes." She leaned down and kissed Gillian's cheek. "We'll see you in the morning."

Chapter Thirteen

HE HAD TAPPED ON THE HOTEL room door. From within, Lucian heard a female voice call, "You're not supposed to see the bride..." Ada Belden said as she jerked open the door. Lucian Damron waited sheepishly in the dimly lit hotel hallway.

Although he certainly felt more than a bit of trepidation, he said calmly, "I know this is unconventional, but may I come in?"

She stepped aside and allowed him to slide through the open doorway. Closing the door quickly, she grumbled, "It's about time."

Lucian took a few steps into the room before stopping, turning in place twice before looking about, confused by what he had hoped to accomplish. "Is she here?" he asked as he ran his fingers absent-mindedly through his hair.

"Down the hall." Ada folded her arms across her chest. "Where in the hell have you been?"

"In a cabin in rural British Columbia." He continued to turn in place as if he thought about how best to make his escape. "Is she all right?" His voice showed his agitation.

"Do you care? You left her to fend on her own. I thought you loved Gillian," Ada accused.

"I do," he insisted. "I was attempting to protect her."

"You didn't even say farewell."

"I was afraid, Ada. My God, Gillian had them check on me. Then the truth came out about what I did. How could I explain the mistakes in my life?" How could he tell her that what others saw as mistakes, he had seen as a lifeline? Gillian wouldn't understand his desperation. How could he explain that living with Lucian Damron was the first time he had a home. The first time someone would have missed him if he had disappeared? He couldn't explain it to himself, as well as to the woman he loved. In his mind, Gillian would go away, and he would be alone in the world again. It was better not to know if she could forgive him than to face the truth of Gillian's resolve. He could not face the possibility so Lucian had avoided the confrontation. However, here he was hanging on to the slim hope of Gillian's benevolence.

"You don't have any idea about her courage. Her strength. You certainly don't deserve Gillian." Ada stood at the end of the bed. Her arms across her chest and a scowl on her lips.

His eyes dropped to the floor. "You are correct, but God knows I need her."

With a deep sigh of resignation, she said, "Melinda and I think you ought to tell Gillian the truth. Be honest. Hold nothing back. Then you should beg her forgiveness and tell her how much you love her." Ada ushered him toward the door.

Lucian stood in wide-eyed dismay, anchored in place. "How can I ask Gillian's forgiveness when I've hurt her so much?"

"I certainly don't understand you!" Ada's hands went up in exasperation. "Why did you come here if you weren't seeking forgiveness?" Lucian looked on, knowing what she had asked was meant as a rhetorical question. "Listen, if you want to be miserable for the rest of your life, that's your business, but Gillian Cornell doesn't deserve the same fate. For some unknown reason, that woman loves you completely, and you're going to get your butt down that hall. You're going to beg, and you're going to grovel, and you're going to be happy whether you want to be or not! Now move!" She shoved him quite violently toward the door.

Lucian's spirits rose with her take-no-prisoners attitude. "Yes, Ma'am." He saluted smartly before turning her where he could see Ada's countenance. "Would you help me get into Gillian's room?" he pleaded.

"Why don't you just knock?" she teased.

He reasoned, "She might not let me in."

"I'll get you in, but if you don't make this right," Ada threatened, "British Columbia will not be far enough away. Do you understand me?" Lucian simply shook his head in agreement. "I'll go down to the front desk and get a spare key card. Wait here."

Ada whispered paused before sliding the key card into the lock. "Lucian, did you see the news conference following Mary Nelson's funeral?"

"Mary Nelson passed? When?" His voice held real concern.

"Never mind," she laughed lightly. "You're in for a big surprise." She slid the key card and turned the handle before sauntering away toward her room.

When Ada and Melinda had departed, Gillian felt a sense of relief. She required solitude. Time to think about what she would do without Lucian in her life. Gillian still questioned whether she could have done something different? Had she misjudged his character? Could he truly explain away all her other questions? When she had discovered her father's journals, she had thought herself quite foolish for not trusting Lucian, but now the pendulum had swung in the other direction. She wondered if she was foolish to hold onto the hope that he might return. What if he returned and took up his old life with the likes of Charlotte Blakeley? Gillian didn't think she could survive such humiliation. And hadn't his continued absence predicted such possibilities?

She looked at the digital clock on the bed stand. She desperately required some sleep; it had been so long since she allowed herself to sleep and to not think of Lucian. "I must take control of my life," she said aloud. "I must think of this baby I carry. Starting now, this child...Lucian's child...will be my only concern. The wedding will be a long day of smiling for the cameras, but then I can return home and do what is best for my baby and for me. Without a father and husband in our lives." Reluctantly, she had called the front desk for a wake up call. Making her way to the bathroom, Gillian instinctively turned the handle to allow warm water to reach the spigot before she striped down for a shower. Stepping into the stall, she permitted the water to run over her body. Her hand drifted to her abdomen, the baby bump already evident. Her fingers lingered on the increase in her body, and the tears escaped. She had cried so much of late; yet here she was crying again. Gillian rolled her head back and allowed the water to run down her neck and chest. Finally, she gave up. What was one more good cry in the scheme of things? Resting her elbow and wrist along the fiberglass wall, she eased her forehead to her arm. Sobs racked her body as the water streamed down her back. He was gone.

How long she remained as such even Gillian had no idea. Eventually, the sobs ceased, and she instinctively finished her ablutions. Stepping from the tub, she wrapped the oversized towel around her, taking another one for her hair before combing it out to let it dry naturally. She stood quietly listening, seeing her own reflection in the mirror—the comb poised at the root of her part. Had she heard something? Definitely the door opened and closed. "Ada," she called. No answer. Had she imagined it?

Clutching the towel to her, Gillian moved tentatively into the main room. "Sweetling," he whispered as he stepped into the bedroom, "it's me." The sound of his voice and the sight of him seemed so real; yet, Gillian knew she had imagined him just like she always did. A shiver of anticipation ran down her spine. "Gillian?" he said again when she didn't respond.

"Lucian?" The word barely escaped her lips. She couldn't remove her eyes from him; she had missed him so much that she actually ached from wanting to touch him.

"Yes, Sweetling." His voice caressed her tenderly.

Still not certain whether she dreamed a different reality, Gillian whispered, "How did you get in my room?"

"Ada is quite adept at breaking and entering." A smile turned up his mouth's corners.

He was there before her. Really there. Gillian didn't know what to do. Should she slap him? Something she had wanted to do for several weeks now. Or kiss him? Something she had also wanted desperately to do. Or order him from her life? Something she had never considered. The tears returned to her eyes, but Gillian swallowed hard to force them away. She didn't want Lucian to know how much he had hurt her.

Lucian took another step forward. "Gillian, I've missed you." His eyes darkened pleadingly.

"I've been right here, Lucian, waiting for your return. Your explanation." Her own voice echoed in her mind as rage slipped into her tone. Gillian needed for him to know her despair. Her loneliness.

"It's okay," he shrugged, accepting her censure. "I deserve your anger. I've been a coward." He edged closer still. "But remember, Sweetling, if you don't forgive me, we can never be together again, and we're good together, Gillian. We're more than good; we're perfect, and I'm not just talking about the sex, although we both know it's spectacular." By now, his voice was hoarse with emotion. "But know this, Gillian Cornell, I love you more than life. The thought that I might lose you forever frightens me beyond reason." He continued to move toward her in a slow, sensual way. "I never wanted to hurt you; I thought if I went away, you wouldn't be involved in this mess."

"We're supposed to be a couple–a united front, and you shut me out." The hurt had lodged deeply in her voice as she chided him.

His eyes never left hers. "I'll tell you everything if you're willing to listen." He stood directly before her, and Lucian reached out tenderly to cup her cheek. His thumb traced circles on her temple. "I know you've been miserable because I've been more than miserable," he whispered softly. "If you never want to see me again, I'll understand, but I couldn't disappear from your life without trying for a second chance at happiness."

Hesitatingly, Gillian edged closer. "I don't know what to do, Lucian."

"I know what I want you to do." His lips hovered a few inches from hers. "I want us to start over right here. Right now." His lips' corners crept upward into a full fledge smile when she sighed with resignation. Those dimples that she loved so much had returned.

Gillian didn't know why she fought it. She could protest; she could fume; she could rant, but her heart belonged to the man standing inches from her. Her heart needed him before it could beat. To live again, truly live, she would need to forgive him. "For both our sakes," she murmured softly, and then she went on her tiptoes to caress his lips with hers.

From the moment he had stepped into her brightly lit hotel room, Lucian had wanted to clasp her to him. To feel her warmth within his embrace. Instead, he had allowed Gillian to set the pace; the kiss soft and gentle at first, and then she deepened it, and moved into him, melding her body to his. Lucian's tongue moved along the line of her mouth as he dropped his hand to her hips and pulled her to him. She opened to him, and the kiss became passion unleashed.

Lucian shook physically. Beneath the towel, Gillian's exquisite body awaited his touch. "May I?" he choked out the request as he took the clasp of the towel in his hands.

An imperceptive nod brought him relief. Gillian wouldn't turn him away; a chance at happiness remained. Before he loosened the knot, he pressed a kiss in the valley found between her breasts. Then he let the linen drop, and Gillian stood before him in all her glory. He let out a rush of air as the emotion escaped him.

Lucian's hands skimmed over her back and hips as he pulled her to him. Their breathing became quick and rapid. "You have on too many clothes," she teased. Her gasp hardened him instantly; she began to unbutton his shirt, pulling it from his slacks. Shoving it from his shoulders, Gillian pressed her breasts to his chest.

He slid his hands up her body, weighing her breasts and satisfying him for a moment. "You're so beautiful," he whispered in her ear.

After so long a separation, it was exciting to finally fill his hands with her breasts. His thumbs circled the nipples, bringing them to a hard peak. Lucian braced her as he leaned took her nipple into his mouth, laving the tender skin with his tongue before he suckled her in a slow, deliberate desire. She moaned, igniting his passion further. Lucian moved to her other breast while Gillian ran her fingers through his hair, holding him to her swollen mounds.

He straightened to return to her mouth. "You're going to marry me, aren't you?" he gulped as she began to unfasten his belt and waistband. She freed him by seductively sliding his slacks down his legs before he stepped from them. Standing again, she took the length of him in her hand and began to stroke the soft, velvety head. Lucian groaned as he edged her toward the bed. "Ah, Gillian," he growled.

They tumbled into the bed, arms and legs entangled in a search for completion. As he pressed her back, Lucian's mouth returned to her breast while his hand slipped between her legs, fingers massaged that point of sexual sensitivity and the folds of her desire. She was already wet with longing. Gillian cried with pleasure as her body arched toward him. His fingers slid into her while his thumb continued to circle the nub, increasing the rhythm until she was slick with exquisite sensations. Passion rushed through her, her breathing becoming pants of delirium. Beneath him, she struggled for a breath, and Gillian's body quivered with intoxicating shudders of a love fulfilled. Lucian held her tight as her breathing returned to normal. Then he moved between her legs, guiding his erection into the folds saturated with Gillian's female scent. His penis jerked with desire as he touched her. Consumed by the tightness, he filled her. He held for a moment; then Lucian withdrew slowly before returning, sliding in further. He repeated this, each time seeking more; Gillian tilted her hips to allow him deeper access. "Oh, God, Sweetling," he moaned close to her ear.

Lucian knew it was coming before the climax broke across her body. They moved together in a rhythmic dance, hips arched to meet an unnamed hunger. He lost himself in the sensation of their bodies becoming one. Lucian thrust harder, and Gillian crested once more, holding herself against him, letting her body jerk with pleasure. He held still until she began to recover, and then he moved in her with an intensity, a need, as the blood roared in his ears. A groan rattling his chest announced his release.

For a long time, their bodies, damp with perspiration, clung to each other, hearts thudding in the other's chest. "You aren't to stay away so long." Gillian nibbled on his ear as he kissed her temple and along her chin line.

"Never again." Lucian pulled her onto her side as he slid from her, settling his breathing once again. They lay as such for several minutes, both lost in the sensation of being desired. Lucian gently stroked her arm and brushed kisses across her temple and forehead. Yet, Gillian possessed other ideas. Flushed with love, she wrapped her arms around Lucian's neck as she pressed her body to his. "Are you trying to seduce me again?" he chuckled when he kissed her upturned mouth.

"Again?" she teased. "You seduced me the last time." She rotated her hips, giving Lucian a nudge with her damp triangle. A quick hardening of his flesh rewarded Gillian's overtures. "So soon? You want me again?" The breathy seductiveness of her voice clouded his brain. A low moan escaped when he prodded her with his erection. "You do want me." She kissed down his neck and in the soft indentation of his shoulder.

"Yes, you, minx, I want you," he growled. "I want you again, and again, and again." Lucian rolled her to her back, following her as their kiss went straight to the next level.

This time they settled into a quiet intimacy. Lucian held her close in his embrace, her head resting easy on his shoulder. Gillian traced circles across his abdomen with the pads of her fingertips. Eventually, he cleared his throat. "Sweetling, we should talk."

Gillian shifted nervously against him and started to sit up. Lucian, instinctively, pulled her to him. He whispered, "I don't want to see the hurt in your eyes. I can't bear it right now. If I'm to say these things aloud, I would rather say them to the air."

Gillian kissed his arm, and Lucian caressed her shoulder. "Tell me what you want to say," she encouraged. "I already know some things, but I still have lots of questions."

"If I don't clear up all your concerns, then you must promise me that you will ask me after I finish this. I want you to choose to spend your life with me, and I don't want any deceit between us, no matter how difficult this might be." Lucian focused on a spot on the ceiling; he couldn't look at her until he finished.

"I lied to you when I told you that I had parents who ignored me. That was Lucian Damron's childhood. His parents were quite wealthy, but the real Lucian Damron was raised by a series of nannies and then by private schools. He was a lonely, solitary child. My real name is Marcus Chambers; I never knew my father; my mother, a morphine addict, had no idea who he was. When I was four, she signed away her rights, and I entered the foster care system." Gillian stroked his arm in understanding, and Lucian interlaced their fingers in a solid grasp for reality.

"I'm afraid I was a bit of a hellion. Maybe it was because my mother was high through most of her pregnancy. Anyway, I caused lots of trouble. I set my bedroom on fire twice, before, at the age of six, I was sent to live with a very special couple."

"My parents," she whispered.

Lucian tightened his hold on her. "I swear, Gillian, I had no idea at first. It was only after I researched you on the internet, that time when Jackson tried to get us to agree to do the show, that I make the connection. I was already interested in you, and, at first, my thoughts were 'how ironic.' I adored living with your family. It was the only time as a child I ever felt loved."

Gillian traced his lips with her fingertip. "My father loved you; he wrote of his affections for you in his journal."

Lucian turned his head to look at her. One brow lifted a fraction. "Your father kept a journal?"

"He made notes on all the children they took in. I read about you a few weeks ago. My Papa wanted to adopt you. He wanted you. Both my parents wanted you to be their son." Her voice was so quiet Lucian had to strain to hear her.

"Then Barb came to them. I remember the night your father told me they couldn't keep me. I promised him I would sleep on the floor and eat half of what I already did. That way there would be enough for both Barb and me, and I could stay. It seemed so logical to an eight-year-old child, but, of course, your parents would not allow any to child suffer. That's why I wanted to stay. I was safe there."

Tears trickled down Gillian's cheeks. "Papa hated it. Except what could he do? Barb would have died if he left her to the State's care."

"Of course, I know that now, but it seemed so unfair at the time. He was going to be my father." Lucian swallowed hard, forcing the despair away. "I guess I should be thankful, at least, in retrospect. It would certainly make our current situation seem lewd if I ended up as your adopted brother. I suppose son-in-law is as good as son in many ways."

"I doubt if we could be here right now in that case." She laughed lightly, but Lucian doubted that she had found any humor in what happened.

"Anyway," he returned to his story, "I drifted from family to family. I stayed with one family throughout high school. They kept me because I worked part time and paid for a lot of my own things. They made money off me. They didn't mistreat me, but neither did they make me a part of their family. I was more like a boarder.

"It wasn't until after I graduated high school that I found a place where I felt a part of the family. I wanted to go to medical school, but I couldn't afford it. I secured a loan and went to the local community college. I reasoned that I could become a male nurse, which are always in short supply, so I took the nursing assistant's training.

"The school placed me with Lucian Damron. It would be an understatement to say that Lucian was unusual. By the time I came to work for him, he was a total recluse. I would ascribe him to being a Howard Hughes, but maybe not so peculiar. He inherited his parents' wealth and was quite eccentric. Yet, the man was an absolute genius. A renowned scientist. A computer mastermind. A mystifying magician. A promising artist and a talented musician. There wasn't a thing that he couldn't master. Lucian was only twelve years older than I, but he became like a father to me. Out of loyalty, he paid for my education. He is the one who encouraged me to consider psychology; he said I would understand other people because I had suffered too. I wouldn't be the type to prejudge.

"I stayed with Lucian for nearly six years. During that time, I rarely left his penthouse unless I ran an errand for the man. I attended him twenty-four/seven. The longer he withdrew from society, the more unconventional became his lifestyle. I took care of all his hygiene needs, and I was also his companion."

Lucian heard her catch her breath and hold it. "I suppose you know that Lucian became obsessed with homosexuality?" She nodded and looked away from him. "Well, I wasn't involved, Gillian. You have to believe me."

"I do," she whispered. "I've lain with you, and I know that is not part of the man I love."

"Lucian and I never had that type of relationship," he assured her. "Sometimes I think when I first came to stay with him, he might have considered it a possibility, but we soon became the other person's only friend. We were both so lonely for a family. It was a natural trip to companionship. I never condoned his lifestyle, but I also never condemned him for it. He was so much more than his sexual preferences."

"Then how did *you* become Lucian Damron?"

"When Lucian died some ten years prior, I held no idea what to do with my life. I had lost a dear friend and the only family I had ever known. Then his attorney contacted me. Good old, unconventional Lucian Damron had remembered me in his will. I would receive fifty thousand dollars per year for ten years if I changed my name to Lucian Damron. The man was an eccentric, and he wanted to live forever. So, if I became Lucian Damron, his name lived on. What did I have to lose? Marcus Chambers barely existed. I had no family. Nothing. Lucian even transferred his copyrights and patents to me. If I made the change, then I could have a new start in life. Lucian was uncommon, but he cared enough for me to provide me a future."

"You're kidding me?" Gillian gasped. "That's why you changed your name?"

"It seemed logical at the time. I had no other family; he was the only person who had seen the part of me that craved an identity. He was willing to give me his name, literally," Lucian reasoned.

Gillian began to laugh. "A person couldn't write this story line!"

"I suppose you're right," he chuckled. "That's why I've been so motivated to succeed. First, the endowment had a time element, and I needed to make something of myself before the guaranteed funds ran out. Lucian left me a buffer zone so I could establish my own practice. Secondly, I wanted to bring some 'fame' to his name. A tribute to a man who thought I was worthy of that name."

"Then why couldn't you tell everyone?" Gillian seemed confused.

"That was part of the will. I couldn't tell anyone the conditions until the ten-year period ended. Lucian had told his attorneys that I must prove my loyalty to our agreement with my silence. The time expired last week." Realizing his story hadn't sent Gillian scrambling for the door, Lucian sat beside her. He propped himself on the pillows while Gillian sat cross-legged in the bed's middle.

"So, we can now answer some of the media questions as to how you became Lucian Damron?"

"I assume so. That is if you're still willing to stand by me." Lucian caught her hand and brought the back of it to his lips.

"I've always been on your side, Lucian," she stated simply; then Gillian turned her entire focus on him. "Tell me what you expect of me. Where do you want our relationship to go?" Her eyes locked on his, demanding the truth.

"The many times I have pictured this moment over the past few months we have never been naked and in a bed. Later maybe, that's where we are, but I never expected to ask you to marry me while we're recovering from a lovemaking session." His eyes sparkled with the humor of the situation. "I planned to ask you first and then seduce you, but it seems I placed the cart before the horse."

She smiled. "Are you asking me to marry you?"

"That was my intention when I came through the door awhile ago." He leaned forward to cup her chin. "Is there any chance you're saying *yes*?"

"I'm saying *hell yes.*" And like that, she was in his arms again, devouring his mouth. Desire spread quickly–hands touching, fingers searching, and bodies meeting. "I love you, Lucian Damron." Gillian crawled on top of him and kissed his chest. "And I plan to make you love me as much as I love you."

"Oh, Sweetling, you make me happier than I could ever imagine."

Exhausted, Gillian laid across the bed doing her best spread eagle imitation. Lucian returned from the bathroom with a damp cloth and began to wipe her clean. "You, my Love, are going to be sore tomorrow," he teased.

"It's a good thing I don't have to move very fast down the aisle." She rolled onto her side as Lucian came to lie beside her. He was too damn handsome for her sanity. "May we tell everyone we'll be getting married soon?"

"Michael Hood will like that." Lucian lazily twisted one of her curls in his fingertips. "It'll boost the ratings for next season's show."

"I don't care about that," Gillian incredulously added. "They don't deserve our assistance with the show's success. In reality, I think we should consider a lawsuit, especially if they try to renege on our other contracts. We just need to get the truth out. It'll be a national format to restore your reputation. To me, that's what is important."

"Yeah, I guess you're right. I no longer have my inheritance from Damron's will. I must bring in enough money to support you in the style you deserve."

Gillian protested, "I can make money, too, you know. Besides I don't care how rich you are."

Lucian kissed the tip of her nose. "Of course, Sweetling. Heck, you'll probably end up supporting me in the style to which I would like to become accustomed." He teasingly kissed behind her ear. "If I'd been smart enough to ask you to marry me when I first thought of doing so, I could've had you pregnant by now, and I would inherit all of Lucian Damron's wealth." Lucian distractedly nibbled on her ear lobe.

Unexpectedly, Gillian shoved him away before bolting up to crouch between his legs. "What are you talking about?" she demanded.

Lucian used his thumbs to massage away her frown lines as he spoke. "Part of Lucian's will stated that if I fathered a child within the ten-years' period, his entire assets would be mine. Of course, I had never thought much about that as a way to have it all. He and I always talked about how hard it would be to build a family. I promised him that I wouldn't marry without love. Even with the promise of wealth, I never betrayed him. The man gave me an education and a home and an identity. I wouldn't marry simply for his money."

"Did you have to be married before the time limit?" Gillian shoved his hair from his forehead.

"Lucian didn't insist on marriage. Although, I, personally, think it has its advantages, Lucian's lifestyle confirmed marriage didn't necessarily make a family." He gave Gillian a wicked grin that told her where his thoughts lay.

Gillian giggled–actually giggled before she took Lucian's hand in hers, splaying his fingers across her abdomen, pressing the hand to her skin and holding it in place. "Dr. Damron," she laughed lightly, "may I introduce you to your first child?"

Lucian had always enjoyed touching her, and for a moment, the meaning behind her words hadn't registered. Then an acknowledgment of her reality played across his countenance. "Gillian?" A smile went all the way to his eyes' corners. "Are you? I mean, are we? For real? How far along?" Confusion mixed with absolute joy. All at once, he remembered Ada's words: *You're in for a big surprise.*

"A little over three months." Her voice trembled.

Lucian clasped her to him in an embrace of pure ecstasy. "Are you okay? You've seen a physician?"

"I haven't set up my regular check ups, but I assure you I'm healthy." Their mouths rested inches apart. "Are you happy? You don't want to change your mind about marrying me?

"Happy? My God, Gillian, I'm going to have a real family. I'll have the woman I love and a child. I'll be a father!" He kissed her deeply before rolling her to her back. "You, Sweetling, have given me the world." His mouth returned to hers. She was the most remarkable woman of his acquaintance.

"Lucian," she laughed lightly, true mirth bubbling from her. "Our child was conceived before the deadline."

The words ricocheted through him. "Lord, you're phenomenal. I didn't even think about that; I was just so happy to have you and a baby in my life." He kissed her again, but the delight gurgled within him.

"What? What is it?" she insisted.

"If it's a boy, we have to name him Lucian Damron so the name lives on. So Lucian lives on. I have no doubt that somewhere in Heaven that Lucian is enjoying manipulating St. Peter. The man planned all this! I told you he was a genius." A smile overspread Lucian's countenance

"Not simply your scientist friend," she corrected. "You might believe Lucian Damron maneuvered us into this, but, personally, I think my father decided you were to be a part of his family, after all. He'll have his son and a child to replace the one he lost all those years ago."

His mirth brought the unaccustomed smile to his lips. "Maybe we should contact John Edward and see if Lucian and your father are working together. Possibly Edward can see into the after life for us. I told you from the beginning, we're destined to be together. See how smart I am."

"You're not going to take credit for all this, are you?" she taunted.

Lucian's body finally eased from the tension he'd known for so long. The emotions rolled through him. "I can't believe how incomplete my life's been and how full it'll be now that I have you." Relief and gratitude radiated into his response. Lucian had never expected to feel such bliss—such deep, powerful contentment. "Someone must've watched over me to lead me to the right woman. Love truly changed everything for me." He had said those words before, but it was the first time he could honestly say that he believed them. It would be too painful to lose Gillian at this point. She was his world.

"You're what makes me happy." Her expression sobered as she captured his hand in hers.

With a powerful shifting of his weight, he maneuvered her beneath him. He stared down at her, the passion darkening his eyes. He whispered her name before kissing her intimately; Lucian worshipped her with his hands, and the desire rushed forward. Then he entered her, thrusting hard and demanding a response. "Tell me you want this," he rasped out.

His heart pounded erratically as she declared, "I want this. I want you. I love you," she moaned. Lucian seduced her into madness as he poured his life and his soul into her.

Finally spent, he cradled her to him; Gillian rested her head in the indentation of his shoulder. He reached for the crumpled sheets and pulled them over their bodies. Lucian's arms tightened around her as a slow evenness highlighted her breathing; she slept, completely sated. Lucian had built a wall of detachment around his heart, but Gillian Cornell would have none of it. From the first time he had looked into her cobalt blue eyes, she had shattered that wall, demanding that he share an intimacy and a love he was hard-pressed to understand. Sleep came slowly to him, but, at last, a smile of enchantment found Lucian envisioning his future.

A light tap on the door sent Gillian scrambling to answer it as Lucian stirred, instinctively reaching for her. She cracked an opening to find Ada and Melinda on the other side. "Did we wake you?" Melinda whispered while taking note of Gillian's disheveled appearance.

"I was awake but not moving." A blush spread to her face.

Ada laughed lightly. "Are you happy?"

Gillian glanced to the bed, noting Lucian stirred from his slumber. She just nodded in response.

"Tell Lucian to make himself decent and then let us in," Melinda insisted.

"Just a minute." Gillian eased the door closed. Turning to Lucian, she asked, "Did you hear?"

He rolled to the side of the bed, straightening the bed linens as he moved. "Give me a second." He sat on the bed's edge and pulled on his wrinkled slacks.

When they were acceptably dressed, Gillian opened the door to her two friends. "Dr. Damron, I've seen you more properly attired," Ada teased as she strolled past him. He picked up his clothes and Gillian's towel and dumped them in a nearby chair.

"We won't keep you," Melinda began. "It will be a hectic day for us all."

Gillian moved to stand by Lucian; she slid an arm around his bare waist. "Is there something wrong with the ceremony?"

Ada chuckled, "Actually, I think Dr. Damron's reappearance is what we require to make this perfect. That's why we're here. We decided Lucian should be part of the wedding party."

"How?" Gillian looked confused. "Everything is set."

"We thought that we could surprise Hood and the American public if Lucian makes an appearance at the wedding. No one else, besides Gary and Andrew, knows he's here. The TV staff is setting up the venue, and all we have to do is find Lucian a tux." Ada laid out the plan.

"Gary has already checked the local mall, and there's a tux rental place there," Melinda added. "It doesn't matter about the style as long as it fits. We didn't choose to have everyone matched in dress for the ceremony. Gillian is in blue, while my sister is in peach, and Ada's sister is in a lemon yellow gown."

Ada leveled a serious look at Lucian. "You've a lot of explaining to do. You've, obviously, convinced Gillian of the truth of what you have to say, and you have given her a logical explanation for your disappearance. Gillian is our friend, and we want what is best for her. If we add you to the wedding party, it will show the public that we're solidly behind you. It'll also provide the two of you a framework to clear the air of these rumors."

"Are you certain?" Lucian was flattered by their confidence in him. "This is your day, Melinda; I don't want to intrude."

"Lucian," Gillian explained, "Melinda and Gary won the dream wedding, but they defied the show's producers and are sharing the day with Andrew and Ada. Everything Cuttles planned has been changed."

"I bet he's fit to be tied." Lucian laughed lightly. "That's what he deserves for choosing such independent thinking women." He affectionately kissed the tip of Gillian's nose.

"Personally, I don't care," Melinda stated matter-of-factly. "I don't even really care about this wedding; I would just as soon use the money more wisely, but it was part of the commitment we made. So, my dream is to share my wedding day with those people who assisted Gary and me to get back together. That includes you, Dr. Damron."

Ada shared, "Our idea is to keep Lucian's appearance secret until he steps from the alcove to escort Gillian down the aisle. What do you think? Are you willing to shock the heck out of Sam Cuttles? To thwart the bastard's plans one more time?"

Lucian smiled. "If the rest of you agree, it would be my pleasure. Afterwards, Gillian and I can announce our own nuptials."

"Have you set a date?" Melinda took a piece of paper from the desk pad to write down the name of the rental place.

"It must be soon," he insisted. "But we haven't chosen a date."

"You must wait until we return from our honeymoons," Ada insisted. "Gillian and I are going to raise our kids together after all."

Lucian looked surprised. "You're pregnant?"

Gillian chuckled. "Ada and Andrew enjoyed the sensate sessions quite literally."

"Who would think a reality TV show could so change our lives!" Melinda teased.

"All right, enough of this," Ada became all business-like. "We have a wedding to attend. Gillian and Melinda, we're still meeting at one. I'm starving; I require breakfast. Let's go, Melinda."

"If we're hiding Lucian, I suppose we'll order room service." Gillian held the door for them.

"Lucian," Ada turned to him with a question, "if you didn't know Melinda and I were sharing this day, how did you know where to find us?"

He looked on innocently. "I read an article about the wedding in an entertainment magazine. It announced the venue so I checked the hotels nearby. I knew you and Gillian shared secrets during the show; that's why I came looking for you. I assumed as the runners-up that Cuttles would insist that you'd be involved."

"Good detective work, Doc." She turned to the open door. "We'll see you this afternoon. I can't wait; it'll make for an interesting story to tell my grandchildren."

When they departed, Lucian donned his shirt. "I assume it's okay if I stay with you."

"Where else would you stay?" Gillian seemed amused with his ploy.

He gave her a seductively raised eyebrow. "I could probably convince someone to take me in."

She threw a pillow at him as she pretended anger. "You, Lucian Damron, are going to make an honest woman of me. Now, retrieve your belongings from the rental car and get your butt back in here before someone sees you. I'll order room service."

"Yes, Ma'am." He saluted teasingly. "Not even married, and I'm already hen pecked."

"And very lucky to be so," she countered.

He cupped her chin and kissed her tenderly. "Absolutely," he murmured. "The luckiest man in the world."

No one had expected Lucian to make an appearance at the televised wedding so when he stepped through the side door to accompany Gary and Andrew to the altar, an excited buzz ran through the audience. Show staffers and technicians scrambled to make adjustments in camera angles and in the accompanying commentary. Sneaking him through the back entrance to the venue had been easier than anyone expected. He simply walked in with the banquet's servers.

"Where the hell did he come from?" Hood came to life as the staff converted the script to include Lucian.

Hood's assistant chastised himself. "We should've expected something with Miss Cornell as part of the wedding party. The man can't stay away from her!"

"Well, the show just got interesting!" Hood clicked on the phone to speak to Cuttles. "Hey, Sam, take a look at your monitor." He paused for Cuttles's response. "Got it! We'll make time at the end of the program for a statement from him. Won't it be great if he finally admits that Marcus Chambers' debacle and his relationship with Gillian Cornell? It certainly will help the ratings."

Meanwhile, Lucian's attention rested totally on Gillian's entrance. She had followed Ada's and Melinda's sisters. Mimicking the pattern established by the sisters' husbands, he met her at the head of the aisle, placing her hand in the crook of his arm and cupping it with his free one. "You're so beautiful," he whispered when they parted to take their positions on either side of the altar. Waiting for Ada's and Melinda's entrances, his and Gillian's eyes never left one another.

He heard Hood speaking through the earphones they all wore for the program's cues. "Come in for close ups of both Miss Cornell and

Damron." Immediately, Lucian recognized the mischievous glint in Gillian's eyes. Quite provocatively, she licked her lips slowly, and Lucian answered with a wink. The red lights on the camera said they had captured both gestures. It was all Lucian could do not to burst into laughter. He loved Gillian Cornell, and Lucian also loved how they had controlled the situation.

Once the vows were exchanged, the wedding party followed the couples up the aisle. Lucian again placed Gillian on his arm as they made their way through the pressing crowd. "Are you ready for the questions?" Gillian asked quietly.

"As long as you're with me, I'm ready for anything." Lucian kissed her cheek as she moved closer to him, wrapping her arm around his waist. Needing her as he always did, he draped an arm about her shoulder to keep Gillian beside him.

Gillian smiled up at him, and Lucian instinctively lowered his mouth to hers for a quick taste of sweetness. "I want to enjoy this celebration; let's mingle."

Hood screamed into the headphones. "Somebody tell me you got that kiss." He adjusted his camera cues once again as he watched Lucian brush the back of Gillian's hand with his lips before leading her through the crowd.

Thus began their open declaration of love. Regularly, throughout the evening Lucian and Gillian shared intimate moments–sweet caresses, lingering kisses, and open closeness. They danced, arms wrapped tightly–having eyes only for each other. She rested her head on his chest, and Lucian pulled her hips to him. They made no effort to hide what currently existed between them. Within minutes, Hood devoted one camera purely to their interactions.

He sent Daniel Lewis to see if Daniel could ply a comment from them. "Gillian," Daniel called as he stepped before them, "are you enjoying yourself?"

Gillian allowed her eyes to drift to Lucian's countenance before scanning the crowd. "It is a spectacular evening, Daniel."

"It's nice to see you and Dr. Damron together. Is there anything the American public should know?" He shoved the microphone in her face.

Gillian offered him one of her winning smiles. "Oh, Daniel, that's enough of that," she chided. "This evening is about Ada and Andrew and

Melinda and Gary. We'll see you later." With that, she and Lucian moved off into the waiting throng.

As the festivities wound down, Cuttles appeared at their table. "May I?" he gestured to an empty seat.

Lucian lounged lazily in his chair. His arm snaked around Gillian's shoulder while her head rested at the indentation of his neck. His finger traced circles on her upper arm. Lucian nodded toward the chair, but he didn't change his position.

"Well, you two certainly pulled off a coup tonight," Cuttles warranted. "I have to hand it to you"

"Were we trying for a coup, Sweetling?" Lucian drawled.

Gillian shifted slightly where she might caress his chin line. "That was never my intention," she purred. "I just wanted to celebrate the show's success. Wasn't that the purpose of this evening, Mr. Cuttles?"

The man actually looked irritated, something one would never expect from a top negotiator. "Quit playing innocent, Miss Cornell," Cuttles warned. "It is not becoming in a woman of your intelligence. Let's get to the point."

"By all means." Lucian gently lifted her head from his shoulder before sitting forward where he could confront Cuttles. "The point, Mr. Cuttles, is that you libeled my reputation by terminating my contract with the show without due cause. You allowed erroneous information to be leaked to the news media. This leak has caused both me and Miss Cornell unjustified stress. Now, you expect us to provide you with an exclusive interview. Am I getting close?"

Cuttles chuckled to himself. "Although I had thought you to be the perfect intellectual–society's pretty boy, I see that you have balls after all, Dr. Damron. Well, I understand your anger. What can we do to make this right?"

Gillian too had "balls" as Cuttles was soon to find out. "You, Sir," she began, "will first make certain our original contracts are filled. Dr. Damron will receive his opportunity for the TV show, and I will complete my publishing deal." By now, she also leaned forward in her seat. Gillian dropped her voice, forcing Cuttles to attend to her carefully. "Secondly, someone–you or one of your underlings–will make a public apology to

Dr. Damron. I expect that apology to play on all the major entertainment shows. A release to *Variety* will be inadequate."

"What do we receive for meeting your demands?" Cuttles bit out the words.

Lucian picked up the conversation from there. "Gillian and I will announce our upcoming marriage exclusively to you and the network that you represent. In doing so, you will provide me a format to clear my name with a thorough explanation of my circumstances. The entire explanation will play without editing."

"That's unheard of," Cuttles insisted.

Gillian added quickly, "I am certain, Mr. Cuttles, that the opposing networks would gladly oblige us."

"I don't like being threatened, Miss Cornell," he warned.

"Is it the threat or the fact that I am a female?"

He leveled an angry glare on her. "Both."

"Then from me it will only be a threat." Lucian's voice took on an undercurrent of annoyance. "We'll take our story elsewhere while slapping this network with a gigantic lawsuit. That's the truth; it's far from a threat." With a renewed possessiveness, he clasped Gillian's hand in his.

Cuttles drummed his fingers on the table. Eventually, a plastered-on smile overtook his frown. "Well, I guess, I'm at your disposal. Could we do the interview after this place clears out from the wedding?"

"I don't think so." Lucian said dismissively. "I don't wish your word on this; I want it in writing. We'll sign the statement of understanding tomorrow at noon, and Gillian and I will be prepared for our sit-down shortly afterwards. I'll call you in the morning with the details. Now, if you'll excuse us, I believe the wedding party is due for a final dance before the happy couples set off on their honeymoons." Lucian assisted Gillian to her feet. "Come, Sweetling."

"You were brilliant," Gillian whispered with true regard as Lucian pulled her within his embrace. "Quite husbandly," she teased.

Lucian released the breath he did not know he held. "Acting the part of the caveman is not usually part of my repertoire, but it was very satisfying to see Cuttles sweat. Very satisfying indeed."

Epilogue

"SWEETLING, I'M HOME," he called as he came through the door. "Where are you?" He surveyed each room as he worked his way through the townhouse. Married for a little over four months, Lucian relished each of the commonplace, everyday activities associated with being married and being a part of a family. Just coming through the door made him happy. "The network called today to set up the promos for the show," he shared while heading toward their bedroom. He loosened his tie as he walked. "Gillian? Are you back here?" A touch of panic laced his tone. She always met him when he arrived home.

Entering the bedroom, Lucian scanned the area, frantically looking for her. "Gillian!" His voice rose in volume. "Where are you, Sweetheart?" A light trickled from under the door to the master bath. "Gillian!" He pushed against the door, but it didn't give completely. Then in the crack, he saw her lying on the floor. "Gillian!" His voice exploded in the silence of the room. This time he laid his shoulder to the door; her body blocked the opening, and he forced the space by shoving her limp form toward the wall so he could squeeze into the room.

Lucian dropped to his knees beside her. "Gillian?" His words came out as a plea. Immediately, he checked for a breath and a pulse. Although weak, it fluttered beneath his touch. She lay in a watery jumble of arms and legs. "I'm here, Sweetheart," he assured her as he whipped open his cell phone to dial 9-1-1.

Making the call, he returned to her side. "Gillian, stay with me," he begged as he cradled her head in his lap. "I can't...I can't lose you." He guided a strand of hair into place. She still didn't respond, her eyes remaining closed. "Damn it, Gillian, don't do this!" He argued against the insanity of what was happening. "Please!" Tears formed in his eyes as he cooed words of love close to her ear.

Finally, he heard the sirens in the distance. "I'll be right back, Sweetheart." He gently lowered her head to the floor again. Scrambling to his feet, in seconds he led the paramedics to where his wife laid. "She's a few weeks from her due date," he explained as the medical personnel began to work on her.

"Has she said anything?" A medic asked as he hooked up an I-V.

"Nothing." Lucian looked on in disbelief. The scene played out like some terrible tableau.

"We've got her." The female medic demanded his attention. "Are you coming with us?"

He nodded quickly and followed them to the squad. Walking beside the stretcher, he clutched her hand in his. "We'll have you at the hospital in minutes, Sweetheart. Just stay with me, Gillian." The words were as much for him as for her.

The next few hours blurred as the hospital staff worked feverishly to save both her and the baby. He had no one else to bring him comfort; Lucian's whole family resided in the operating room. Unable to sit passively in the waiting room, he found his way to the hospital chapel.

The candles flickered at the front as he slid into a nearby pew. A figure of the Blessed Mary holding the baby Jesus stood to one side of the central cross, riveting Lucian's eyes to the Madonna's face. The statue's gaze rested on the child she held. "That's what I ask, God," he whispered. "Take everything else, but give me that. Give me my Gillian and the baby. I've made my mistakes, but Gillian's done nothing more than open her heart to those who need love the most." Tears rolled down his cheeks. "It's in your hands." He wasn't certain whether he said the words out loud. "God," the sobs now consumed him, "don't take them from me. Everyone we ever loved is gone. It's only Gillian and I, but if one of us must leave, take me. Leave Gillian. She is the best. The absolute best person you have ever created. She has the most loving heart, and there's no known value for a loving heart. It exists as its own entity."

A nurse stood at the door. "Dr. Damron," she cleared her voice, "they've moved your wife to recovery. If you'll come with me, I'll show you the way."

Using the back of his sleeve, Lucian wiped his tear stained face as he stood. "How is she?" He asked as he turned to follow her.

"I'm not certain," the woman said as she wove her way through the intersecting corridors. "They just ask me to find you."

Consumed with dread, Lucian stumbled along beside her, attempting to steady his thoughts and steel his heart against the chaos surrounding him.

"Dr. Damron," the attending physician approached when he saw Lucian rounding the corner to the nurse's station.

"How is my wife, Dr. Stevenson?" Lucian beseeched him.

"We came close to losing her twice on the table. She certainly had us going there for a while, Dr. Damron." Lucian felt a glint of hope invade his heart. "Does Mrs. Damron know that she has the early stages of diabetes?"

"A diabetic?" Lucian gasped. "I should've recognized the symptoms."

Dr. Stevenson plied his best bedside manner. "We don't always see what's right before our eyes. Mrs. Damron is lucky that you arrived when you did. We'll require a couple of days to stabilize her, but your wife will pull through just fine."

Lucian rolled his eyes in supplication. "Thank God!" he murmured. "And the baby?" Concern returned to his voice.

"Your son's in the nursery. You may see him there. Once your wife is awake, we'll bring him to her room."

Lucian's knees went weak. "They'll both make it?" he barely whispered.

Stevenson smiled. "You'll be able to take your son home tomorrow if you wish. Your wife will require an extra day before she can join you. You may wait and take them both together; we like for newborns to bond with their mothers right away."

"How may I thank you?" Lucian extended his hand to the man.

"No need," Stevenson added. "We'll let you know when Mrs. Damron is awake."

⌒

Gillian turned over in bed to see Lucian's side empty. She smiled, knowing where she could find him. Padding down the hall, her bare feet lightly brushed against the shag carpeting. She paused in the doorway to the nursery.

"You should have woken me," she whispered upon seeing her husband rocking their son to sleep after giving him a bottle of her breast milk.

Lucian's face changed from loving contentment to concern. "You needed your rest."

"I'm not an invalid, Lucian," she half teased.

"You have him to yourself all day," he reasoned. "This is my time with my son." The baby's hand clung to his index finger. Lucian's eyes rested on his child. Gillian seemed to find his obsession with his son amusing, but Lucian could care less. This was his family. "Sweetling," he addressed her in hushed tones, "we make beautiful babies together. He'll be fighting off the women when he gets older."

"Our Marcus will be just like his father then." She came to stand behind him where she too could admire their child. The baby's eyes drifted closed, and Lucian shifted him in his arms to cradle its head. "Let's put him down and go back to bed, Love."

Lucian returned Marcus to his crib. Giving the baby one last touch, he turned to his wife. Catching her hand in his, he led the way to their bedroom. "Now, you, Mrs. Damron, are to get your rest." He reached to turn the linens back on her side of the bed.

Stepping away to allow her easier access, Lucian had never expected her to shove him down on the bed instead. "Gillian," he laughed, as she followed him to straddle his body, "what do you think you're doing?"

"I think I'm seducing my husband." Her husky voice encased him. Gillian closed the distance between them with a kiss. "I don't want to sleep." Her raspy voice made his arousal harden. "Tell me you want me."

Her lips returned to his, and Lucian answered with an unmistakable moan. He pulled her into his embrace while he deepened the kiss. Their tongues dueled in a merry dance of pleasure as she voraciously devoured his mouth. Lucian returned her ardor before forcing his mouth from hers. "Are you certain, Gillian?"

"I am fine, Lucian. The baby is nearly two months old. You don't have to treat me as if I'm a porcelain doll. Make love to me; I've missed having you inside of me."

He paused to judge for himself how fit she might be. Then his hands moved feverishly over her body's curves, divesting her of the nightgown she wore.

There was little foreplay and no time for finesse. As she had recovered from the surgery, he had denied himself the pleasure of touching her. Now, they wrestled and tumbled, laughed and fought against the desire consuming them. Lucian wedged his hips between hers and entered her with one powerful thrust. A groan filled the room. The passion consumed them as they clung to each other. Fracturing their senses with the movement, stripping them of their self-imposed separation. They spiraled into the ecstasy.

Arms and legs entangled, their breathing slowly returned to normal. He noticed of late that Gillian possessed that secretive, Madonna-like smile he had observed carved into the hospital statue. Daily, he thanked God for sparing his family. "I can't believe how much joy you bring me," he murmured against her ear.

"Then you do love our life together?" she asked as she burrowed into his chest.

Lucian's wry smile should've told her that hers was a merit less question. Of course, he was happy–for the first time in his life. The love he felt for her quite simply radiated from him. His hand traced the outline of her cheek. "I'll tell you if you give me a kiss." He winked at her before pulling Gillian closer. Her tongue traced his lips' outline. "Do you call that a kiss?" he taunted.

"No, my Love, I call that a tease." She half giggled.

"Tease away, Sweetling," his tone admitting his love for her. Lucian's lips brushed hers. "I was thinking," he began again, raspier this time, "we should take a long weekend, maybe to the beach–some place isolated."

"Some place isolated?" She let her hand drift down his body. "Whatever could we find to do to occupy our time?"

He rolled her to her back. "Let me give you a preview of coming attractions," he taunted as his mouth traced kisses along the pulse points in her neck.

"Does the story we write have a happy ending?" Her hand played with the hair at the nape of his neck.

"For our story," he swallowed hard to find his voice, "before the words *The End*, it will say 'they lived happily ever after.'"

Resources

Adkins, Trace. "This Ain't No Thinkin' Thing." *Greatest Hits Collection, Volume I.* Capitol/EMI Records, 2003.

Adkins, Trace. "You're Gonna Miss This." *American Man: Greatest Hits Volume II.* Liberty, 2007.

Aiken, Clay. "I Survived You." *Measure of a Man.* RCA Records, 2003.

Berman, Laura, Dr. "Scientists Discover Secret Sex Nerve." *Today Show.* 25 Mar. 2008. MSNBC. 27 Mar. 2008. {http://www.msnbc.msn.com/id/13781652/from/RSS/}.

Clifford, Paul F. "Mambo Dance Steps and Timing." November 2000. *XPert.Site.com.* Street Dance: Australia's Dance Survival Guide. 9 Jul 2008. {http://www.Geocities.com/sd_au/mambo/sdsmambo.htm}.

Costello, Elvis. "She." *Notting Hill Soundtrack.* Island, 1999.

Forester Sisters. "Men." *Talkin' Bout Men.* Warner Bros., 1991.

Hill, Faith. "If I'm Not in Love with You." *Breathe.* Warner Bros., 1999.

Jones, Tom with Mousse T. "SexBombs." *Reload.* Git/V2. 1999.

Keating, Ronan. "When You Say Nothing at All." *Notting Hill Soundtrack.* Island, 1999.

Kerner, Ian, Ph.D. "Love at First...Scent?" *Today Show.* 24 Jan. 2008. MSNBC. 27 Mar. 2008. {http://www.msnbc.msn.com/id/22825753/}.

King, Ann. "Herbs and Things to Increase a Woman's Sex Drive." *Associated Content.* 2008. Associated Content. 19 Apr. 2008. {http://www.associatedcontent.com/pop_print_shtml?content_type=articl e&content_type_id=36769}.

Knight, Terry and the Pack. "I Who Have Nothing." *Lucky Eleven from Cameo Parkway 1957-1967,* 1966.

Lost, Caroline. "To Be with You." *Chasing Liberty Soundtrack.* 2004.

McGee, Mike. "Foods That Increase Sex Drive." *Associated Content.* 2008. Associated Content. 19 Apr. 2008. {http://www.associatedcontent.com/ Pop_print_shtml?content_type=article&content_type_id=36578}.

Menzel, Idina and Kristin Chenoweth. "For Good." *Wicked.* Decca Broadway, 2003.

"Parks: Humbug Spires." *GORP.* 1999-2008. Orbitz Away, LLC. {http://gorp.away.com/gorp/resource/us_wilderness_area/mt_humbu.htm }.

Richie, Lionel. "Hello." *Can't Slow Me Down.* Motown, 1984.

"The Role of Sex Therapy." *Harvard Health Publications.* 23 Jan. 2007. The Faculty of the Harvard Medical School. 19 Apr. 2008. {http://body.aol.com/learn-about-it/women's-sexual-health/the-role-of-sex-therapy?cc70}.

"Sensate Focus: The Foundation of Sex Therapy." *Harvard Health Publications.* 23 Jan. 2007. The Faculty of the Harvard Medical School. 19 Apr. 2008.{http://body.aol.com/learn-about-it/womens-sexual-health/the-role-of-sex-therapy/sensate-focus-the-foundation-of-sex-therapy?cc=70}.

"Sex Therapy: All You Wanted to Know." *IndiaDiets.* 1999. {http://indiadiets.com/sex_guide/Sextherapy/Sex_therapy.htm}.

"The Single Most Important Dimension for Making a Relationship Work."
  eHarmony. 11 May 2008.
{http://advice.eharmony.com/?page=articles/
view&AID=1882&cid=23602&aid=1006}.

Starr, Jasmine. "The Top Ten Sexual Turn Offs for Men. *Associated
  Content, Inc.* 2008.
{http://associatedcontent.com/pop_print.shtml?content_type=article&cont
  ent_type_id=10464}.

Vassar, Phil. "Amazing Grace." *Shaken Not Stirred.* Arista Records
  Nashville, 2004.

Vassar, Phil. "I'll Take That as a Yes." *Shaken Not Stirred.* Arista Records
  Nashville, 2004.

"What is an Outward Bound Course?" *Outward Bound.* 2008. {http://
outwardboundwilderness.org/whatis.html}.

"What to Expect During Sex Therapy." *Harvard Health Publications.* 23 Jan.
  2007. The Faculty of the Harvard Medical School. 19 Apr. 2008.
{http://body.aol.com/learn-about-it/womens-sexual-health/the-role-of-
sex-therapy/what-to-expect-during-sex-therapy?cc=70}.

About the Author

Regina Jeffers, a public classroom teacher for thirty-nine years, considers herself a Jane Austen enthusiast. She is the author of several Austen-inspired novels, including *Darcy's Passions, Darcy's Temptation, Vampire Darcy's Desire, Captain Wentworth's Persuasion, The Phantom of Pemberley,* and the upcoming *The Disappearance of Georgiana Darcy.* She also is a Regency romance author: *The Scandal of Lady Eleanor, A Touch of Velvet, A Touch of Cashémere,* and *The First Wives' Club.* A Time Warner Star Teacher and Martha Holden Jennings Scholar, Jeffers often serves as a consultant in language arts and media literacy. Currently living outside Charlotte, North Carolina, she spends her time with her writing, gardening, and her new grandson.

www.ingramcontent.com/pod-product-compliance
Lightning Source LLC
Chambersburg PA
CBHW051454170626
46811CB00002B/476